SUSQUEHANNA UNIVERSITY STUDIES

Politics, Gender, and the Arts

Susquehanna University Studies is an interdisciplinary scholarly volume published as part of the Susquehanna University Press. Each issue is devoted to a theme or themes of academic interest. The editors invite manuscript submissions prepared in accordance with the *Chicago Manual of Style*, 13th edition.

Contributors should send manuscripts with a self-addressed, stamped envelope to Editor, *Susquehanna University Studies*, Susquehanna University, Selinsgrove, Pennsylvania 17870.

MEMBER

Council of Editors
of Learned Journals

SUSQUEHANNA UNIVERSITY STUDIES

Politics, Gender, and the Arts

Women, the Arts, and Society

Edited by
RONALD DOTTERER and SUSAN BOWERS

 SUP

SELINSGROVE: SUSQUEHANNA UNIVERSITY PRESS
LONDON AND TORONTO: ASSOCIATED UNIVERSITY PRESSES

Associated University Presses
440 Forgate Drive
Cranbury, NJ 08512

Associated University Presses
25 Sicilian Avenue
London WC1A, 2QH, England

Associated University Presses
P.O. Box 39, Clarkson Pstl. Stn.
Mississauga, Ontario,
L5J 3X9 Canada

The paper used in this publication meets the requirements
of the American National Standard for Permanence of Paper
for Printed Library Materials Z39.48-1984.

The Library of Congress has catalogued this serial
publication as follows:
Susquehanna University
Susquehanna University studies. v. 1- 1936–
Selinsgrove, Pa., Susquehanna University Press
[etc.]
v. diagrs. 23-31 cm.
Annual
Indexes.
Vol. 1–5, 1936–56, in v. 5; Vols. 1–8, 1936–70, in v. 8.
ISSN 0361-8250 = Susquehanna University studies

LH1. S78S8   082   38-14370
                                  MARC-S
Library of Congress   [8708-87]rev2

ISBN 0-945636-30-X
Printed in the United States of America

Contents

Preface

The papers in this three-volume series grew out of an idea at an editorial board meeting of *Susquehanna University Studies*. The idea for a regional celebration of women and art ultimately became the national Conference on Women, the Arts, and Society, 3–5 November 1988, on the Susquehanna University campus. Sponsored by the University and *Susquehanna University Studies*, the conference was funded by the President's Fund for Excellence at Susquehanna University, the Pennsylvania Humanities Council, and the Pennsylvania Council for the Arts. Some 800 college and university faculty, independent scholars, and members of the public participated.

The essays in these volumes were selected from the 171 conference presentations.

RONALD DOTTERER AND SUSAN R. BOWERS

SUSQUEHANNA UNIVERSITY STUDIES

Politics, Gender, and the Arts

Definition of Feminist Art or Feminist Definition of Art?

Selma Kraft

My title is more than a play on words: it states a distinction critical in determining how to bring about overdue recognition of women's art. A feminist definition of art is better suited to this goal than a definition of feminist art.

The call for a feminist definition of art arose in the context of explaining the problem of undervaluing past and present women artists on the basis of the male bias of traditional criteria used to attribute artistic value.[1] This approach does not apologize for the art of women, explaining away their "lack of greatness"[2] in inequitable social conditions. Instead, it locates the problem of women's exclusion from serious recognition as artists not in their art but in the very definition of art. According to this view, the problem does not reside in the art women have created; it lies in the conditions of viewing visual works as art in the Western tradition.

A successful feminist definition of art would replace the traditional definition of art. Philosophers, however, have increasingly questioned whether it is possible to locate a set of necessary and sufficient conditions for calling something art, i.e., for defining art. More than thirty years ago Morris Weitz established the framework for this questioning when he stated: " 'Art,' itself is an open concept. . . . The very expansive, adventurous character of art, its ever-present changes and novel creations, makes it logically impossible to ensure any set of defining properties."[3] Because of this, "If we actually look and see what it is that we call 'art,' we will find no common properties—only strands of similarities."[4] Since that time a new way of defining art, George Dickie's institutional theory of art, has become widely accepted. In 1974 he wrote: "A work of art in the classificatory sense is (1) an artifact; (2) a set of the aspects of which has had conferred upon it the status of candidate for appreciation by some person or persons acting on behalf of a certain social institution (the artworld)."[5]

The kind of definition Weitz found impossible is a normative definition—one which provides a criterion, or criteria, for aesthetic judgment. As Weitz puts it, any evaluation of the statement, " 'This is a work of art' implies 'This has P,' where 'P' is some chosen art-making property."[6] Without the belief that not only is such a definition possible but is, indeed, in use and biased against the art of women, there would be no need to seek a feminist definition of art.

The kind of definition that Dickie provides, however, is descriptive rather than prescriptive. It provides no standard for including or excluding anything as art. It states a fact upon which there is widespread agreement, i.e., that the determination of art is a social process. It is the social process that needs change, not the definition.

Despite Weitz's objections to the contrary, art historians, museum curators, gallery owners, critics, and collectors use a criterion that is agreed upon for making value judgments about art every day, a criterion not the subject of argument or discussion but simply assumed: stylistic originality is the definitive characteristic of art. Visual works that do not meet this standard are taken to be craft, "motel art," commercial art, or anything considered to be less than art.

Stylistic originality is not a quality found in any work per se. Looking at a Roy Lichtenstein comic strip painting and a newspaper comic strip frame, or an all-over painting by Lee Krasner and another by Jackson Pollock, one could not tell by any perceptible qualities which one or ones are formally innovative. The determination of stylistic originality can only be made by knowing something about the background of a work, which is the historical circumstances of its creation. One must know to what tradition it belongs and how it is connected in time to the elements of that tradition. No amount of looking, even of sensitive looking, could reveal whether Lichtenstein's or the newspaper's comic strip frame, Krasner's or Pollock's painting, were more stylistically original or even stylistically original at all. Without knowing the circumstances of the creation of, say, two identical-looking Brillo boxes, it would not be possible to differentiate between one that is a mere object found in a grocery store and a work of art by Andy Warhol. Stylistic originality is, then, an attribute added to a work of art from other information, not one derived from it.

A paradigmatic assumption of stylistic originality as the definitive characteristic of art is made by H. W. Janson in his immensely
influential art history textbook: "Originality, then, is what distinguishes art from craft. We may say, therefore, that it is the
yardstick of artistic greatness or importance."[7] It is clear that what
Janson means by originality is innovation in style, not meaning.
For example, when he evaluates the *Nike of Samothrace* as "the
greatest masterpiece of Hellenistic sculpture," he speaks of the
formal element of space: "There is an active relationship—indeed
an interdependence—between the statue and the space that en-
velops it, such as we have never seen before."[8]

It is this assumption that is implicitly agreed upon by art critics.
The particular aesthetic characteristics they refer to in evaluating
art (e.g., powerful, deliberate, complicated, motionless, au-
thoritative, intense, beautiful, seductive, potent, eerie, visionary,
gorgeous, severe, forceful, perishable, vulnerable, ghostlike)[9]
may be seen as positive, negative, or neutral attributes by different critics or even by the same critics regarding different works.
Depending on context, any of these words can be and are used
with different evaluative meanings. A work of art might be interpreted, for example, as overly complicated or interestingly complicated; as flashily gorgeous or sublimely gorgeous; as fancifully
perishable or incompetently perishable; as boringly motionless or
breathtakingly motionless. The attribute of stylistic originality,
however, is always positive and that of stylistic derivativeness is
always negative.

This distinction is true even in our postmodern era, when
stylistic originality seems threatened to suffer the fate of other
earlier valued attributes of art, that of being outmoded. Artists
currently are doing blatant copies of earlier artists' works or un-
abashedly replicating their styles. These kinds of gestures, however, are considered to be manifestations of originality by virtue of
their turning away from the originality of modernism. For example, the reviewers of a recent show by Mark Tansey in a New York
gallery remark that what Tansey is involved with is "rejection of
formalist strategies."[10] Thus the fact that his "figures are redolent
of Eakins in their academic realism, the space and dramatic lighting borrowed from the Baroque," does not diminish their appreciation of his art, because "Originality is everywhere denied."[11]
Tansey, in other words, is not unoriginal; he is stylistically original
in denying formalistic originality. This denial is, of course, not to
be found in the work itself. It is attributed to the work on the basis
of the place of the work in the tradition of formalist art. When

compared to formalism, the stylistic characteristics of academic realism and Baroque art are formal innovations. Therefore, this artist is worthy of having his work shown in a prestigious New York gallery and of being reviewed in *Artnews*.

So pervasive is the acceptance of stylistic originality as the defining characteristic of art that even feminist art historians use this criterion of artistic value. In evaluating the work of Lavinia Fontana, Ann Sutherland Harris and Linda Nochlin remark: "Her major handicap . . . is being one of the last representatives of a conservative *maniera*. . . . Thus her work has an old-fashioned air that is unfortunately not redeemed by either a novel personal interpretation of *maniera* or by a consistently high level of quality."[12] The clear implication here is that a novel personal interpretation of a style, whatever the deficiencies of her art, would have been sufficient to redeem Fontana's artistic reputation. In another book compiling past women artists, Wendy Slatkin states that the artists she includes are not "women artists of mere competence," and the first criterion for inclusion she lists is "technical or formal innovations."[13]

Among aestheticians, too, there are those who have explicitly taken the position that originality is a necessary condition for something to be called art, or as Arthur Danto puts it, "an analytical requirement of being a work of art."[14] David Goldblatt deduces from this belief that an artist repeating his own style is guilty of self-plagiarism, i.e., ceases to count as an artist.[15] What is even more revealing about the deep belief of the connection between art and originality, however, is the implicit assumption that originality is a sufficient condition for art. Some aestheticians interested in defining art, such as Weitz, Dickie, and Danto,[16] do not start with definitive characteristics of art which can account for works that are original. Instead, they start with the notion of originality and try to find definitions that can include a wide variety of original works. Instead of using prevailing conceptions or their own definitions of art to question the artistic legitimacy or value of such works as the most famous example of all, Marcel Duchamp's *Fountain*, they use such works as unquestioned examples of art that their definitions must meet. Marcel Duchamp's *Fountain*, Andy Warhol's Brillo boxes, Claes Oldenburg's filled-in hole-in-the-ground, Chris Burden's locking himself in a foot-locker for seven days—what common quality do these disparate items have in common that makes it necessary to account for them in any definition of art, before any definition of art is forthcoming, other than their novelty in how they are done?

Counterexamples to stylistic originality as art's assumed central defining feature are to be found in artistic traditions outside Western art. When looked at from within these cultures, as opposed to looking with Western aesthetic expectations, the aesthetics of African, Chinese, and American Indian art, to name some examples, do not require originality. This is not to say that these cultures don't require creativity or individualized expression for their art, simply that stylistic innovation is not assumed to be a sufficient or necessary condition for art, or even held in high esteem at all. Of course, the artworks produced by these cultures are generally excluded from consideration by traditional Western aesthetics.

The exclusion of women from the canon of Western art also stems from this assumption. In historical terms the visual works women have made have not met this requirement. Although those women artists who have been valued most highly in Western culture have been creative and highly personal in their individual expressions, they made no significant stylistic innovations. Artemisia Gentileschi worked in the style created by Caravaggio; Mary Cassatt's style was derived from the Impressionism developed by Claude Monet et al.; Georgia O'Keeffe's style was influenced by that of Arthur Dove. The fact that no woman artist has been recognized for having made a stylistic breakthrough in and of itself does not mean, however, that the very notion of stylistic originality is inherently exclusionary toward the art of women.

A closer look at the radical innovativeness involved in achieving significant stylistic originality indicates that it has not been a goal for women artists. To replace intentionally an accepted style with one significantly different requires a certain antagonism to what exists, aggressiveness in overthrowing it, and a willingness to take risks in destroying what stands in the way.[17] While men in Western culture have been socialized to these qualities, women have been taught to be accepting, docile, and passive.[18] This is not to imply in any way that these differences are biological in origin or inevitable for the future. In the past, however, women have stressed the need to connect to the past and to accept life as it is given them. No male artist has been known to have said, "I try to see through the eyes of many others,"[19] or, "[My art] is the thread of my connections which makes the world intelligible to me."[20] No woman artist has been known to have talked about art as "a difficult feat of bravado,"[21] or "the love of danger,"[22] or to have said, "I feel no tradition . . . I'm disconnected."[23]

Furthermore, whatever women artists may or not have created, or have been motivated to create, it has not been possible to see women's art as stylistically original. A requirement for stylistic originality is the context of tradition. Only a work that is different vis à vis something that came before it in the tradition can be determined to be original. Women, prevented from receiving traditional training or having access to membership in recognized artists' organizations or to important patronage, have worked outside the traditional male artworld. In addition, because they have been isolated from each other and dependent on male mentors, they have not been able to form an independent tradition of their own (except in nontraditional artforms such as quiltmaking).

Perhaps in the future stylistic originality will become a goal for women artists, and they will be able to make revolutionary stylistic innovations because there will be no obstacles against their working in the mainstream tradition. Perhaps. For this to happen, however, much of what has been valuable in women's art would be lost. Stylistic originality for the sake of originality, art-for-the-sake-of-art would replace the richness of meaning and social context found in women's art. To retain the special qualities of women's art and have it judged by a standard to which these qualities would be relevant requires a new definition of art. Such a definition would replace the present limited aesthetic standard mistakenly assumed to be universal by the white male power group of the artworld. This feminist definition would provide a basis for unbiased evaluation of women's art, as well as of minorities whose origins are non-Western.

Creating a definition of feminist art, on the other hand, would not achieve this result. Defining feminist art, like defining feminine art,[24] centers on the question of whether there is something distinctive about women's art. Both formal/stylistic features (e.g., soft, centered, repetitive, diffuse, intimate, and so on) and features referring to meaning (e.g., birth, motherhood, rape, autobiography, menstruation, domesticity, and so on) have been suggested. When used in reference to feminine art, such terms are generally considered to be negative, and in reference to feminist art, positive. Whether such terms praise or damn women's art depends on who is using them and for what purpose. Because they have no independent evaluative meaning, they are not normative terms. They can be considered descriptive terms only, albeit richly revelatory. However useful these terms may be in providing new insights into women's art, they are not definitive terms. At present there is no agreement that any such terms are implied when using the term *feminist art*.

Weitz's characterization of art as an open concept is at least as applicable to women's art as to men's. In addition to the ever-changing nature of its aesthetic characteristics, women's art is complicated by shifting relationships to men's art. Some women's art looks very much like men's art. As Nochlin has pointed out, there is more similarity between the art of men and women of the same culture than between that of women of different cultures.[25] Some women's art, like that of Judy Chicago or Miriam Schapiro, is intentionally different from men's art. Other works, such as patterned quilts or china painting, are unintentionally different from men's. Some work, such as that of Georgia O'Keeffe, has been viewed as prototypically female, but with strong denial by the artist. There has been no agreement, nor is there promise of one, of a definitive criterion of women's art. The problem is compounded in the case of feminist art, because there is no agreement on what feminism means. Furthermore, while a classificatory definition of women's art as art done by women might be agreed upon, it is not clear that it is true that feminist art is that which is done by feminists.

Two components are involved in defining feminist art: feminist and art. No matter what would be posed as the defining characteristic of feminist art (e.g., art expressing a feminist outlook), for feminist art to be accepted as art, it would have to meet the implicitly accepted standard of art—stylistic originality. But stylistic originality has not been a central concern of feminist artists. Indeed, it is this very demand that has served so effectively in the devaluation of women's art up to now. It is time to provide a new definition of art that is inclusive rather than exclusive, broad rather than narrow—a feminist definition of art.

Notes

1. See, for example, Gisela Ecker, "Introduction," *Feminist Aesthetics*, trans. Harriet Anderson (Boston: Beacon Press, 1986), 15–22; Thalia Gouma-Peterson and Patricia Matthews, "The Feminist Critique of Art History," *Art Bulletin* 59, no. 3 (September 1987): 326–57.

2. For a significant statement of this view, see Linda Nochlin, "Why Have There Been No Great Women Artists?" *Artnews* 69, no. 9 (January 1971): 22–39, 67–71.

3. Morris Weitz, "The Role of Theory in Aesthetics," *The Journal of Aesthetics and Art Criticism* 15 (1956): 31.

4. Ibid., 92.

5. George Dickie, *Art and the Aesthetic: An Institutional Analysis* (Ithaca: Cornell University Press, 1974), 34.

6. Weitz, "Role of Theory," 93.

7. H. W. Janson, *History of Art* (Englewood Cliffs: Prentice-Hall, 1977), 14.

8. Ibid., 142.

9. These terms were chosen at random from five reviews of current exhibits by five different critics, appearing in the following order: Richard Huntington, Peter Clothier, Sue Taylor, David Benetti, and Pamela Hammond, *Artnews* 87, no. 1 (January 1988): 175–78.

10. Susan Kandel and Elizabeth Hayt-Atkins, "Mark Tansey," *Artnews* 87, no. 1 (January 1988): 152.

11. Ibid.

12. Ann Sutherland Harris and Linda Nochlin, *Women Artists 1550–1950* (New York: Knopf, 1981), 122.

13. Wendy Slatkin, *Women Artists in History* (Englewood Cliffs: Prentice-Hall, 1985), xiii.

14. Arthur Danto, "Artworks and Real Things," *Theoria,* 39 (1973): 1–17.

15. David Goldblatt, "Self-Plagiarism," *The Journal of Aesthetics and Art Criticism* 42, no. 1 (Fall 1984): 71–77. See my *Afterword* to Goldblatt's article: Selma Kraft, "Content, Form, and Originality," *The Journal of Aesthetics and Art Criticism* 44, no. 4 (Summer 1986): 406–9.

16. Danto, "Artworks," n. 7; see Dickie and Weitz above.

17. These characteristics are taken from Renato Poggioli, *The Theory of the Avant-Garde,* trans. Gerald Fitzgerald (Cambridge, Mass: Harvard University Press, 1968).

18. See, for example, Carol Gilligan, *In a Different Voice* (Cambridge: Harvard University Press, 1982), and Eleanor M. Maccoby and Carol N. Jachlin, *The Psychology of Sex Differences* (Stanford: Stanford University Press, 1974).

19. Pat Steir, quoted in Paul Gardner, "Pat Steir: Seeing through the Eyes of Others," *Artnews* 84, no. 9 (November 1985): 84.

20. Robin Lehrer, quoted in Carrie Rickey, "Decorating, Ornament, Pattern and Utility: Four Tendencies in Search of a Movement," *Flash Art/Heute Kunst* 90–91 (1979): 23.

21. Roy Lichtenstein, quoted in Ellen Johnson, ed., *American Artists on Art* (New York: Harper & Row, 1982), 103.

22. T. Martinetti, quoted in Herschel B. Chipp, ed., *Theories of Modern Art* (Berkeley: University of California Press, 1986), 286.

23. David Smith, quoted in Johnson, *American Artists,* 13.

24. For explication of this definition, see Ecker, "Introduction," 15–22.

25. Nochlin, *Artnews,* 24.

Recovering Feminist Aesthetics by Reading a Reaction on the Left

Phyllis Culham

E lisabeth Vigée-Lebrun's *Souvenirs* claimed that women reigned in eighteenth-century Paris, until the Revolution overthrew their regime.[1] Vigée-Lebrun had won admission to the Academic Royale and lived to see women excluded from the subsequent Institut des Arts. Women had been deprived of civil rights, forbidden to form clubs and associations, and banned from demonstrating in the streets and wearing the cockade.[2] It is disconcerting that republicans, who professed belief in the inalienable rights of mankind, could be oblivious to considerations of elementary equity, but it is more surprising that some leftists of later generations plumbed new depths of antifeminism.

In particular, the anarchist Pierre-Joseph Proudhon (1809–84) outdid his merely patriarchal and antifeminist conservative and reactionary mid-nineteenth-century contemporaries by espousing doctrines that were actually misogynistic.[3] Proudhon wanted to exclude women not only from politics but from culture. Women, he argued, should neither make nor appear in art; nor could any good come of their serving as patrons. Although there were republican and even revolutionary precedents for Proudhon's resentment of women as artists, or just as active participants in social and cultural life, this extreme reaction from the anarchist left begs for an explanation. Why would a radical have outdone the reactionaries of his day on this one issue? Exploring Proudhon's frequent, vehement rejections of women as artists and of women in art illuminates a classicizing feminist aesthetic in the Paris salons of the late-eighteenth and early-nineteenth centuries. In this case the cultural program of these women artists and their patrons was most thoroughly documented by their most hostile critic. Unlike the sympathetic David, Greuze, and Vernet, Proudhon had to try to articulate what these women were doing to demonstrate how dangerous they were.

Proudhon's aesthetic manifesto, *Du Principe de l'Art*, attacked at length both romanticism and neo-classicism.[4] One judgment pronounced in passing is startling to the twentieth century reader. Near the end of a hostile discussion of David, in a chapter devoted to neo-classicism's sins, Proudhon finally said that he could not work up any intellectual interest in David, Lebrun, or in anyone else of that genre.[5] What genre, the reader wonders, could be made to include both the stark, tightly constrained world of David's Romans and the warmly lit intimacy of Vigée-Lebrun's portraits? To understand Proudhon's sensibility it is necessary to read the *Du Principe* in light of his journals and of that other unfinished treatise, *La Pornacratie, ou les Femmes dans les Temps Modernes.*[6]

Proudhon was, above all, a moralist.[7] Art, it followed logically, was good to the extent that it contributed to society's health.[8] Thus Proudhon's politics produced an aesthetics more concerned with subject matter than with style or composition. For Proudhon classicism consisted not only of formalism, simplicity, and balance but also of Greeks and Romans. He was unable to separate style from topic. The only things that Vigée-Lebrun and David had in common were that they had done portraits; they had depicted humans in classical garb; and they used paint. Nonetheless, for Proudhon they were both bound in with a nexus of related ideas: women in flimsy drapery were prominent in depictions of Greek and Roman antiquity; the Greeks and Romans became decadent and died; classicism was decadent; some women associated themselves with the decadent, classical part; women were decadent; decadence is dangerous. Proudhon's cultural package might not have been logical, but it was capable of a certain coherence best summarized in the concept of *pornocratie*, derived from the Greek *porne*, whore. Proudhon saw women's cultural participation, or even their presence, as tending toward the creation, or recreation, of pornocracy, the reign of whores.[9]

Nothing good, Proudhon maintained, could come from painting the ancient examples of virtue. To illustrate Susanna's beauty and the perfidy of the elders, one had to show her in her bath, not confounding them later while clothed. Even if Lucretia were depicted killing herself, she would have to display the effects of rape with her lasciviously torn clothing and exposed body.[10] If neither of these moral exemplars was a safe topic, ancient religious worshippers such as bacchants were unthinkable.[11] The visual force of such pornocratic agents (*agents pornocratique*) was such that the traditional moral point of a topos was lost.[12] It was impossible to represent the only appropriately feminine virtue, namely, chastity.[13]

Nor was it possible to claim that depiction of women in classical drapery represented a search for pure beauty. In the first place, from the context of Proudhon's lifelong conviction that morality was the end of art, making beauty the end of art was unthinking idolatry.[14] Second, women were not beautiful when compared to the greater physical perfection of males. The otherwise repellant (to Proudhon) pederastic ethic of the Platonic school grew from that kernel of true perception.[15] It seemed undeniable to Proudhon that most classical topoi intrinsically involved erotic adventure, and that, in both art and life, classical garb provided women greater physical freedom (an evil in itself) and put more of their charms on display.[16] The Greeks and Romans, in fact, were empirical proof of his thesis that it would suffice to destroy a civilization if women were as prominent in its culture as were men; if ever they achieved dominance, the end would be quick.[17] Proudhon disapproved of religion and despised the Catholic church, but he believed that Christianity had originally constituted a stage of progress beyond classical civilizations, whose very gods practiced the gamut of sensual pleasures, including bestiality.[18]

It was even worse, predictably, when women made art rather than simply sitting for it. Proudhon did not distinguish between the visual and literary arts. Women, he insisted, were hostile to anything that was intellectually demanding and merely toyed with various topics in their art.[19] Because art was an important prop for the morality of society, any culture treating it playfully was on its deathbed.[20] Women could not invent; they could only reinvoke, produce analogies, work baroque variations, and trace.[21] Women's art was given over to the luxurious and the erotic.[22]

The phrase "women's art" is not so much ambiguous as it is all-inclusive. Proudhon was one of those people who talked about Woman or even about The Woman. Whether women were on the canvas, painting the canvas, or commissioning the canvas, it was all equally bad; there was nothing to choose between those women who identified themselves with Aspasia and Sappho and those who identified others with Aspasia and Sappho by painting them in that guise. Aspasia and Sappho, a courtesan and a lesbian, were enemies of marriage and the family, the basic units that provide social order in an anarchist society.[23] It didn't matter whether a woman was taking a position on political issues, or whether her portrait was on display, or whether she was well-known as an artist; a woman in public was a whore.[24]

The unfinished *Du Principe* is more vehement than precisely logical, but it is clear that Proudhon despised most of his female contemporaries, not only the few female artists, and blamed them, as public and as patrons, for much that had gone wrong with art. *Du Principe*, as it was put together after his death, is violently interrupted at one point by one of its infrequent footnotes, this one well over a page long, on *la jolie femme*.[25] *La jolie femme* had taken over French society, pursuing pleasure, to the exclusion of more suitable concerns, by adopting exotic costumes, Chinese, Arabian, and classical. This *fleur des salons* adopted the new styles of dress to facilitate her promiscuity. Classical tableaux provided her with an excuse for adorning and then displaying herself. *Du Principe* later supplied a slightly older, more wealthy companion for *la jolie femme* in the person of the female patron who exemplified everything rotten in art and society by commissioning giant, historical paintings with nudes for her bedroom.[26] Women's art from this point of view blurred sexual distinctions at the same time that it displayed them. The erotic iconography aroused similar responses in both male and female viewers; once these passions were evoked they might be directed at the opposite sex or the same sex, depending on the availability of an object, or might find relief in masturbation.[27] Proudhon's description of these effects is reminiscent of the pithy phrase with which he dismissed Ingres: voluptuous yet sterile.[28] His intuitive perception that this art simultaneously asserted women's cultural presence and denied contemporary gender constructs requires examination. The results should justify the study of some misogynistic cultural documents by demonstrating that those who hate and fear women most may pay the closest attention to what women are actually trying to do and may feel the greatest need to document their findings.

Women artists' special need for and reliance on patrons led to their disproportionate relegation to portraiture as opposed to landscape or to the most prestigious form of art, history painting. Women artists were frequently and popularly assimilated to patrons who commissioned portraits and who were disproportionately female. Female patrons, conversely, disproportionately chose, or were assigned, women portraitists.[29] This undoubtedly lay behind Proudhon's casual amalgam of women artists and women in art. Vigée-Lebrun herself was associated in the public mind with Marie Antoinette to such an extent that she had to go into exile during the revolution.[30] A later instance was Benoist, neoclassical portraitist to the Bonapartes, who was publicly identified with her classicizing portrait of Pauline Bonaparte.[31] Such examples would have been triply offensive to a Proudhonian sensibility: they simultaneously displayed the wealth and power to command of the patron; they conferred on the artists social prestige and admission to elite circles; and they presented influential women to the public for admiration and emulation.

The identification of portraitist with patron was not a figment of Proudhon's rhetoric nor of his imagination. The artists announced their own epiphanies in the sub-genre of self-portraiture that was especially popular among women artists.[32] Vigée-Lebrun indulged enthusiastically and prolifically in self-portraits. Some of these showed her decked in lace collars and satin sashes in intimate, dim interiors similar to those in which her patrons appeared. No one could ever actually have worked with oils in those clothes or in those salons. Self-adornment, of course, was one means of self-assertion and self-expression women had been allowed, and Vigée-Lebrun seems to be suggesting that it deserves commemoration and exploration as much as men's political self-assertion.[33] In others she assumed the standard poses as well as the finery of her patrons.[34] In two notable instances, she painted herself with her daughter. In both cases, she toyed not only with the genre of royal mother and child scenes but even with the iconography of Christ and the Virgin. *The Artist with Daughter* in particular was a playful treatment of Raphael's *Madonna of the Chair* and made a point of substituting a female child for the infant Jesus.[35] In all of these portraits, Vigée-Lebrun went even farther in idealizing her own youth and beauty than she normally did for her patrons.

A more complicated example of this sub-genre was Lemoine's depiction of herself with Vigée-Lebrun, *Interior of the Atelier of a Woman Painter*. This neoclassical portrait of the two women in what purported to be Vigée-Lebrun's studio had Lemoine sitting attentively at her feet, while Vigée-Lebrun painted a classical scene with, perhaps, Minerva and a worshipper (she is not known ever to have attempted such a thing). It has been plausibly suggested that the painting, done in Vigée-Lebrun's absence, was an effort to secure her return from exile by suggesting that she too could participate (or allegedly had participated) in the artistic program of the revolution and that she was more than simply Marie Antoinette's favorite artist and friend. Lemoine's explicitly disciple-like posture emphasizes Vigée-Lebrun's stature as an artist. This is especially significant, because there is no reason to believe that Lemoine ever actually studied with Vigée-Lebrun, who notoriously hated to take students and who was actually slightly younger than Lemoine.[36]

Vigée-Lebrun's eminent contemporary Adelaide Labille-Guiard managed to go from portraits of royalty and nobility to portraits of revolutionaries, including Robespierre. She also engaged in self-portraiture. One of these self-portraits, *Madame Labille-Guiard and Her Students, Mademoiselle Capet, and Mademoiselle de Carreaux de Rosemond*, typically emphasizes the luxurious dress of the artist, who is wearing a huge, plumed, beribboned hat while painting. Even more striking is the reverent expression of the students who are intent on Labille-Guiard's canvas, while she looks at the viewer with warm but regal pride. Labille-Guiard did apparently take women students and tried in general to advance the careers of women artists.[37]

Labille-Guiard's emphasis on her own and her students' femininity and on their resemblance to their patrons in life-style and manner supports Proudhon's belief that there was such a thing as women's art, but Lemoine may be an even better case in point. Lemoine had not studied with Vigée-Lebrun, nor is there much in her art that suggests the stylistic or technical influence of Vigée-Lebrun; nonetheless, she clearly placed herself in a succession of artists within some tradition. The question is the nature of that tradition. If Proudhon was correct in thinking that there was such a thing as women's art, he might even have got its main characteristics right.

Proudhon suggested that women's art featured women and the portraits seem to make his point, but he also identified women with a decadent and uncreative reliance on a lurid, classical past. Proudhon's worst fears were embodied in women's portraits of women in classical roles. Sapphos were rife, and so were literary heroines such as Dido.[38] Bacchants like those who horrified Proudhon were common; the neo-classicist Benoist did one and so did Vigée-Lebrun, who spent part of her exile prefiguring the Italian travels of de Stael's Corinne. In Naples she met Emma Hamilton and painted her in a number of guises including as a sibyl and as a bacchant.[39] If Proudhon's *pornocratie* is a slighting reference to Vigée-Lebrun's reign of women, we can assume his knowledge of her popular memoirs and of her meeting, becoming friends with, and painting Hamilton, whom Proudhon would undoubtedly have labeled a whore. Hamilton was famous for her historical "attitudes," which probably inspired Vigée-Lebrun's portraits. Proudhon may well have been thinking of Hamilton and of these particular portraits when he commented that women used historical tableaux simply to display their erotic charms.

Feminist critics and others have echoed unwittingly Proudhon's insistence that classicism amounted to eroticism in women's art. Feminists in particular have sometimes been puzzled by women artists who went farther than their male contemporaries in painting women as explicitly sexual beings.[40] One frequently cited example is Bouliar's *Aspasia*, which has sometimes been thought schizophrenic in its view of women. Aspasia held a scroll in apparent reference to her rhetorical skills, but her Grecian drapery fell away, completely exposing one breast.

Actually, Proudhon was the one social critic who had some inkling of what these women were doing—trying to appropriate western culture and to make it their own. To do that, they had to stress the presence in the earliest tradition of women as females, distinct from men and with their own desires, more natural and vital than contemporary constructs of a feminine gender allowed. Some of their male predecessors provided partial precedents. David's women in the *Brutus* were deliberately highlighted as more human and more sympathetic than the protagonist. Benoist and David collaborated, after a fashion, working on problems of depicting women.[41] Nonetheless, paintings like *Aspasia* lay claim to the classical past by insisting that clichés such as the muses were not signs without meaning until an artist (usually male) assigned them meaning but were instead true statements about female ability to create and inspire both art and life.[42] As Parker and Pollack commented in another connection, they were confronting a problem "of meaning, of what images signified and what could or could not be represented."[43]

The painting that most clearly exemplified this programmatic aspect of women's art is Vigée-Lebrun's portrait of *Mme. de Stael as Corinna*, in which woman as artist and woman as art are made identical. Even feminist critics have dismissed Vigée-Lebrun's later portraits of women in classical roles as frivolities inspired by socializing during her travels, a departure from her solid accomplishments in the tradition of French portraiture. The treatment in Vigée-Lebrun's own memoirs of these paintings, of the ambiance, and of Hamilton suggests that these paintings be taken seriously as thoughtful, if experimental, rethinkings of the role of women in culture and society.[44] Vigée-Lebrun valued one of these portraits of Hamilton so much that she carried it about with her in exile as part of her necessarily very limited private collection. Her painting of de Stael was not a product of the enforced leisure of the exile but the result of a trip to Switzerland deliberately undertaken after her return to Paris. We may not like what she did, but she seriously meant to do it. Proudhon despised de Stael's novel *Corinna;* he hated its classical content, and he thought the author's life immoral.[45] He must have loathed the product of her meeting with Vigée-Lebrun, the portrait of de Stael as the Greek poet Corinna, the namesake of her own heroine, holding a lyre marking her as a successor to Homer. The intellectual female author who commissioned an embarrassingly revealing portrait of herself qua author even inspired a 1844 Daumier caricature.[46]

The apotheosis was complete, the woman writer made timeless, her own creator and her own product. It is undeniably an easy painting to loathe and a difficult one to defend. The intimate, revealing treatment of de Stael's face shows her as warmly human and vulnerable, yet amid the coldly classical drapery and stark landscape she is as embarrassing to look at yet as impossible to look away from as a rococo commode in a Danish modern living room. The deadly earnest desire of both de Stael and Vigée-Lebrun to be taken seriously is palpable and sad. The painting is almost as difficult to bear now as the novel. We no longer communicate in either of the idioms of Vigée-Lebrun was trying to command, neither in the feminine intimacy and vulnerability nor in the topoi of neo-classicism, but we can recover her aesthetic program and describe it with the adjective feminist, although it was a very narrow feminism aspiring to gain its wealthy, talented, and highly trained adherents membership in a cultural elite. *Corinna* and *Aspasia* are two of the most explicit attempts to stake out simultaneous claims to the pen and the brush, Art with a capital *A,* and to appropriate symbols of the western tradition, such as the lyre and the scroll.

The attempt of women to edge into the masculine, elite reserve of history painting is an attempt to review, if not revise, history and to command the rhetoric with which the past was described. Portraiture featuring classical topoi broke boundaries of genre and restored women to the center of the field rather than treating them as bystanders who merely reacted. It asserted the essential equality of portraiture and history painting, claiming that this one genre in which women had recently excelled was worthwhile and not to be denigrated. Vigée-Lebrun's preceding, more playful attempts to subvert the mother-and-holy child topos are more to the modern taste, but that should not blind us to the explicitly programmatic nature of her later work nor to what Lemoine, at least, could read even earlier. It was, nonetheless, left to younger neo-classicists like Constance Marie Charpentier, in her *Mademoiselle Charlotte du Val d'Ognes*, and Eulalie Morin, in her *Portrait of Madame Recamier*, and Benoist, in *Portrait of a Negress*, to express the intimacy and interest in women as individuals of Vigée-Lebrun's portraits in the forceful rhetoric of neo-classicism.[47]

Proudhon was not alone in believing that women's art made for dissolute lives as well as a decadent culture. The critic Portalis commented that women artists inevitably became unchaste.[48] He may not have been thinking of Vigée-Lebrun's notorious Greek dinner,[49] but there were plenty of contemporary examples of the interaction between life and art that might have inspired his statement. Gerard's illustration of *Les Liaisons Dangereuses*, for example, made a new art object from that book and presumably exposed her to reading it. Perhaps a similar concern accounts for Proudhon's complete neglect of Bonheur, although she was doing just the kind of popular, realist work he claimed to value. She, after all, had been forced to cross-dress to observe the scenes she painted.[50] It says something about the force of the feminist classicizing aesthetic developed at the turn of the century, which Proudhon diagnosed, that it blinded him even to his close contemporary Bonheur and left him seeing Sapphos and bacchants everywhere. His remarkably vitriolic hatred for women's art reflected his accurate understanding of what women were trying to do and what was at stake. They were trying to capture the classical heart of western culture and to put female content back into empty topoi men had been able to use as they wanted. Proudhon was not one to underestimate the continuing force of classical symbols and classical rhetorical structure in literature or in art, because he manipulated them very well himself.

Notes

1. Marie Louise Elisabeth Vigée-LeBrun, *Souvenirs*, vol. 1 (Paris: Charpentier, 1835), 35.

2. On the antifeminism of the Revolution, see as basic, not exhaustive, references, Jane Abray, "Feminism in the French Revolution," *American Historical Review* 80 (1975): 43–62; Harriet B. Applewhite and Darlene Gay Levy, "Women, Democracy, and Revolution in Paris, 1789–1794," *French Women and the Age of the Enlightenment*, ed. Samia I. Spencer (Bloomington: Indiana University Press, 1984), 84–79; Applewhite and Levy, "Women and Political Revolution in Paris," *Becoming Visible: Women in European History*, 2d ed., ed. Renate Bridenthal, Claudia Koonz, and Susan Stuard (Boston: Houghton Mifflin, 1987), 279–306; Applewhite and Levy, *Women in Revolutionary Paris 1789–1795* (Urbana: Univer-

sity of Illinois Press, 1979); Olwen H. Hufton, "Women in the French Revolu-tion," *Past and Present* 53 (1971): 1–22. On the exclusion of women artists from the new academies, see Danielle Rice, "Women and the Visual Arts," in *French Women*, 242–44. Joan B. Landes, *Women and the Public Sphere in the Age of the French revolution* (Ithaca: Cornell University Press, 1988) is an exhaustive treatment of the redefinition of "public" to exclude women.

3. On patriarchal tendencies of the post-revolutionary period, especially among conservatives, see Clare Moses, *French Feminism in the Nineteenth Century* (Albany: State University of New York Press, 1984), 151ff. For those on the left, see Charles Sowerwine, *Les Femmes et Le Socialisme* (Paris: Fondation Nationale des Sciences Politiques: 1978), 10–19, 156ff. Ideological attempts to reinforce unquestioning patriarchy can be traced in popular art also, cf. Michel Melot, "La Mauvaise Mère, *Gazette des beaux Arts* 79 (1972): 167–72. On republican ideolog-ical reasons for excluding women, see Landes, *Public Sphere*, 69, 172, and passim.

4. Pierre-Joseph Proudhon, *Du Principe de l'Art et sa Destination Sociale*, 2d ed. (Paris: Picard, 1865).

5. Ibid., 113.

6. Published by friends posthumously, available in *Oeuvres Completes* (Paris: Lacroix, 1876).

7. See most recently K. Stephen Vincent, *Pierre-Joseph Proudhon and the Rise of French Republican Socialism* (Oxford: Oxford University Press, 1984), 21-123, 179–80; and the useful chapter "Art and Women" in Edward Hyams, *Pierre-Joseph Proudhon: His Revolutionary Life, Mind, and Works* (New York: Taplinger, 1979), 26–74.

8. Proudhon, *Du Principe*, 258–80 and passim.

9. Proudhon, *Pornocratie; Du Principe*, 255. Others also used the term; cf. Koenraad W. Swart, *The Sense of Decadence in Nineteenth Century France* (The Hague: Martin Nijhoff, 1964), 453–55.

10. Proudhon, *Du Principe*, 252–53. On treatments of Susanna, see Mary D. Garrard, "Artemisia and Susanna," in *Feminism and Art History: Questioning the Litany*, ed. Norma Broude and Garrard (New York: Harper & Row, 1982), 147–71.

11. P.–J. Proudhon, *Carnets de P.–J. Proudhon*, vol. 4, ed. Pierre Haubtman (Paris: Marcel Rivère, 1974), 11.

12. Proudhon, *Du Principe*, 255.

13. P.–J. Proudhon, *Carnets de P.–J. Proudhon*, vol. 1, ed. Pierre Haubtman (Paris: Marcel Rivère, 1960), 256. On the cultural history of chastity as a feminine virtue in France, see Jeanette Geffriaud Rosso, *Etudes sur la Feminité aux XVIIe et XVIIIe Siècles* (Paris: Golliardica, 1984), 165–87. Edwin Mullins, *The Painted Witch* (New York: Carroll and Graf, 1985), 64, argues that male artists had indeed subverted the original significance of Susanna and other exemplars so that they were made sexually provocative. (Mullin's interest, however, is nearly the op-posite of Proudhon's.)

14. Proudhon, *Du Principe*, 193.

15. Proudhon, *Carnets*, vol. 4, 10–11.

16. Proudhon, *Du Principe*, 306–8.

17. P.–J. Proudhon, *Carnets de P.–J. Proudhon*, vol. 2, ed. Pierre Haubtman (Paris: Marcel Rivère, 1961), 12. Contrast recent treatments such as Mullins, *Witch*, 92, who recognizes that the frequent occurrence of women in neo-classicism usually flatters powerful men, because women are shown as atten-dants and worshippers.

18. P.–J. Proudhon, *Les Femmelins: Les Grandes Figures Romantiques* (Paris: Nouvelle Librairie Nationale, 1912), 73.

19. Proudhon, *Carnets*, vol. 2, 11; vol. 4, 63.

20. Ibid., vol. 64, 63–84.

21. Ibid., 11. Cf. Carl Baldwin, "The Predestined Delicate Hand, Some Second Empire Definitions of Women's Role in Art and Industry," *Feminist Art Journal* 2 (1973/74) 14–15.

22. Ibid., 61. For the background of such ideas, see Pierre Darmon, *Mythologie de la Femme dans l'Ancienne France XVIe–XIXe Siècles* (Paris: Editions du Seuil, 1983), 74–81, 178–93.

23. Ibid., 197.

24. Proudhon, *Carnets*, vol. 1, 373.

25. Proudhon, *Du Principe*, 131–33.

26. Ibid., 260. Although Proudhon's views of these issues were surprisingly consistent from his earliest journals through the posthumous works, the virulence of *Du Principe* undoubtedly owes something to his contempt, which was widely shared, for the luxury of the July Monarchy, as my colleague Anne T. Quartararo pointed out to me.

27. Proudhon, *Carnets*, vol. 4, 63.

28. Proudhon, *Du Principe*, 129.

29. See especially Rozsika Parker and Griselda Pollock, *Old Mistresses: Women, Art, and Ideology* (New York: Pantheon, 1981), 32–33, on preference for permitting women artists access to royal women and on their subsequent inclusion in the social life of the court. On the constraints on women artists so placed, see Jean Cailleux, "Portrait of Madame Adelaide of France, Daughter of Louis XV," *Burlington Magazine* 111 (1969): v. It has sometimes been suggested (e.g., Parker and Pollock, ibid.) that women did not receive sufficient formal training in composition and in figures to enable them to undertake the complicated canvases of large-scale history painting, but David's many female students and associates should have been able to overcome those obstacles.

30. Vigée-LeBrun, *Souvenirs*; the basic biographic treatments are Ann Sutherland Harris and Linda Nochlin, *Women Artists 1550–1950* (New York: Knopf, 1978), 190–96; and Karen Petersen and J. J. Wilson, *Women Artists: Recognition and Reappraisal From the Middle Ages to the Twentieth Century* (New York: Harper & Row, 1976), 49–54.

31. Petersen and Wilson, *Women Artists*, 61.

32. Parker and Pollock, *Old Mistresses*, 33–34.

33. Lemoine's portrait of Vigée-Lebrun at work shows her wearing the simply sashed muslin that she refers to in her *Souvenirs* as working clothes. Some self-portraits also show her simply dressed, but see Petersen and Wilson, *Women Artists*, 51. She also leveled out the differences between herself and her patrons by urging them toward greater simplicity and less fussiness of dress in their portraits. I owe this discussion of self-adornment to my colleague David Peeler, who also suggested that the same motive (i.e., validation of traditionally feminine pursuits) also functioned in the effort discussed later in the text to assert the equivalence of portrait painting and history painting. On the cultural significance of using clothing to assert one's personal existence and independent judgment, see M. E. Roach and J. B. Eicher, "The Language of Personal Adornment," in *The Fabrics of Culture: The Anthropology of Clothing and Adornment*, ed. J. M. Cordwell and R. A. Schwartz (New York: Sewell, 1979), 9ff; and J.-T.

Maertens, *Essai d'Anthropologie des Inscriptions Vestimentaires* (Paris: Gerard, 1978), 10ff. Cf. R. Barthes, *Systeme de la Mode* (Paris: Gerard, 1987), who analyzes "vestemes" as units of rhetoric that can be found in what texts say about clothes, an approach that presumably could be applied to depictions of clothes.

34. The portraits with her daughter are especially reminiscent of her paintings of Marie Antoinette with the royal children, in that they romanticize parental attachment but always keep the mother central and highlight her beauty.

35. E.g., Germaine Greer, *The Obstacle Race: The Fortunes of Women Painters and Their Work* (New York: Farrar, Straus, Giroux, 1979), 272–73.

36. Harris and Nochlin, *Women Artists*, 188–89. David Ojalvo, "Musée des Beaux-Arts D'Orléans: Peintures des XVIIe et XVIIIe Siecles," *Revue du Louvre* 22 (1972): 333, claims that the influence of Vigée-Lebrun is obvious in the work of Lemoine, but he seems to work backward from current, if implicit, constructs of femininity.

37. Ibid., 186; Rice, "Women and the Visual Arts," 250; Anne Marie Pattez, *Adelaide Labille-Guiard* (Paris: Arts et Metiers Graphiques, 1973), 32ff. Labille-Guiard supported the Revolution, but she certainly did not see herself as a typical Parisian working woman.

38. For example, Benoist and Vallain did Sapphos. Anzou did Dinomache, the mother of Alcibiades, as well as a baccant and a Daphnis and Phyllis. Mongez did Orpheus with Eurydice and a Perseus and Andromeda.

39. Vigée-Lebrun, *Souvenirs*, vol. 2, 153–60; Petersen and Wilson, *Women Artists*, 54.

40. E.g., Parker and Pollock, *Old Mistresses*, on the "contradiction" of sexuality in Vigée-Lebrun, whose paintings illustrate the "constraints" placed upon her by her society. For feminist treatments arguing a general connection between eroticism and exploitation, Anne Beatts and Lowena Hymovitch, "Paintings You Never Studied in Art 101," *Ms.* 4 (1975): 80; Linda Nochlin, "Eroticism and Female Imagery in Nineteenth Century Art," *Women as Sex Object: Studies in Erotic Art 1730–1970*, ed. Thomas B. Hess and Nochlin (New York: Newsweek, 1971), 8–15. It is also possible that increasing explicitness in paintings of women by women represents a response to their exclusion from life classes.

41. Harris and Nochlin, *Women Artists*, 210.

42. Cf. Roseanne Runte, "Women as Muse," in *French Women*, 143–45. It is possible that this brand of classically informed, self-conscious visual feminism could be traced at least as far back as Madame Pompadour, and it is also possible that she contributed to Proudhon's conception of *pornocratie*, culture created by and for whores. She has been described as an important classicizing artist herself; for example, A. de La Fiziliere, "L'Art et les femmes en France: Mme. de Pompadour," *Gazette des Beaux Arts* 3 (1859): 129–52. The Goncourt brothers, Proudhon's contemporaries and no strangers to decadence themselves, denied that she had contributed to interest in classical art, but it is significant that they thought a denial necessary; E. de Goncourt, *Madame de Pompadour* (Paris: Firmin-Didot et Cie, 1888), 327. Rice, "Women and the Visual Arts," in *French Women*, 246, notes that the question of Pompadour's influence on the arts requires further investigation. Such a feminist yet classicist influence would have been a significant response to "the all-determining opposition between preciosity and classicism in Old Regime France," Landes, *Public Sphere*, 29.

43. Parker and Pollock, *Old Mistresses*, 115. Landes, *Public Sphere*, 3, notes that the ". . . early modern classical revival . . . invested public art with a decidedly masculinist ethos, thereby illustrating the necessity of reappropriation."

44. Vigée-Lebrun, *Souvenirs*, vol. 2, 310–20.

45. Proudhon, *Femmelins*, 63–73.

46. Jacqueline Armingeat, ed., *Liberated Women: Catalogue and Notes* (New York: Viking, 1982), no. 3 (Daumier, L. Delteil, 1243); cf. no. 2, a homely bluestocking wearing classical garb and a laurel wreath and gazing into a mirror and whom the editor assumes to represent a devotée of de Stael.

47. Vigée-Lebrun herself did anticipate or exceed their accomplishments, when there was less at stake ideologically; witness the elegantly neoclassical yet intimate *Portrait of Angelica Catalani* from her Italian period. One would have expected Vigée-Lebrun's meeting in Italy with Angelica Kauffman to have been momentous in both personal and artistic terms, but even her classicizing work resembles the spare, rigorous neoclassicism of her French contemporaries and displays no trace of Kauffman's grandeur. See Harris and Nochlin, *Women Artists*, 207–10; Parker and Pollock, *Old Mistresses*, 150–51. The attribution of *Charlotte* to Charpentier is relatively recent and not universally accepted; see C. Sterling, "A Fine David Reattributed," *The Metropolitan Museum of Art Bulletin* 9 (1951): 121–32. Sterling has, at least, demonstrated that *Charlotte* is not by David.

48. Cited in Armingeat, *Liberated Women*, 132.

49. Greer, *The Obstacle Race*, 96; on the inflation in gossip of the cost and licentiousness of a simple, if flirtatious, dinner, Vigée-Lebrun, *Souvenirs*, vol. 1, 75–77. See Petersen and Wilson, *Women Artists*, 52, on the success of her salons in general.

50. Dore Ashton and Denise Brown, *Rosa Bonheur: A Life and A Legend* (New York: Viking, 1981), 57; they reproduce one of the police certificates authorizing her transvestism. Admittedly, Bonheur's Saint-Simonian affiliations and her admiration for George Sand would have repelled Proudhon, but that should have subjected her to attack rather than to silence.

The Relation of Suffrage Art to Culture

Alice Sheppard

The twentieth-century campaign for woman suffrage united and mobilized women in a manner unprecedented in western history. In meetings, parades, and demonstrations, through script, canvas, verse, and song, thousands of women across separate continents were linked in their effort to attain political equality. Artists explored diverse means to apply their art to the cause, creating paintings, sculptures, banners, posters, illustrations, and cartoons to promote the goal of suffrage.

Considerable contact existed between women activists in England and America. As a result, artwork created in England might appear on the pages of American periodicals or be displayed and sold by regional suffrage organizations. This essay surveys American and British suffrage art, examining parallels and interaction between the two traditions. It focuses on the origins of suffrage cartooning, the role of suffrage associations, and the contributions of individual artists. Differences in organizational structure, tactics, and social values also are considered.

· Suffrage artists were heirs to two traditions: the fine arts' arena of drawing and painting and the skilled craftsmanship of the newspaper engraver and cartoonist-illustrator. The fine arts tradition offered a further split between those who upheld classical ideals of the academy, and newer, reactionary principles, such as those of Ash Can Realists. We can cluster suffrage graphic art into several groups. The first exemplify classical principles, often influenced by the Pre-Raphaelite School, which offered thematic and stylistic principles. Progressives, reformers, and socialists

This research was partially funded by a Fellowship from the National Endowment for the Humanities. An extended discussion of American suffrage art will be found in the author's book in progress, *Cartooning for Suffrage*.

understood that the use of allegory and inspirational images could arouse solidarity and action. These images often fit archetypal patterns: warrior, crusader, earth mother, virgin, hero, or pilgrim. The second artistic category constitutes realistic representation, an effort to portray conditions as they existed. It differs from the first in its aesthetic aim, as well as in an intention to evoke understanding and sympathy. Social conditions are laid bare, no detail spared. The third style applies cartoonist-illustrator techniques, in which the elements of a print are labeled to represent persons, events, and issues. Its key element is the cartoon symbol.

I

During the nineteenth century, several distinct events proved influential for the development of political art. Some important ones began in England, finding ready disciples across the Atlantic as well. Arising partly as a reaction to the Industrial Revolution, an effort emerged to foster aesthetic values in workers' homes, known as the Arts and Crafts Movement. Its underlying rationale, according to John Ruskin, was that an aesthetic environment played a necessary role in the individual's appreciation and production of art.[1] Another antecedent was the Pre-Raphaelite Brotherhood, a group of painters who sought a return to pristine and spiritual pre-Renaissance forms in their art and who used an iconography replete with female archetypes: angels, goddesses, virgins, and mothers. They relied on allegory and symbolism, while simultaneously attempting to remain true to nature. One political link is found through William Morris, who was attracted to the pre-Raphaelites early in his career, championed the Arts and Crafts philosophy, and eventually became a Socialist. Walter Crane, another Pre-Raphaelite and socialist, furthered art in the service of ideology through his collection, *Cartoons for the Cause*.[2] An additional impetus for the political cartoon's popularity may be traced to the founding in 1841 of the British humor magazine, *Punch*. The magazine soon represented a national tradition of sophisticated visual and literary humor.

In *The Spectacle of Women*, Lisa Tickner has traced the origins and proliferation of art for suffrage in turn-of-the-century England.[3] It began at a time when a British tradition of political art posters existed, to the extent that American journalists of the 1890s were quick to recommend the technique to their own leaders and political parties:

> One effective picture in glaring color or bold black and white may
> bring home a political lesson or point a moral far better than all the
> oratory of the platform or all the appeals of the pulpit.[4]

Banners were an especially dramatic form of propaganda display. Decorative and inspirational, they blended the goals of suffrage with time-honored traditions of women's needlework. The
use of banners, of course, was not without precedent, claiming a
medieval heritage as well as the more recent implementation by
trade unions to advertise their crafts.[5] One notable precursor to
the colorful, well-designed parade banners was the small, calico
"Votes for Women" banner which two militant women smuggled
into a 1905 meeting where candidate Winston Churchill was
scheduled to speak.[6]

Most British suffrage art revealed ties to one of two art societies,
the Artists' Suffrage League and the Suffrage Atelier.[7] The Artists'
Suffrage League was founded first, organized in 1907 by professional artists who were planning a demonstration for the National
Union of Women's Suffrage Societies. The goal of the League was
"to further the cause of Women's enfranchisement by the work
and professional help of artists."[8]

Two years later a second British women's art society was
formed, the Suffrage Atelier. It sought not only to produce usable
suffrage propaganda, but to train artists and craftspersons in
skills and techniques necessary for production. Another difference was that the Atelier proclaimed itself an "Arts and Crafts
Society," whereas members of the Artists' Suffrage League were
fine artists who were highly trained and experienced exhibitors.
Common Cause, the paper of the National Union of Women's Suffrage Societies, summarized the functions of the Suffrage Atelier
as follows:

> Weekly cartoon-meetings are held for illustrations, with practical
> demonstrations of the methods of drawing required for the various
> processes of pictorial reproduction, so that members may be properly
> qualified to turn out work adapted to reproduction as cartoons,
> posters, etc. Hand-painting is also practiced, so that the society can
> produce some of its own publications.[9]

British suffrage art was promoted and produced by centralized
suffrage art societies. Between the years 1908 and 1913, dozens of
posters and more than 150 artistic banners were created by the
Artists' Suffrage League, the Suffrage Atelier, and various individual artists.[10] A few will be briefly described below.

Poyntz Wright. Untitled. Postcard published by Suffrage Atelier. Courtesy of
Michigan State University Libraries.

II

Reminiscent of the Pre-Raphaelite school, allegorical and symbolic figures pervade much suffrage art. "Justice at the Door" was a 1912 British poster designed by Mary Lowndes in which Justice appears, clad in flowing gown and sandals, her sword strapped to her side. The blindfolded figure clutches a placard for Women's Enfranchisement and is mortified to be denied entry to the House of Commons. Justice appears strong and determined, her attire evoking universal, as well as historical, meanings.

Another allegorical figure used in suffrage art was the "Bugler Girl," a poster created by Caroline Watts to publicize a march and mass meeting. This 1908 poster measured 60×40 inches and was printed in bold colors: black, gold, and orange. Its central figure was the resolute crusader, lifting her banner and sounding her trumpet at daybreak. Her robust physical appearance would today be seen as androgynous; her helmet, sword, and body armor reveal spirituality and a bond to mythological heroes.

A design by Poyntz Wright portrayed a female warrior defeating the force of prejudice, her sword held high, "Women's Suffrage" her shield. Behind her head is a circle of light labeled "The Vote," from which bright rays emanate. The same artist, whose pen and ink style incorporated allegorical figures in medieval settings, also portrayed the winged demon of Prejudice overcome by the angel of "Women's Suffrage." The symbols are further differentiated by the sun's illumination of the angel's domain; prejudice, now retreating, is obscured by darkness.

Realistic illustrations represent a second type of artistic appeal. "Convicts and Lunatics" by Emily J. Harding Andrews reflected a popular motif for enfranchisement: the mutual categorization of women, criminals, imbeciles, the insane, and children as non-voters.[11] Published by the Artist's Suffrage League, this 40- $\times$ -30-inch poster presents an attractive, determined twentieth-century woman, forced to stand imprisoned behind a locked metal fence in the company of the criminal and lunatic. She is dressed in her academic gown, which symbolizes education and intellect, and is seeking the key to terminate this wrongful association. "Convicts, Lunatics and Women! Have no Vote for Parliament" proclaims the caption.

Another example of realistic illustration is a poster featuring a solemn-faced working class woman clad in clogs and red shawl, who scrutinizes regulations governing women's factory work posted on the door.[12] The scene represents the exclusion of women from factory decisions and is captioned: "They have a Cheek I've never been asked." This large poster (40 × 29 inches) was drawn by Emily Ford.

Cartoon symbolism, figures, and objects used to represent persons and events pervades other suffrage illustrations. Some date from 1907, the year of the Artists' Suffrage League's first poster competition, won by Dora Meeson Coates. Her design depicted Mrs. John Bull dipping her ladle into the serving dish of "Political Help" to fill her "Votes for Women" bowl. Six young boys, each representing a different progressive organization, were told, "Now you greedy boys, I shall not give you any more [Political Help], until I have helped myself."[13]

Similar artistic conventions were adopted by Joan Harvey Drew, whose central character was John Bull. One poster (40 × 30 inches) portrays Bull plagued with political dilemmas (infant death rate, temperance, food for the school child, old age pensions, factory legislation, and so on), while a woman, labeled "Woman's Suffrage," watches and offers, "Won't you let me help you, John?" A related theme is found in another poster (30 × 40 inches) in which John Bull attempts to mind three children and tend the stove. Distracted by the imposition of free trade, tariff reform, education, poor law reform, and infant death rate, the caption queries, "Why won't they let the women help?"

Another example portrays young Jane Bull, a work by Isobel Pocock. Miss Bull is smartly dressed and wears a "Votes for Women" banner, bringing her feather duster and reform bucket to the People's House. The caption is as follows:

Jane Bull: No Women admitted! No wonder the place is in such a state. High time for a good Spring clean![14]

An intellectually provocative series of postcards featured the Anti-Suffrage Society (the A.S.S.) as a human figure with a large donkey head. The A.S.S. character lectures on how evolution does not apply to women and argues that a dress made on grandmother's pattern must still be an adequate fit. Tickner identified the artist as Catherine Courtauld, a member of the Suffrage Atelier. Courtauld designed several large posters as well as a number of postcards, which reveal an uncluttered, bold, humorous style.

As noted above, banners were integral to suffrage aims, celebrating "a 'women's history' in their iconography, their inscriptions and their collective workmanship."[15] One series of banners

Isobel Pocock. Untitled. Postcard published by Suffrage Atelier. Courtesy of Michigan State University Libraries.

was constructed to honor great women of the past. Many of the banners for this series were designed by Mary Lowndes of the Artists' Suffrage League, a talented artist who upheld meticulous standards of color selection, fabrics, and workmanship.[16] Providing a heritage and a context for the advancement of women, those commemorated in the series included Susan B. Anthony, Jane Austen, Marie Curie, George Eliot, Lucy Stone, Jenny Lind, Elizabeth I, Joan of Arc, Florence Nightingale, and Boadicea.

Occupational banners were another type, used by individual suffrage associations whose members might include artists, actresses, writers, students, educators, and even hunger-strikers. Serving to proclaim a group's identity to crowds of onlookers, they also provided a structure to the procession. The practice was borrowed when American suffragists organized their first parades.

American reformers enjoyed close contact with their British counterparts from the nineteenth century into the twentieth. Among American suffrage leaders, Anna Howard Shaw, Lucy Burns, Harriot Stanton Blatch, and Alice Paul participated in the English movement. Some of the artists who contributed to the American effort had visited or studied in England and were thus well-acquainted with the effectiveness of British suffrage art. Art students from England and America may have established contact in the art salons and academies on the continent. Finally, British suffragists, notably Emmeline Pankhurst and her daughters, made an American tour. Through a variety of means British art became known and available across the Atlantic.

III

Given an American fascination with the political cartoon and the British success with the suffrage poster and banner, it is not surprising that American suffragists would contemplate use of the pro-suffrage art. Between 1911 and 1920 American women drew numerous suffrage cartoons for suffrage periodicals, including the *Woman's Journal, Suffragist, Woman Voter,* and *Maryland Suffrage News.*[17] Their work was also published in national humor magazines: *Judge, Puck,* and *Life.* Additional examples were found in the radical press, especially the *New York Call* and *The Masses.*

The story of suffrage art in America, however, begins not with societies of suffrage artists, but with negotiations between individual artists and suffrage publications. For example, there is the story of Lou Rogers, one of the earliest and most prolific Amer-

Lou Rogers. *He Does the Family Voting. New York Call,* **15 October 1911, p. 6.
Courtesy of the State Historical Society of Wisconsin.**

ican suffrage cartoonists. In an autobiographical essay published in the *Nation*, she described an early venture in which her suffrage cartoon was rejected by the *Woman's Journal*.

> I still knew little about drawing, but I saw that there was not a cartoon on our side, though plenty of fierce ones on the other. I made a sketch in ink of a man standing in a most conceited attitude with both feet on the ballot box holding against his breast a diploma marked "Past master in egotism"; I drew huge donkey's ears on his head and under it I put the caption: "The ballot box is mine, because it's mine." I went with this to suffrage headquarters. Dr. Anna Howard Shaw's experience with cartoons had been very unhappy. I am sure this unladylike picture filled her with horror. It was certainly not welcome, and I took it to the New York *Call*.[18]

Rogers' drawing was too radical for the dignified *Woman's Journal*, which for some time had published suffrage cartoons primarily by Toronto cartoonist, John Bengough. Her struggle reveals her isolation from other artists and reliance on trial and error to discover what was acceptable for the cause. Nevertheless, her rejected cartoon was published in *The Call* and later reprinted in the *Woman Voter.*

A contrasting experience, but also focused on a single individual, concerned the recruitment of Nina Evans Allender for the *Suffragist*, organ of the National Woman's Party. Allender's bold crayon cartoons appeared almost weekly from 1914 to 1919, begun originally at the behest of Alice Paul.

> When Alice Paul asked Mrs. Allender to draw a cartoon for THE SUFFRAGIST in 1914 she didn't know she could. Mrs. Allender said she painted, and preferred to paint. But unconsciously, as she had herself felt the new suffrage spirit, to oblige, she expressed this spirit in the series that suffragists in every state now know so well.[19]

Allender created a young, energetic suffragist as a major character and is credited with providing an alternative to the stuffy, old-maid suffragist that had graced American newspapers for years.[20]

IV

Fitting the definition of allegorical images in the earlier typology are images of goddesses and universalized woman, often in classical or medieval dress. A figure inspired by mythology is

Nina Allender. *Soon the Sun Will Have to Smile. Suffragist,* **21 April 1917.**

"The Dawn of a New Age" by Card.[21] She is attired in a classical robe with sandals, gazing off into the rising sun of 1913 with her oil lamp on the ground beside her. The caption reads: "Womanhood, now fully awake, with awe and joy sees upon the horizon the dawn of a new era. The lamp of knowledge is at her feet."[22] Familiar motifs include the rising sun, the lamp of knowledge, and generalized womanhood.

"Breaking into the Human Race" by Lou Rogers depicts another universalized woman, initially imprisoned in darkness. Wearing clothing similar to that of Womanhood in the previous example, she has used her own resources to form two windows into the world: education and suffrage.[23]

A further example of this style is Fredrikke Palmer's work, "Lucy Stone's Vision."[24] Although a real-life Lucy Stone is shown gazing out her window, the focus of the cartoon is the dreamlike fantasy. In the distant landscape sits a weary pilgrim resting her burden beside the trail. Suddenly a female standard-bearer appears extending a helping hand and carrying the flag of "Woman's Suffrage." The drawing reveals suffrage as a mystical force that would ease the burdens of womanhood.

A final example of allegory is "The Trumpeter Awaking New York." Although this example bears the signature of Martha Byrn,

Martha Byrn. *The Trumpeter Awaking New York. Woman's Journal,* **6 May 1911.**

it can easily be seen that it varies only slightly from a British poster by Carolyn Watts.[25] Featuring the armored crusader with trumpet, sword, and banner arousing the city to action, the image was borrowed to promote the Women's Political Union of New York.

Realist ideals are represented in the illustration style by artists whose themes were poverty, worker exploitation, and child labor. Nina Allender's cartoons fit into this category, especially her earliest depictions of slum dwellings and their youngest inhabitants.

Another example is this devastating portrait of child labor, in which a little girl has been sacrificed to Profit. It was the work of Mary Ellen Sigsbee, whose illustrations highlighting impoverished living conditions appeared in *The Masses*, the *Woman's Journal*, and commercial magazines.[26] Several of Sigsbee's illustrations were printed as suffrage fliers.

Sentimental portraits of children, often associated with women artists, were transformed to sympathetic depictions of the working class children by Alice Beach Winter. One poignant drawing of a girl's face, a factory in the distant background, is captioned, "Why must I work?" Two of her works were published in *The Masses* and later reprinted in the *Woman Voter.*[27]

The majority of American suffrage cartoons demonstrate efforts to make effective use of cartoon symbols. Some significant differences in style can be discerned between individuals who incorporated fine arts principles and self-taught illustrators and cartoonists who relied on cartooning conventions as their models. We shall consider the fine artists first.

Cartoon symbols appear in "Anti-suffrage Parade," which ridicules all of the common, unthinking reasons why women should not have the ballot ("It would unsex women," it's "agin the Constitution," "It would only increase dishonest vote"). It was drawn by Ida Sedgwick Proper, art editor of New York City's *Woman Voter.* The images are bold and integrated into an overall pattern, published as individual panels and a single display.[28]

Works by Blanche Ames were published in the *Woman's Journal* and *Boston Transcript.* "The Next Rung" reveals metaphors of darkness/oppression versus the goal of progress/enlightenment, which appear alongside allegorical demons of prejudice and injustice. "Meanwhile they Drown" used an analogy of the ballot as a self-preservation measure, which men refused to provide for rather unconvincing reasons. Former President Taft referred to this cartoon in the *Saturday Evening Post* as "absurd and unjust,"

Mary Ellen Sigsbee. Untitled. *Good Housekeeping,* **August 1913, p. 168.**

which stimulated the offended artist to submit a second cartoon titled, "Our Answer to Mr. Taft."[29]

Understatement and irony characterize drawings by Cornelia Barns, which offered the provocative titles of "Voters," "Lords of Creation," and "Anti-Suffrage Society." Evolving a particularly distinctive style, Barns was a professional artist who combined a rich sense of humor with a mastery of technique. Most of her pro-suffrage art was published in *The Masses*. She eventually joined Nina Allender as contributing art editor of the *Suffragist* in 1919, although contributing little of her own work.[30]

Using styles found in humor magazines and newspaper car-toons, several American women contributed important suffrage graphics. Rose O'Neill was already famous for her Kewpies, the Cupid-derived characters with rounded bodies and large heads. Her "Votes for Our Mothers" depicted Kewpie-type children pa-rading their message. Another illustration by O'Neill portrayed a girl baby's distressed discovery of "Taxation without Representa-tion."[31]

The Brinkley Girl, a flirtatious, glamorized woman with long eye lashes and masses of curls, also stepped forth from the comic pages to endorse suffrage. Her creator was Nell Brinkley, a syndi-cated cartoonist. Captioned "The Three Graces," Brinkley Girls depicted Suffrage, Preparedness, and Americanism, offering the following message:

> Any man who loves and reveres his mother and his country should idolize, if he worship at all, these three graces Suffrage, Preparedness and Americanism.[32]

Although alluding to the Graces of antiquity, Brinkley's women are thoroughly updated: attractive, fashionable, and patriotic.

A humorous cartoon created by Edwina Dumm symbolized suffrage as an attractive hat. Mrs. Sam jealously regards Russia's first lady, turning to her own husband to protest: "And to think you let her get it first."[33] The same artist likened Ohio's role in the campaign to "A Modern Sir Walter," laying his cloak in the mud for a lady.[34]

Few genres were as easily employed for suffrage as the cartoon. Yet, other forms were attempted in America, including a painting on a suffrage theme by Ida Proper: "The End of the Suffrage Parade, Union Square."[35] Proper was co-exhibitor with sculptor Malvina Hoffman in a show publicized as the work of "suffragist artists." Other American painters and sculptors announced that a substantial share of their sales' profits would be donated to suffrage.[36]

At least three North American women created sculptures to endorse or commemorate suffrage. Using allegorical images, Canadian-born Ella Buchanan executed "The Suffragist Trying to Arouse Her Sisters" in 1911. It contained five female figures, whose symbolism she carefully explained. The large standing central figure of a woman sounding a clarion is the Suffragist. Vanity is seated at her right, head erect; to her left Conventionality slouches as she dozes. The figure of Prostitution lies at her feet oblivious to the call; the Suffragist's free hand reaches out to the kneeling Wage-Earner at the left-rear.

Also allegorical was Gertrude Boyle's sculpture of a naked woman spreading her wings to fly to freedom. Titled "Woman Freed," it was photographed for the *Suffragist* at the close of the campaign. Links between life, art, and government were affirmed as follows:

> Let woman follow nature more closely and understandingly than man has done in the world she is about to enter. Let her use her new freedom to find truth and dare to give the truth she finds fearless expression. Government will then become, as she moulds it, not an instrument with which man represses man, but an instrument that will aid life to become art—art, life.[37]

V

Finally, a realistic style was used for Adelaide Jonson's figures of three famous suffrage leaders. Completed to celebrate ratification of the Nineteenth Amendment, these monumental figures of Susan B. Anthony, Lucretia Mott, and Elizabeth Cady Stanton are now displayed at the Smithsonian Museum in Washington.

Suffrage art represented a major effort by women artists worldwide to use a symbolic vehicle to promote political action. Countering the common conception that women rarely produce political art, the campaign for woman suffrage was advanced through the works of dozens of dedicated artists, whose historical role has generally been undervalued by historians and artists alike. Contributing to a tradition of feminist creativity, analysis of the sources and functions of suffrage art can provide insight into the processes underlying women's political art.[38]

The women artists who produced art for suffrage contrasted in nationality, ideologies, age, marital status, art background, and preferred genre. They ranged from near-celebrities to women whose lives are so obscure that they cannot be found in any biographical source. Yet, there is a common thread (one beyond their presumed white, middle-class status) in that all of them used their profession and their talents to advance the cause of women.

English and American suffrage art shared a fundamental commonality in purpose and incorporated similar arguments to advance women's status. Each emerged in an era of progressive reform, demanding an end to women's oppression. They reminded citizens that Justice, Democracy, and humanitarian principles all demanded women's voices in public affairs, and that women's unique skills would benefit the government.[39]

Three graphic styles—allegorical representation, realism, and cartoon symbolism—characterized suffrage art on both sides of the Atlantic. The styles themselves, however, were influenced by their cultural context. British women were chiefly heirs to Pre-Raphaelite imagery and Arts and Crafts techniques. American women relied more frequently on principles of Ash Can realism and conventions of the popular cartoon.

American and British suffrage organizations attracted a cluster of women who had obtained extensive art training, as opportunities expanded during the nineteenth century.[40] From the information available, the American cluster appears slightly more homogeneous in age, the majority being born in the 1870s, therefore just entering middle-age at the height of the campaign. British women were a somewhat older group; several leaders of the Artists' Suffrage League were born in the 1850s.

The British preference for the large, dramatic poster and the artistic banner was unmatched in the United States. These productions were artistic and compelling, requiring cooperative effort to translate a design into stitched or printer form. Artistic techniques involved were also time-consuming and expensive. Nevertheless, British women did not produce the mass of cartoons published by American women. Americans relied on inexpensive, mass-distribution forms, obtaining new examples for each weekly or monthly issue. Cartoons were printed in black ink on newsprint paper, in sizes ranging from about two to ten inches. Because of the cheap paper used, copies survive, if at all, in poor condition. Original artwork, often drawn on available scraps or with pasted corrections, generally has been lost.

The British suffrage movement was perceived as a political struggle—its tactics, strategies, and objectives following from this premise. The government bodies, political leaders, and images defined a political arena in which Parliament, Prime Minister Asquith, and John Bull/Jane Bull figured prominently. The American campaign was a decentralized one, following a state-by-state strategy advocated by the National American Woman Suffrage Association. Only late in the struggle do Congress, the President, Democrats, and Republicans appear in suffrage art. The vocabulary of the movements differed, too. British activists accepted the label "suffragettes" and worked toward "women's suffrage." Americans were "suffragists" dedicated to "woman suffrage."[41]

British artists understood the possibilities of collective action, resulting in the organization of suffrage art societies before the production of propaganda art. Both the collaborative effort on banners and the frequent anonymity of artist/designers suggests the elevation of group aims over individual accomplishments. Americans continued to rely on individual talent and effort, for example, never organizing themselves into artist societies. They did, however, recognize social influence as a motivating factor by appointing art editors for the journals and art committees within suffrage societies.

Women artists of the suffrage movement, bonding together in a massive political attempt, contributed the women's perspective in political art. It was based on psychological and social qualities of women, on her historical and contemporary condition, and on the female life cycle. Even cartoon character women, when drawn by women, evidence enhanced dimensionality. Women were conceptualized and portrayed with great stylistic diversity, yet they revealed inner strength and multiple aspects of their lives. The woman artist was working to change the political, social, and psychological status of women. Within that endeavor she extended the boundaries of women's art, as well.

Suffrage art by women can be best understood and appreciated in its historical and social context. Through interdisciplinary approaches, historical images projected by women are reconstructed, providing insights into psychological perceptions, social values, and artistic goals. Posters, banners, and cartoons produced by American and British suffrage artists reveal a view of creativity as clearly dependent on culture.

Notes

1. Eileen Boris, *Art and Labor: Ruskin, Morris, and the Craftsman Ideal in America* (Philadelphia: Temple University Press, 1986), 4.

2. Walter Crane, *Cartoons for the Cause* (London: Twentieth century Press, 1896).

3. Lisa Tickner, *The Spectacle of Women* (Chicago: University of Chicago Press, 1988).

4. "The Poster in Politics" *The Review of Reviews* 12 (1895): 285.

5. See Tickner, *Spectacle*, 60–73. The Union banners did not use needlework, but were painted on fabric.

6. Josephine Kamm, *Rapiers and Battleaxes: The Women's Movement and Its Aftermath* (London: Allen & Unwin, 1966), 145–46.

7. I am indebted to Lisa Tickner for her research on British art societies and the biographies of suffrage artists. I also have relied on the collection of British poster and documentation from the Schlesinger Library.

8. Tickner, *Spectacle*, 16.

9. Ibid., 21.

10. Ibid., 69, and Appendix 3.

11. It was used pictorially in the United States as early as 1893 in "American Woman and Her Political Peers" by Henrietta Briggs-Wall. Women's Rights Collection, Sophia Smith Archives.

12. See Tickner, *Spectacle*, 50–51, for a description of the dress of the English mill girl.

13. Ibid., 17. The printed poster measured 30×40 inches. Organizations symbolized were the Primrose League, Women's Liberal Association, Independent Labour Party, Social Democratic Federation, Women's Liberal Federation, and Trade Unions.

14. Most suffragists believed that women would bring a unique contribution to politics, based on experience as mothers, homemakers, and moral educators. The image of "cleaning up politics" is commonly portrayed as scrubbing, sweeping, dusting, vacuuming, and so on.

15. Tickner, *Spectacle*, 60.

16. Ibid., 262–64.

17. The relationship of suffrage humor to social attitudes has been documented in a study by William Frauenglass, "A Study of Attitudes Toward Woman Suffrage Found in Popular Humor Magazines, 1911–1920" (Diss., New York University, 1967). Unfortunately, he fails to consider any characteristics of the cartoonist, such as gender and beliefs, nor did he investigate the women's press in his sample of periodicals.

18. [Lou Rogers], "Lightning Speed Through Life," *Nation* 124 (1927): 395–97. The essay was part of the series, "These Modern Women," published anonymously. See Elaine Showalter, *These Modern Women* (Old Westbury, NY: Feminist Press, 1978), for identification of the authors.

19. *Suffragist* 6 (2 March 1918): 6.

20. Boardman Robinson also presented a flattering image of the American suffragist. See New York *Tribune* 24 February 1911; 4 May 1913.

21. No identification has been possible regarding this artist.

22. *Woman's Journal*, 43 (1912): 409.

22. *Woman's Journal* 42 (1911): 377.

24. *Woman's Journal* 46 (1915): 255.

25. Tickner, *Spectacle*, plate VIII.

26. See Lois Banner, *Women in Modern America* (New York: Harbrace, 1974), 113. For documentation of Sigsbee's socialist activities, see Katrina Sigsbee Fischer, *Anton Otto Fischer, Marine Artist* (Brighton, UK: Teredo Books, 1977). Socialists conducted an active press early in the century, to which radical artists contributed, especially New York City's daily, *The Call*, and the monthly intellec-

tual magazine, *The Masses*. See Rebecca Zurier, *Art for the Masses* (Philadelphia: Temple University Press, 1988) for a discussion of Winter's cartoons and illustrations in *The Masses*.

27. *Masses* 3 (May 1912); 4 (Feb. 1913): 8.

28. Ida Proper, "Anti Suffrage Parade," *Woman's Journal* 43 (1912): 297.

29. *Woman's Journal* 46 (1915): 295. Ames' other contribution to suffrage history was that she and husband Oakes Ames subscribed to a newsclipping service that provided a collection of suffrage cartoons from across the country. These scrapbooks are currently at Radcliffe and Smith Colleges.

30. Barns graduated from the Pennsylvania Academy of the Fine Arts and is best known for her *Masses* cartoons. See Zurier's excellent discussion.

31. According to Shelley Armitage, Rose O'Neill spent some years overseas, which permitted her to work closely with the British suffrage movement.

32. *Boston American,* 1 July 1916.

33. *Columbus Monitor* 30 March 1917.

34. Ibid., 15 January 1917.

35. Zenobia Ness and Louise Orwig, *Iowa Artists of the First Hundred Years* (Wallace-Homestead, 1939).

36. *Woman Voter* 6 (1915): 10.

37. *Suffragist* 9 (1920): 63.

38. Alice Sheppard, "Suffrage Art and Feminism," *Hypatia* 5 (Summer 1990): 122–36.

39. See Aileen S. Kraditor, *The Ideas of the Woman Suffrage Movement, 1890–1920* (New York: Norton, 1981) for a discussion of historical shifts in the arguments advanced by women's rights activists.

40. See Anthea Callen, *Women Artists of the Arts and Crafts Movement* (New York: Pantheon Books, 1979); and Diana Korzenik, "The Art Education of Working Women 1873–1903," in *Pilgrims and Pioneers,* ed. Alicia Faxon and Sylvia Moore (New York: Midmarch Arts Press, 1987).

41. Cott has emphasized the importance of terminology, particularly the historic change from "woman" to "women" in the twentieth-century women's movement. See Nancy Cott, *The Grounding of Modern Feminism* (New Haven: Yale University Press, 1987).

Herland: Utopic in a Different Voice

Minna Doskow

From earliest times, humanity has longed for a perfect world, one in sharp contrast to whatever its particular surrounding reality happened to be. Such utopian longings are still prevalent, still written about in our literature, and still, as always, un-realized. Expressed in the story of the Garden of Eden or a lost golden age, in classic works such as Plato's *Republic* or More's *Utopia,* in nineteenth-century socialist visions or twentieth-cen-tury behaviorist ones, man's longing for the ideal has been seen through many eyes and taken many shapes. Yet, it has always been man's view; "man" used in the generic sense, of course, but unavoidably expressing the male perspective and carrying with it limitation in the sexual sense as well. Nowhere is this limitation more apparent than in the contrasting vision of Charlotte Perkins Gilman's feminist utopia, *Herland.* The differences in her ap-proach and angle of vision underscore the lacunae in and one-sided development of the utopian literary tradition. These dif-ferences, moreover, correspond closely to what Carol Gilligan describes as a historically female approach to self-definition and moral decision-making in her book, *In a Different Voice.*[1] Gilligan's analysis thus suggests a gender-based rationale underlying Gilman's approach.

Written in 1915 and serialized by Gilman in her magazine, *The Forerunner, Herland* was not published in book form until 1979.[2] It has been, for the most part, ignored by histories of utopian literature.[3] Yet Gilman's book deserves the attention of modern readers. Engrossing, satiric, and cogent, the book, like other literary works in the utopian genre, establishes a standard by which to judge contemporary society.[4] For the present reader, however, it does more than that, because it not only aims its criticism at the position of American women in 1915, it also satirizes our contemporary views and practices. Seen within the context of the Utopian literary corpus, it provides, in addition, a striking contrast in approach and perspective to male-authored utopias.

Most male-authored utopian literature concentrates on political, economic, social, or religious structures as the foundation of the utopian state and assumes that these institutions shape the relationships and feelings of the respective inhabitants. Gilman reverses the procedure. She founds her utopia on a basic human relationship—motherhood—and an emotion—the love that accompanies it, and assumes that these shape appropriate and equitable institutions. Instead of concentrating on *how* the society functions, on particular social structures and their operation, as the male utopian authors do, Gilman focusses on *why* the society functions as it does, because of the motivations, feelings, and relationships of the utopian inhabitants. In this respect, as several critics have pointed out, Gilman sets the pattern for much contemporary feminist utopian science fiction writing.[5] Gilman thus reverses the normal figure and ground of utopian literature. Male authors trust to institutions to shape consciousness in appropriate utopian ways. They hardly mention the interpersonal relationships of the inhabitants or analyze the nature or basis of those relationships. Gilman, on the other hand, directs attention inward to consciousness and assumes its outward reflection in suitable institutions and events. The particular forms that the outward reflections should take are left vague with hardly a passing reference to political, economic, or legal institutions, much less full descriptions.[6]

If we look for political structures in *Herland*, we find that the entire book yields but a single sentence devoted to that topic, and even there the reference is tangential, lodged within a discussion of proper names. We are told that sometimes a woman's name is lengthened to reflect her particular individual merit. "Such as our present Land Mother—what you call president or king, I believe" (75). This passing reference furnishes us with all the political information the novel grants. Even the tantalizing promise: "You shall meet her," (75), is never kept. Nor is she mentioned again. We never learn how she is chosen, what her responsibilities are, what powers she has, or whether she has assistants or auxiliaries.

Although the Land Mother appears to be *Herland*'s philosopher queen, she differs greatly in her role and treatment from Plato's philosopher king in the *Republic*. Plato's figure is the apex and culmination of the entire hierarchical structure of the *Republic*. He is the crux of the vision and the person whom the entire elaborate and fully delineated structure relies upon and leads up to, whose wisdom controls the state and keeps all elements in balance there as the faculty of reason does within the individual soul. All the elements (or classes) of the state (or soul), their nature, characteristic functions, hierarchical relationships, and subordination to the philosopher king are described at length. In contrast, any description of hierarchical structure as a whole, or its particularities in form and content at any level, is completely absent from *Herland*. Instead, there is that single passing reference to a "president or king," an intentional ambiguity between two different types of rulers. So casual is Gilman's interest that she devotes only a single fourteen-word sentence in a 146-page book to political rule, and even then does not distinguish between the two very different types of rulers.

Hierarchies are absent from all spheres of life in *Herland*, not only the political. Instead, a relationship—sisterhood—is substituted. Competition as a motive for action is also absent and replaced by caring or love. "They had had no kings," Gilman tells us, "and no priests, and no aristocracies. They were sisters, and as they grew, they grew together—not by competition, but by united action" (60). An egalitarian basis of existence is substituted for a hierarchical one in all spheres of life, and the organic metaphor of growth merges with it to depict nurture rather than struggle. Gilman is concerned with the relationship of sisterhood, growing out of common descent, that leads in her utopia not to sibling rivalry but to cooperation and "united action." She does not describe how the non-hierarchical society functions, but simply why it does—because of sisterhood—and leaves the picture of the resulting institutions to the reader's own imagination.

If we next examine economics, we find the same lack of attention to structure, hierarchical or otherwise. The reader can gather from indirect references that there is some kind of communal economy in operation, that there are centralized eating facilities, and that the entire population works at various specialized occupations for which they are somehow trained according to their particular abilities. We know that Herland has foresters, educators, carpenters, masons, and part-time priestesses (that is, wise elders who are summoned for consultation and comfort occasionally, but who do some other unnamed work most of the time). But how all this is organized, how houses get built, roads paved, clothing produced, crops raised, what systems of production and distribution are employed, how labor is assigned or carried out remain a mystery for the reader. On this topic, too,

Gilman grants us a passing reference in a single sentence: "I see I have said little about the economics of the place; it should have come before, but I'll go on about the drama now" (99). So much for economics.

Even the little Gilman claims to have said about economics in the first ninety-eight pages of her book is incidental and disconnected. Glimpses of economic institutes or structures emerge from the plot, from what the three male adventurers encounter as they eat their meals, are clothed, housed, educated, and meet the natives. No overarching system is described, however, and no general plan laid out. Only unconnected particularities and individual instances are mentioned. This is in sharp contrast to the systems of production, labor credits, and centralized warehouses for distribution of goods described at length by Edward Bellamy in *Looking Backward.* Or, to cite a pre-industrial vision, it is in equally sharp contrast to Sir Thomas More's description of the economic organization of Utopia, its agriculture, trades, and labor system, as well as its political and social structures. Even B. F. Skinner, whose main concern in *Walden II* is behaviorist conditioning, pays more attention to economics than Gilman. Indeed, it is difficult to think of a male-authored utopia in which the description of economic structures gets as little attention as in *Herland.*

One more example of Gilman's omissions will suffice: the absence of legal and judicial structures. Gilman seems as unconcerned with these systems as she is with political and economic ones. Of course, as Ellador, one of the Herlandian trio of heroines, tells Van, the male social scientist from America, it has been "quite 600 years since we have had what you call a 'criminal' " (82). This situation does make judicial structures a bit less crucial in Herland than in contemporary American society. Yet, there are in Herland instances in which women are deemed unfit to raise children. How and by whom? Gilman never says. Further, there is an actual crime committed during the novel by one of the male interlopers, Terry. He attempts to rape Alima, another of the Herlandian trio, and is tried for his crime. As we are told, "There was a trial before the local Over Mother" (132). The description takes four short paragraphs (less than half a page), although:

> It was a long trial, and many interesting points were brought out as to their views of our [the Americans'] habits, and after a while Terry had his sentence. He waited, grim and defiant. The sentence was: "You must go home!" (133)

Presumably the "Over Mother" pronounced sentence. However, because the text uses the passive voice to describe the action,
the reader merely infers this and does not know for certain. The
use of the passive also suggests that the voice pronouncing sentence is not individualized but speaks for the entire community. It
appears from this incident that Over Mothers act as judges. How
they do so, who appoints them, and what their duties are remain
shrouded in Gilman's silence. All we are told of Over Mothers is
that they are the best and wisest women in the country, who are
rewarded and honored for their abilities not by Supreme Court
appointments but by being allowed to have more than one child.
They are "the nearest approach to an aristocracy" that exists in
Herland, and the closest thing inhabitants can claim to noble
descent.

Again, the contrast with other utopias is striking. We need only
recall, for example, the system of magistrates More creates in his
Utopia, his concern with crime, punishment, and law to become
conscious of Gilman's omission.

What then does Gilman substitute for all of the unmentioned
structures, the missing political, economic, and legal systems? On
what foundation does she build her utopia, if not on formal
systems? On one giant building block, and one only—motherhood, the relationship of mother and child. But for Gilman, a
great deal is implied in this single basic relationship, and these
implications reach out to define and color the entire world of the
novel. As the narrator sees it, "motherhood was the dominant
note of their whole culture" (58). "A motherliness . . . dominated
society, which influenced every art and industry, which absolutely protected all childhood, and gave to it the most perfect care
and training . . ." (73). Or again, as Moadine, one of the wise
elders, explains the concept to the three male adventurers,

> "Motherhood means to us something which I cannot yet discover in
> any of the countries of which you tell us. You have spoken"—she
> turned to Jeff, "of Human Brotherhood as a great idea among you, but
> even that I judge is far from a practical expression?"
>
> Jeff nodded rather sadly. "Very far—" he said.
>
> "Here we have Human Motherhood—in full working use," she
> went on. "Nothing else except the literal sisterhood of our origin, and
> the far higher and deeper union of our social growth.
>
> "The children in this country are the one center and focus of all our
> thoughts. Every step of our advance is always considered in its effect
> on them—on the race. You see, we are Mothers," she repeated, as if in
> that she had said it all. (66)

In Gilman's utopian version "a fully awakened motherhood plans and works without limit, for the good of the child" (102). It is unselfish, loving, and all-encompassing. Basing her characterization on the positive virtues of mother love as she has seen it, Gilman extends these further in *Herland,* washing off the dross of faults and revealing the pure shining ideal of "fully awakened motherhood." This extension reaches even to the image of God herself.

Any selfish, possessive, or restrictive aspects of motherhood are eliminated from this portrait. Only the love, aspirations, care, and nurturing, and the concern and responsibility for children's interests that characterize a mother's love for her particular child are evident, and these are applied to the entire population. Each individual mother, therefore, is interested not only in her biological child, the particular miraculous baby-bundle to whom she gave birth, but also in those of all her countrywomen. Concentrating natural maternal feelings on all children as her own, she plans and works for the good of all. As one commentator explains it, "because they were not confined within the isolation of the private selfish home, women could use their nurturant capacities for social and community service."[7] Communal child-rearing enhances this generalized interest, and a concern for the nation's children becomes the motivating force behind all actions and institutions in Herland. "You see," the reader is told, "children were the raison d'être in this country" (51). The reader is also given good historical reasons for the development of this concern for children. The original formation of Herland was the result of prolonged, devastating wars and natural cataclysms that eliminated the male population. Only the miraculous appearance of parthenogenesis in ancient times enabled the inhabitants to continue their race when all hope seemed to be lost. The first virgin birth was, therefore, the hope of the entire race and the energies and care of the entire population were lavished on mother and child. The allusion to the Christian virgin birth is implicit, of course, as is the contrast in the subsequent histories of the two cultures. Christ's teachings have historically been as much ignored as followed, more distorted in war and enmity than followed in peace and love, whereas the virgin birth in Herland changed everything forever after. Subsequent births in Herland, increasing exponentially by five in each generation, strengthened the inhabitants' hopes and care and assured the continuance of the race. Each time the nation's hopes for survival were pinned on the new generation, and each time the new generation was loved and protected by all. The nation, therefore, developed a co-operative society to nurture and advance the interests of its children, which were identical with national interests. Patriotism, the collective selfishness of a nation,[8] which Gilman claims is largely pride and "has a chip on its shoulder" (94), was replaced by matriotism, the generalized love and unified action of a sisterhood.

Descended from one original mother, the entire population is literally related in sisterhood as well as motherhood, "One family, all descended from one mother!" (57). Although similar in myth to our own Biblical common descent from Adam and Eve, the Herlanders seem to take their common descent more to heart, and, being absolute literalists of the ideal, to act on it accordingly. When, for example, a crisis occurs in which the land is threatened with overpopulation, they all come together and solve their problem by a common decision to limit childbearing rather than compete in a struggle for existence. Here we see sisterhood and united action at work. This decision serves to compound their common interest in all children as the sublimated mother-love strengthens national bonds and common interests: "With this background, with their sublimated mother-love, expressed in terms of widest social activity, every phase of their work was modified by its effect on the national growth" (102).

The extension of motherhood and accompanying sisterhood into social organization has multiple consequences. Connected by bonds of affection and kinship, the inhabitants of Herland develop their peaceful, nonhierarchical and noncompetitive society. To reiterate, "They were sisters, and as they grew they grew together—not by competition but by united action" (60). The organic concept of growth, rather than struggle for survival, is used here, as it is throughout the book. Gilman's organicism runs counter to the social Darwinism popular in her day and articulated earlier by Van, the male social scientist in the novel.[9] Indeed, the incredulity of a skeptical male American adventurer whose capitalistic background makes him unable to envision work or progress without the motivating force of competition is faced head on and answered with the all-purpose relationship of motherhood. "Do you mean," he is challenged, "that with you no mother would work for her children without the stimulus of competition?" (60). Even he is forced to admit the possibility of other motivations. Once admitted as a possibility within the context of family relationships, motherly love in a society that resembles an extended family may then be generalized to encompass national motivation as well.

The extension of the family to the state harkens back to an older morality evident in myth and folklore based on family ties rather than political allegiances. We see this older morality in conflict with and being superseded by the newer one in ancient Greek tragedy. When Agamemnon chooses to sacrifice his own daughter, Iphigenia, to advance political ends and pursue the war in Troy, we see the clear choice made. Or again, in the *Oresteia* when the tribunal is established at the end of the trilogy and the Furies are transformed into the Eumenides, included but subsumed under the *polis,* the shift from family allegiances and blood ties to abstract allegiances, principle, and political ties is completed. Gilman goes back to the earlier tradition, but rather than seeing family allegiances at war with political ones, she extends them to include the political, the exact reverse of Athena's action at the end of the *Oresteia* when she includes the Eumenides within the Athenian state.

In Herland not only politics but religion, too, grows out of the basic relationship of motherhood: "Their great Mother Spirit was to them what their own motherhood was—only magnified beyond human limits" (111). A projection of their own motherhood, their god is an active, in-dwelling spirit of love within each person who works for good and is evident in their love of one another. As Ellador explains, "You see, we recognize in our human motherhood, a great tender limitless uplifting force—patience and wisdom and all subtlety of delicate method. We credit God—our idea of God—with all that and more" (112). They thus recognize no independent and external deity separate from their own indwelling spirit, which gains its necessary outward expression in their actions and institutions. Their religion is thereby woven into the fabric of their entire society, their personal development, and their relationships. Here we see the enactment of "God is motherlove" on a national scale.

Certainly Gilman presents an idealized version of motherhood. But in a utopian work such as hers, this is no problem. Utopian literature is, after all, a workshop for human ideals to be cast in whatever mold most pleases a particular author's imagination. What seems to please Gilman is an idealized love expressed as glorious motherhood and sisterhood. She relies on inner states and relationships to reflect themselves outward in institutions and form the utopian world, rather than the usual utopian mode of relying on various institutions to shape character.

This unusual reversal of figure and ground appears strange to the reader of utopian literature and may even, at first glance, seem misguided or soft-headed. But in dealing with utopian literature, hard-headedness is not a necessary quality, nor one that comes immediately to mind when analyzing the genre. We are still in the land of nowhere, albeit perhaps in a good place as well. With Gilman there has simply been a shift in the foundation of goodness from abstract principles, hierarchies, and formalized structures to feelings and relationships.

This attention to feelings and connections as motivating moral forces shaping decision-making is described as a typically feminine way of defining the self and structuring moral action by Carol Gilligan in her book *In a Different Voice*. Writing sixty-seven years after Gilman's book and concerned with a different subject, Gilligan nevertheless systematically analyzes and describes those qualities forming the basis of Gilman's ideal state and distinguishing her literary utopia from those of her male predecessors or successors in the genre.

Gilligan distinguishes between historically male and female modes of personality development and moral decision-making, noting that masculinity is traditionally defined through separation and individuation while femininity is defined through connection and attachment or relationship.[10] Following Piaget (1932) and Lever (1976), she further characterizes male development as based on abstract principles, rules, and various formal structures and female development as having a "greater orientation toward relationships and interdependence [implying] . . . a more contextual mode of judgment and a different moral understanding."[11] This difference between male individuation and measurement against an abstract ideal and female connection and measurement through activities of care also describes the basic difference in approach between the male-authored utopias I have mentioned and Gilman's *Herland*. It is the difference between the emphasis on abstract systems expressed in formalized political, economic, social, and legal structures, and the emphasis on caring and connection between mother and child, or sister and sister. As a female-created and female-inhabited utopia, *Herland* reflects remarkably closely the principles of the psychology of women described by Gilligan and suggests a gender-based utopian literary distinction that demands further study.

The underlying logic of each gender-based approach is further characterized by Gilligan as follows: "Thus the logic underlying an ethic of care is a psychological logic of relationships, which contrasts with the formal logic of fairness that informs the justice approach."[12] Again, Gilligan's analysis is suggestive in illuminating the contrast between Gilman's and the male-authored utopias mentioned above. Taking as part of any working definition of literary utopias the fact that they are written in an attempt to create a just state, if only on paper, we can recognize the male emphasis on equitable structures as a reflection of the formal logic of fairness, while we recognize Gilman's emphasis on connections as a reflection of the psychological logic of relationships.

If, as Gilligan's studies seem to indicate, the moral imperative for women is by and large the ethic of care, then it is logical that their emphasis will be on connections between self and other, the central operating principle in Gilman's utopia. Because all are descended from the Ur Mother and are related to each other, the connections are structural and inevitable. The ethic of care thus prevails, and the society necessarily produces the appropriate institutions to embody that ethic.

On the other hand, if the moral imperative for men is by and large the ethic of fairness, then it is logical that the emphasis will be on separation, individual rights, codes of abstract principles, and institutions to ensure fairness. Again, this is reflected in the attention to laws and structures that prevail in the male-authored utopias.

A glance at the informing myths of two utopias, Gilman's and Plato's, is illustrative in this context. There is a sharp contrast between the historical-mythic tale of a common ancestor that molds Herlandian society and the myth, or noble lie, of class distinctions in spite of a single earth mother that Plato uses to explain the hierarchical order of his republic. Descent from a single mother stresses connection in Gilman but is overshadowed by distinctive, separate, and hierarchical descent from gold, silver, or iron that stresses individuation in Plato. Each carries the logic of its own truth into the nature of the society that it undergirds. Each illustrates the distinctive vision of its author.

Gilligan notes two recurrent gender-based images—the web and the hierarchy—in the texts of women's and men's responses, thoughts, and fantasies that she analyzes. These images describe the two kinds of utopias I have been discussing as well. The nonhierarchical society of Herland is perpetuated by the interconnected web of relationships among its inhabitants. The utopias of Plato, More, and Bellamy, on the other hand, depend on various hierarchical structures for their establishment and continued existence.

Although Gilligan calls for an androgynous balance between separation and connection in individual development, utopian authors are under no such compulsion to find balance and may be allowed their one-sided imaginative reaching after an ideal. It is, nevertheless, significant that in doing so they are far from haphazard in their choices and reflect the particular gender-specific psychological mode of imagination that Gilligan systematically analyzes.

In the context of utopian literature, therefore, it is crucial to pay particular attention to Gilman's contrasting utopian approach. Rather than criticizing her for certain omissions, we need to seek her out for the different notes she sounds in the chorus of utopian literature and the particular harmony she provides. Recognizing Gilman's divergent approach, the particular key she plays in, we suddenly become aware of its absence elsewhere in the utopian chorus reverberating across the ages. With Gilman, the distaff side is sounded, and we are presented with a utopia that is truly "in different voice."

Notes

1. Carol Gilligan, *In a Different Voice* (Cambridge: Harvard University Press, 1982).

2. Charlotte Perkins Gilman, *Herland* (New York: Pantheon, 1979).

3. See, for example, Lewis Mumford, *The Story of Utopias* (New York: Viking Press, 1962) and Frank E. Manuel and Fritzie P. Manuel, *Utopian Thought in the Western World* (Cambridge: Harvard University Press, 1979).

4. Northrop Frye, "Varieties of Literary Utopias," *Utopias and Utopian thought*, ed. Frank E. Manuel (Boston: Beacon Press, 1967), 31.

5. Several critics have commented on the similarities between Gilman and post-1970 feminist science fiction novels in their common abolition of conventional sex roles and emphasis on changed consciousness and relationships as the basis of a changed civilization—e.g., Lucy M. Freibert, "World Views in Utopian Novels by Women," *Journal of Popular Culture* 17 (1983): 49–60; Patricia Huckle, "Women in Utopia," *The Utopian Vision: Seven Essays on the Quincentennial of Sir Thomas More*, ed. E. D. S. Sullivan (San Diego: San Diego University Press, 1983), 115–36; Lee Cullen Khanna, "Women's Worlds: New Directions in Utopian Fiction," *Alternative Futures* 4.2–3 (1981): 47–60; and Carol Pearson, "Coming Home: Four Feminist Utopias and Patriarchal Experience, in *Future Females: A Critical Anthology*, ed. Marlene S. Barr (Bowling Green: Bowling Green State University Popular Press, 1981), 63–70.

This discussion of whether science fiction, such as these critics discuss, should be classified as utopian writing or reserved as a separate genre is left for another time and place. So is the similar discussion of fantasy in which category Susan Gubar in "*She* and *Herland*: Feminism as Fantasy," in *Coordinates: Placing Science Fiction and Fantasy*, ed. George E. Slusser, Eric S. Rabkin, and Robert Scholes (Cardondale: Southern Illinois University Press, 1983), 139–49, places *Herland* while noting its "utopian strain of feminist rhetoric" (148). For the purposes of this essay, I utilize an enlarged utopian classification that includes all these categories.

6. Even if we place *Herland* within the male satiric rather than utopian

tradition, as Keyser argues (Elizabeth Keyser, "Looking Backward: From *Herland* to *Gulliver's Travels,*" *Studies in American Fiction* 11.1 [Spring 1983]: 31–46), this distinction obtains, differentiating Gilman from Swift as much as from the male utopian tradition. Keyser describes Gilman as doing with the sexes what Swift does with status and perspective. However, we should note that Swift goes into detail describing the various institutions, laws, and governments of Lilliput, Brobdingnag, and so on, while Gilman glosses over such descriptions with little comment.

7. Mary A. Hill, "Charlotte Perkins Gilman: A Feminist's Struggle with Womanhood," *Massachusetts Review* 21.3 (Fall 1980): 523.

8. Leo Strauss, *Thoughts on Machiavelli* (Glencoe, Ill.: Free Press, 1958), 23.

9. Rather than blindly accepting social Darwinism, Gilman questioned the social application of the theory of evolution and eagerly endorsed sociologist Lester Ward's gynecocentric addition to evolutionary theory (Lester Ward, *Dynamic Sociology,* 1883). Ward believed that the female sex was primary and the male secondary, that the main function of the male was to enable the female to reproduce. Gilman said of Ward's ideas, "nothing so important to humanity has been advanced since the Theory of Evolution, and nothing so important to women has ever been given to the world" (quoted in Hill, 524, n. 47).

10. Nancy Chodorow, *The Reproduction of Motherhood: Psychoanalysis and the Sociology of Gender* (Berkeley: University of California Press, 1978), defines these differences in psychoanalytic terms as follows: "From the retention of preoedipal attachments to their mother, growing girls come to define and experience themselves as continuous with others; their experience of self contains more flexible or permeable ego boundaries. Boys come to define themselves as more separate and distinct, with a greater sense of rigid ego boundaries and differentiation. The basic feminine sense of self is connected to the world, the basic masculine sense of self is separate" (169).

11. Gilligan, *In a Different Voice,* 22.

12. Ibid., 73.

Technology and the Female in the *Doctor Who* Series: Companions or Competitors?

Katherine Stannard

The relationship between women and the accomplishments of science and technology has long been marked by ambivalence. Schiebinger reviews the attempts to catalogue the scientific accomplishments of women from the fifteenth to the eighteenth centuries. Although a number of achievements were reported, in the nineteenth century there were still arguments concerning the capability of women to engage in scientific pursuits.[1] The role of women in technology has been examined by McGaw, who observes that women's participation in technology during the last half of this century remains largely unexplored.[2] Schiebinger records some of the efforts to change the conventional "male" approach to the history of science, with proposals that would "reevaluate science in order to appreciate fully women's contributions."[3]

She reports the emphasis of Christine de Pizan, who not only noted the role of women in such fields as law, writing, and numbers, but also cites the importance of what we consider domestic arts: Isis as innovator in gardening and planting, Ceres in food preparation, and Arachne in textile manufacture. The images of the goddess break through into technology.

Rossiter found that conservative vocational guidance "advises women at every level to head for safe, familiar, 'feminine' fields,"[4] an approach implying that there are some careers more suitable to women than to men, and that "feminine" characteristics are a determinant of entry into certain occupations. We will examine some concepts of depth psychology in relation to these aspects of the feminine.

Jung, Hillman, and Archetypal Psychology

Jung distinguished two levels of the unconscious: the personal containing individual memories; and the collective, transpersonal depth containing "the primordial images common to humanity," or "archetypes."[5] An important archetype is that of the anima, the formless pattern of the feminine that lies in the collective unconscious of men.

Lauter and Rupprecht see the need for revising Jung's theory because his ideas became codified among the first generation of his followers.[6] His theory of archetypes, for example, became unchangeable. Lauter argues that the archetype is not "frozen," and we can move beyond the configurations of Jung and his immediate followers to search for new archetypal images of women.[7] Because images in which the formless patterns of the archetypes appear will vary with time and culture, we should expect to find new manifestations of ancient primordial patterns. Such manifestations need not arise only in response to unconscious models in the male psyche but may describe conscious female experience as well.

Jung and the post-Jungians, in their use of mythic gods and goddesses as prototypes for psychology, have given us an alternative lens through which to view our own condition. Hillman proposes a polytheistic view of the human psyche, with archetypal images that seize consciousness realized in the ancient images of gods and goddesses.[8] Certainly the anima, as the unconscious in the male and as the consciousness of the female, has many variations. Hestia, goddess of domesticity, is valued for her ability to focus intently on the present and to turn inward to her own resources. Athena is valued for her clear logic, technical competence, and clever strategies. Artemis is valued for her strength, courage, and loyalty. Bolen points out that women need to look carefully at their own characteristics to see what may be lacking, and to consider what each of the goddesses may offer to complete the personality.[9] When women value themselves for their unique goddess qualities, we can hope for a science that allows unique female expression.

Keller argues for a feminine/erotic approach to science as well as that of the masculine/logos. She sees, not necessarily a difference between the sexes' scientific views, but a dual theme of objectivity and subjectivity. According to Keller, a feminist critique of science can be transformative, bringing "a whole new range of sen-

sitivities, leading to an equally new consciousness of the poten-
tialities lying latent in the scientific project."[10]

In respect to the relationship between women and science,
Hillman stated in 1972, "The image of female inferiority has not
changed, because it remains an image in the masculine psyche."[11]
He further observed that we know next to nothing about how
feminine consciousness regards scientific data, and the very questions science asks have been formed through the specific modern
masculine mind. It is from the perspective of archetypal images of
the goddess that we will examine the relationship of women and
technology and use as our exemplar that unique science fiction
drama, the *Doctor Who* television series.

The Doctor Who Series

Popular culture often provides a mirror for our own psyches. I
have shown elsewhere[12] that *Doctor Who* abounds in archetypal
images and that it may be this perennial mythologic quality that
has been responsible for its twenty-five years on British television
and its immense popularity in the United States. Doctor Who, a
Time-Lord whose mission is to prevent the collapse of cultures
into domination by the evil Master, is the prototype of the hero,
and his female companions, who change with a fair degree of
regularity, represent the Doctor's anima.

The Doctor's companions travel with him through time and
space in an ancient vehicle of uncertain reliability (the TARDIS, or
Time and Relative Dimension in Space machine). They depend on
the Doctor for help and occasionally rescue him. Are these
women only companions, fulfilling the unconscious anima function, or are they also conscious competitors, to some extent
usurping the masculine prerogatives of the Doctor? These women
have appeared to be both, and thus symbolize the general ambivalence in the larger culture concerning women's roles in technology and science.

Images of the Goddesses in the Female Companions

Over the twenty-five years of the *Doctor Who* series, there have
been nineteen females playing companion to seven doctors.[13]
(The Doctor is capable of regenerating into a new individual
twelve times, so in addition to variations in women, there is a
variation in the male role.) Four of the early companions were
children or adolescents, and their roles as young dependents are

not relevant here. However, the remaining fifteen female companions were adults with varying occupations, whose relationship
with the Doctor was that of affectionate friend. All these adult
women may be seen as personifications of the three Greek goddesses who shared the prerogative of chastity: Hestia, Artemis,
and Athena.[14]

We will examine the occupation assigned to the companions by
the decade in which they appeared. From 1963 to 1970 there were
five adult female companions whose respective professions were
public school history teacher, handmaiden during the time of
Troy, space agent, assistant to a computer programmer, and li-
brarian. All but the space agent had roles of service, secondary to
a male, and the agent was portrayed as subordinate in relation to a
Solar Guardian. These traditional and subordinate female roles
suggest the image of Hestia, keeper of the hearth, innovator of
domestic technology, and the focus of the household. Bolen observes that in her focus on the family welfare and her domestic
tasks, Hestia never uses technology to lighten her workload, but
rather to increase the quality of family life. The Hestia woman is a
quiet and unobtrusive person, and is not rewarded by the competitive workplace. She "is likely to be found holding a traditional
woman's job . . . where she is either . . . taken for granted, or
appreciated as a 'jewel' who works steadily and dependably."[15]

During the 1960s, Doctor Who was played first by a somewhat
grumpy and arrogant grandfather type, and second by an inter-
galactic hobo who portrayed the Doctor as a jolly fellow that
attracted the interest of children. In both of these personas the
Doctor maintained a position of superiority over his female traveling companions. There was a general effect of a domestic group,
with the frequent presence of children in the series. In such a
setting in the 1960s, it is not surprising that the companions were
formed in Hestia's image.

From 1970 to 1981, the Doctor was portrayed by two actors: one
with the personality of a dandy encouraging his companions to
use their scientific skills, the other a droll wit with insatiable
curiosity. With the advent of these doctors the first companions
appeared who demonstrated some aspects of the women's movement that in the early 1970s had captured popular attention.[16] It
may well be that the change in character of the Doctor and the
professional upgrading of his companions were related to the
decade's activism.

The five companions of the 1970s included a scientist, an accident-prone assistant trained in espionage, an investigative jour-

nalist, a female Time Lord fresh from the academy, and a stone-age warrior (about whom we will speak later). The first four of this group were represented as persons at least potentially competent to hold their own in the technical activities of the Doctor. Even the assistant was encouraged by the Doctor to develop further scientific ability. In these companions we see images of Athena.

Guiron describes Athena in her pacific aspect as preeminently the working woman.[17] According to Bolen, Athena, goddess of crafts, stands for will and intellect, presides over battle strategy, and forms mentor relationships with strong men who share her own interests. Athena is the prototype of the competitor, and Athena-like women traditionally select conventional male careers.[18] The scientist, journalist, and Time Lord joined in the Doctor's struggles with evil, often taking the initiative and protecting the Doctor. The accident-prone assistant may be seen as a "failed Athena." She had been placed in her position by an influential uncle and struggled valiantly to aid the Doctor. Unfortunately, her special abilities were left unfulfilled.

Stone-age warrior Leela, although sharing some of the attributes of Athena, is more accurately characterized as Artemis, goddess of the hunt. Dressed in a tunic and armed with primitive weapons, she is the image of this goddess. Artemis acted swiftly and decisively to protect and rescue her friends and was quick to punish enemies. However, Guirdon reports that Artemis's "heart was stirred by the hunter Orion,"[19] and Leela left the Doctor to marry a soldier of the Doctor's home planet. According to Bolen, Artemis is "a personification of the independent feminine spirit. The archetype she represents enables a woman to seek her own goals on a terrain of her own choosing."[20]

From this roster we see that, in the 1970s, the companions of Doctor Who were transformed in four of the five instances into potential competitors. As the decade went on, the companion became more the equal of the Doctor. After the cooperative scientist came the journalist, who frequently made her own way; then the warrior, who protected the Doctor even to death; and finally the Doctor's equal, the Time Lord who had graduated with honors, in contrast to the Doctor's more modest academic accomplishments.

We also may view these female figures as anima images of the Doctor. He no longer must represent masculine reason as compared with the feminine eros. The woman is allowed to express her own logic, while the Doctor can afford to express uncertainty and even affection, which was not the case in the previous decade.

As the series moved into the 1980s, we see some intriguing developments. In 1981 the regenerated Doctor was extremely youthful and often quite helpless, requiring the assistance of his companions to survive. There were two major female companions of the Doctor from 1981 to 1983. The first was the daughter of a noble family and a competent scientist and mathematician, continuing the Athena tradition of the 1970s. The second, an Australian flight attendant, was an unwilling member of the crew, having stumbled into the TARDIS by accident. Her role was that of critic and complainer, contributing little to the solution of problems faced in the adventures. It seems appropriate to view this companion as a displaced Hestia. Her vocation had been to provide for the well-being of others dependent on her ministrations. As a companion she was surrounded by clever and independent people who made her appear even more inadequate. Psychologically, this demonstrates the unfortunate consequences of being forced into a role for which one is temperamentally unsuited. The reappearance of Hestia also suggests a return in this television series to an ambivalent position concerning women and their technological competence.

The ambivalence is confirmed by the appearance of another companion, a student on holiday, whose main function appeared to be that of a woman in need of rescue by a strong man. That man was the most gentle of the Doctors in the initial episodes, but he was replaced by the sixth incarnation of the Doctor in 1985, an irascible and short-tempered personality who has little sympathy for the incompetence of his companion. It appeared that there had been a completed circle. Once again the companion was just that; there was no sign of competition in technological know-how, and the Doctor was again the dominant figure. It is probably no accident that the student companion was followed by a young lady whose most pressing concerns seemed to be to convince the Doctor to follow an appropriate diet and to engage in aerobic exercise.

Public television in the northeastern United States has recently acquired the episodes of the seventh regeneration of the Doctor. In this last regeneration the Doctor's irascibility has been replaced with remarkable gentleness and a tendency to mix metaphors. It is uncertain if the change in the Doctor's personality is the result of social factors, ratings issues, or availability of the actor. However, this change forced his aerobic Hestia companion to become more assertive; unfortunately her major talent has been the ability to shriek for help when confronted with threat. In any case, it was clear in the first episodes of the new combination of Doctor and companion that the addition of some tough-mindedness would be necessary for the story lines to develop in their usual danger-and-rescue pattern.

In the last episode shown in New England in fall 1988, the screaming companion left the Doctor to share in the establish-ment of a new colony with a brawny conman-cum-hero. She was replaced by a sixteen-year-old refugee from a regressed tech-nological society with the suggestive name of "Ace." No screamer she, but a technically competent companion who literally blasts her way to safety with her own dynamite. In addition young Ace appears to enjoy human companionship with none of the suspi-cions of the former Artemis-type companion nor the aggressive competition of Athena. The reasoning behind this change of pace at the beginning of the twenty-fifth year of the series is not clear. The implications seem to suggest that the Doctor can be comfort-able with his anima; his gentle feminine attributes seem at peace in his male body. And reciprocally, although Ace has appeared only briefly, it appears that she may combine the courage of an adolescent Artemis, the warmth of Hestia, and the technological know-how of Athena.

Recognizing the variety of expressions found in the goddess-images in one bit of science fiction, we may hazard a suggestion that this popular art may indicate something of the nature of future society. A feminist science may well be marked by many new possibilities embodied in the attributes of the three goddess images described. These, when joined to conventional mas-culinized science, should help reduce the ambivalent roles of women in science and produce a richer and more integrated field of inquiry. At the end of a quarter century of sex-role ambivalence in the *Doctor Who* series, we may at last be seeing two androgynes who share a common and cooperative mission. Stay tuned.

Notes

1. Londa Schiebinger, "The History and Philosophy of Women in Science: A Review Essay," in *Sex and Scientific Inquiry,* ed. Sandra Harding and Jean F. O'Barr (Chicago: University of Chicago Press, 1987), 7–34.

2. Judith A. McGaw, "Women and the History of American Technology," in *Sex and Scientific Inquiry,* 47–78.

3. Schiebinger, "History and Philosophy," 17.

4. Margaret W. Rossiter, "Sexual Segregation in the Sciences: Some Data and a Model," in *Sex and Scientific Inquiry*, 40.

5. C. G. Jung, *Two Essays on Analytical Psychology* (Princeton: Princeton University Press/Bollingen, 1972), 65.

6. Estella Lauter and Carol S. Rupprecht, *Feminist Archetypal Theory: Interdisciplinary Re-Visions of Jungian Thought* (Knoxville: University of Tennessee Press, 1985), 5.

7. Estella Lauter, "Visual Images By Women: A Test Case for the Theory of Archetypes," in *Feminist Archetypal Theory: Interdisciplinary Re-Visions of Jungian Thought*, ed. Estella Lauter and Carol S. Rupprecht, 46–92.

8. James Hillman, *Revisioning Psychology* (New York: Harper, 1975), 26–27.

9. Jean S. Bolen, *Goddesses in Everywoman: A New Psychology of Women* (New York: Harper, 1984), 276–77.

10. Evelyn F. Keller, "Feminism and Science," in *Sex and Scientific Inquiry*, 233–46.

11. James Hillman, *The Myth of Analysis: Three Essays in Archetypal Psychology*, (New York: Harper, 1972), 249.

12. Katherine Stannard, "Archetypal Images in a Contemporary Television Series: The Mythology of Doctor Who," *The Humanistic Psychologist* 16, no. 2 (1988): 361–67.

13. Peter Haining, *Doctor Who: A Celebration / Two Decades Through Time and Space* (London: W. H. Allen, 1983); Peter Haining, *Doctor Who: The Key to Time* (London: W. H. Allen, 1984); Peter Haining, *Doctor Who: The Doctor Who File* (London: W. H. Allen, 1986); Lesley Standring, *The Doctor Who Illustrated A–Z*. (London: W. H. Allen, 1985).

14. F. Guirand, "Greek Mythology," in *New Larousse Encyclopedia of Mythology*, new ed. (New York: Crescent Books, 1968), 85–198.

15. Bolen, *Goddesses*, 121.

16. M. P. Burke, *Reaching for Justice: The Women's Movement* (Washington, D.C.: Center for Concern, 1980), 37.

17. Guirand, "Greek Mythology," 107.

18. Bolen, *Goddesses*, 87–89.

19. Guirand, "Greek Mythology," 121.

20. Bolen, *Goddesses*, 49.

The Actress as Social Activist: The Case of Lena Ashwell

Claire Hirshfield

In 1889 London's Royal Academy of Music played host to Ellen
Terry, who had consented to judge the annual elocution contest and to present a medal to the outstanding student. The award
that day went to a young girl who recited a speech from *Richard II*.
"She was a queer-looking child, handsome, with a face suggesting
all manner of possibilities," Terry wrote, struck by an unusual
quality in the girl who "flung away the book and began to act, in
an undisciplined way, of course, but with such true emotion, such
intensity that the tears came to my eyes." Reflecting on the girl's
performance, Terry confided to her diary later that day: "She has
to work. Her life must be given to it, and then she will . . . achieve
just as high as she works."[1]

Terry's words were prophetic, for the young medalist would
become one of England's most accomplished actresses, Lena Ashwell. Interestingly, the intuitive Terry had glimpsed not only a
unique acting talent but a keen intelligence as well: "A pathetic
face, a passionate voice, a *brain*," Terry wrote.[2] That cerebral
quality distinguished Ashwell as an actress and a public personality who chose to involve herself in social and political issues
ranging from worker relief to votes for women.

The politically active or socially committed actress has become
in recent years a familiar icon: today actresses routinely lend
support to candidates for political office, participate in anti-nu-
clear marches, and travel to Third World capitals to promote a
political agenda. In the twentieth century's first decade, however,
it required substantial courage to break the mold of "china tea
cup"[3] and to identify with such unpopular causes as women's
suffrage or the rights of exploited workers. Lena Ashwell, more
conspicuously than any other star of the Edwardian stage, chose
to risk her popularity by sharing platforms with Labour Party
organizers[4] and by endorsing publicly the tactics of militant suf-

fragettes,[5] personifying the "actress-as-activist" model which her spiritual descendants today emulate, wittingly or not.

Ashwell, whose family name was Pocock, grew up in Canada, the daughter of a retired naval officer of limited financial means. Captain Pocock was determined that his daughters should be able to earn an independent livelihood; Lena, he planned, would attend the University of Toronto to prepare for a teaching career. However, following his wife's sudden death, he was forced to move his family to England, where two maternal aunts stood ready to offer financial support.[6]

In London Lena's musical abilities won her admission to the Royal Academy of Music, an institution numbering among its graduates Marie Tempest, Julia Neilson, and Henry Wood. During her second year at the Academy, Lena gave up her musical studies to concentrate upon drama, despite the fact that a tactless teacher had pronounced her too plain to succeed on the stage.[7] Winning the Academy's elocution medal began Lena Pocock's affection for Ellen Terry. Terry put in a good word with producer George Alexander for the raw young actress who adopted the more euphonic stage name of Ashwell,[8] and he hired Ashwell in 1891 for a series of brief walk-ons. After spending several years learning her craft in various touring companies, she was ready to move on.[9]

In 1895 Ashwell was engaged by Henry Irving, actor-manager, for a season at the Lyceum. As Elaine in Comyn Carr's *King Arthur*, she shared the stage with Irving and Ellen Terry. Although she impressed the influential critic, Clement Scott,[10] George Bernard Shaw was skeptical of her talent, describing her as "weak, timid, and subordinate with an insignificant presence and a voice which, contrasted as it was with Miss Terry's, could only be described . . . as a squall."[11] When she reappeared at the Lyceum in 1896, however, playing the Prince of Wales to Irving's Richard III, even Shaw was won over: "She now returns to the Lyceum stage as an actress of mark . . . who is very much her own mistress and treats the boards with no little authority and assurance as one of the younger generation knocking vigorously at the door."[12]

Ashwell followed her triumph in *Richard III* with a series of successes culminating in 1900 with the title role in Henry Arthur Jones's *Mrs. Dane's Defense*. "Lena Ashwell established her right to be classed among the greatest emotional actresses of the day," the stage historian H. B. Baker wrote of her portrayal of Jones's errant heroine.[13] With a theater filled to overflowing each night and

Edward VII and the Prince of Wales in attendance on several occasions, Ashwell had won her place in the front rank of Edwardian actresses at age twenty-nine: "I was a success; I had got there. I was no longer one of the supports in a play but a star."[14]

Next, she appeared as the peasant girl Katusha in Beerbohm Tree's adaptation of Tolstoy's novel *Resurrection*. Ashwell's characteristic style and on-stage persona were well suited to the role of Katusha, whose innocent involvement in a murder and subsequent degradation precede her inevitable redemption in a hospital prison ward and eventual apotheosis as a living saint in Siberia. Ashwell later confessed that she had been powerfully affected by the Tolstoyan theme of resurrection and touched by the revelation that "the weak . . . may be helped to recover from the misery inflicted on them."[15]

There soon followed another success in *Leah Kleschna*, a play written specifically for Ashwell. Again she portrayed a Russian peasant, this one forced into criminality in order to survive. Inevitably typecast as a victimized heroine, Ashwell conveyed in her performances ways in which unconscionable social and economic pressures damaged women, even as they brutalized men. It was the kind of role with which Ashwell became increasingly identified, one "no other actress could play . . . with such thrilling and convincing intensity."[16] In 1904 she added yet another tormented heroine to her list. In Claude Askew's and Edward Knoblock's *The Shulamite* she played the repressed wife of a stern, harsh Boer farmer, torn between her marital obligations and her love for a young Englishman. Produced soon after the Boer War's end, when popular attention was focused upon South Africa, the play became the focus of widespread interest and discussion both in England and in the United States.[17] With *The Shulamite* Ashwell reached her career's peak, one of a handful of actresses so strongly identified with a type of heroine that authors developed parts with them in mind. She was beginning, however, to reach for new challenges. *The Shulamite* was the first play she helped to produce; like a few other female performers, she was beginning to seek for herself a wider sphere in a theater dominated almost exclusively by men.

Ashwell rose to prominence when the "theatre of ideas" was beginning to stir. In 1891 Jacob T. Grein had established the Independent Theatre and soon presented London audiences with plays such as Ibsen's *Ghosts* and Shaw's *Widowers' Houses*. In 1899 the newly established Stage Society offered alternatives to late Victorian melodramas, musical comedies, and drawing room frivolities. Five years later Harley Granville-Barker and J. E. Vedrenne at the Court Theatre presented experimental dramas with controversial themes by such relative unknowns as Shaw, Lawrence, Housman, and John Galsworthy.[18]

To be sure, popular dramatists continued to depict the manners and modes of fashionable London society. Often these drawing-room staples perpetuated submissive or frivolous images of femininity increasingly distasteful to many actresses, who found themselves reinforcing on stage conceptions they had come to regard as demeaning. Already a number of actresses who had performed in Ibsen's plays beginning with the 1889 London production of *A Doll's House* had been converted to feminism as a result—among them Janet Achurch, Florence Farr, Marian Lea, and Elizabeth Robins.[19] Robins, an American-born actress, wrote that her appearances in *A Doll's House* and *Hedda Gabler* had awakened her to the unfair conditions under which women in the theater had to work: "The stage career of an actress was inextricably involved in the fact that she was a woman, and those who were masters of the theatre were men."[20] Robins was a singularly gifted woman who went on to a multifaceted career as actress-manager,[21] playwright, and suffragette. Other actresses, too, were beginning to reject their subordination to the male power elite that controlled the Edwardian theater. Lillah McCarthy, for example, credited her role as Ann Whitefield in Shaw's *Man and Superman* with liberating her from the conventional stereotype of "teacup and saucer" drama and with awakening her feminist conscience: "Women . . . have told me that Ann brought them to life and that they remodeled themselves upon Ann's pattern. . . . She was insistent when she should have been submissive. She had a will of her own. . . . The Court was to become the scene of women's emancipation: a double emancipation, for Ann set the leading lady—and with her all the ladies of the theatre—free,—and she set the world of women free."[22]

Shaw himself was struck by the emerging phenomenon of the actress in rebellion. "The horrible artificiality of that impudent sham, the Victorian womanly woman, a sham manufactured by men for men," he wrote, "had become more and more irksome to the best of actresses who had to lend their bodies and souls to it— and by the best of actresses I mean those who had awakeningly truthful minds as well as engaging personalities."[23] Like Robins and McCarthy, Lena Ashwell was among Shaw's "handful of actresses . . . who had amazingly truthful minds." Although she avoided the "bit of fluff" roles that enraged McCarthy, she was profoundly affected by the outcasts and victims she portrayed. Entering into the soul of a Leah Kleschna or Tolstoy's Katusha had convinced her that the "unfortunates of social life" were in need of compassion and redemption. The empathy uniting her with the weak and abused women she played on stage may well have stemmed from a misery she was enduring in her own private life during these years. During the run of *King Arthur* at the Lyceum, a young doctor had given her a nasal spray containing cocaine, leading to an addiction "which very nearly ruined my life."[24] Soon after, she met and married a fellow actor, an alcoholic who abused her mentally and physically before a painful separation and divorce.[25]

Ashwell, however, survived largely because of her strong commitment to work. Crucial to her evolution as a social activist was her friendship with Shaw, who introduced her to Fabian circles and helped to establish her future directions. "The great problem" she wrote in her memoirs, "then as now was to discover in what way the wealth of the nation could be so distributed that there should no longer be extremes of riches and poverty; and above all that those whose hours of work were longer and duller than those of the better-to-do should have an interesting leisure as well as a daily wage."[26]

An opportunity to implement these beliefs soon presented itself. In 1908 Lena Ashwell became one of a handful of women who attempted the management of a co-operative stage company. With a private subsidy she was able to secure a lease on the Kingsway Theatre and to assemble a company to produce new plays by unknown authors. "Full of the ideals of democracy as promulgated by the red-haired, red-bearded Irish enthusiast, George Bernard Shaw, I could sweep the profession clean of all artificial standards of value, all inhibiting control by the aristocracy of the profession," she wrote. "Room must be made for the unknown author, for experiments with new lighting, for new ideas of scenery."[27]

Despite critical successes, the Kingsway experiment quickly became a financial disaster; the subsidy was withdrawn by the project's benefactress who was annoyed by Ashwell's engagement to Dr. Henry Simpson.[28] Ashwell exhausted her savings on the venture and was forced into unattractive stage roles in order to meet her obligations to the Kingsway's lessor. The financial debacle notwithstanding, Ashwell had attained eminence as actress-manager and had enhanced her influence in the profession. Thus, when a Joint Select Committee of Lords and Commons was established in 1908 to "inquire into the censorship of stage plays" after a series of controversial bannings, Ashwell was the single female witness called to testify among a group that included Shaw, Granville-Barker, J. M. Barrie, Sir Herbert Tree, Arthur Wing Pinero, George Edwardes, John Galsworthy, and Gilbert Murray.[29]

Ashwell had suffered from official censorship on several occasions, and she was convinced that the "interference . . . was often ridiculous."[30] But the paramount issue engaging Shaw's "best of actresses" was female enfranchisement. Elizabeth Robins's pioneering play at the Court Theatre, *Votes for Women*, had demonstrated in 1907 the services the theater could render to the struggle for female equality. Although Robins had designated *Votes for Women* a "dramatic tract in three acts," suffragist cheers punctuating each performance affirmed theater's power to raise a collective consciousness in an audience.[31] Nor was Ashwell slow to follow Robins's lead. Her second offering at the Kingsway in 1908 was Cicely Hamilton's *Diana of Dobsons*. Hamilton, an actress turned playwright, had been unable to secure a production of a full-length play until Ashwell took over the Kingsway. Although *Diana of Dobsons* was not a propaganda play in the style of *Votes for Women*, it convincingly laid bare the double standard women suffered in Edwardian England.[32] Although it manipulated audiences shamelessly, *Diana of Dobsons* was a financial and critical success, heartening those eager to demonstrate that actresses possessed unique abilities to promote and humanize a political cause.

In December 1908 the Actresses' Franchise League (AFL) was launched with the threefold purpose of educating the theatrical profession about female enfranchisement, of taking part in parades and demonstrations, and of making the services of its members available to other suffrage societies for fundraising or propaganda purposes through staging of plays and entertainments. The initial call for suffragist actresses was issued by two performers—Sime Seruya and Winifred Mayo—who had strong associations with the militant Women's Social and Political Union (WSPU). Seeking to attract to the League actresses whose popularity would provide maximum publicity, they prudently played down their militant connections, designating the AFL as "strictly neutral in regard to Suffrage tactics." Minimizing internal differences, the League could entertain at meetings of radical groups such as the WSPU and the Woman's Freedom League (WFL), and moderates such as the National Union of Women's Suffrage Societies (NUWSS) who defined themselves as "constitutional" and used the classic methods of persuasion and lobbying.[33]

Although actual control was vested in a small Executive Committee, Mayo and Seruya enlisted as League vice-presidents a number of famous actresses, among them Ashwell, Irene and Violet Vanbrugh, Lillah McCarthy, Julie Opp Faversham, Lily Langtry, and Eva and Decima Moore.[34] For many the title was largely honorary. But a few including Ashwell took their duties seriously and were active as League spokespersons. Ashwell notes in her memoirs that feminism represented for her an almost automatic response to her dissatisfaction with the male-dominated theater:

> It is impossible to realise now the scorn which women who thought that they should be recognised as citizens drew upon themselves from otherwise quite polite and sensible people. Managers, authors, pressmen became quite passionate in their resentment and [women] wise in their generation, did not associate themselves with this unpopular movement. Once when I went to see Tree, I had in my hand a book called "The Soul of a Suffragette." Tree picked it up and with a magnificent gesture of contempt flung it into the far corner of the room.[35]

The League offered Ashwell an attractive outlet, and she threw herself almost immediately into its activities. In spring 1909, for example, she arranged a production of Cicely Hamilton's sketch *How the Vote Was Won* at the WFL's Green, White, and Gold Fair.[36] She also represented the League at rallies and parades, where elegant and popular actresses helped to defuse the habitual hostility of the public toward suffrage marchers. On 17 June 1911 forty thousand women marched from the Embankment to Albert Hall to demonstrate support of a newly introduced Commons bill. The AFL contingent, including Lillah McCarthy, Eva and Decima Moore, and Olive Terry paraded in white dresses and carried tall staffs adorned with Dorothy Perkins roses. Ashwell cut short rehearsal for a new play and joined the parade before she was able to change her black dress.[37] The press made much of the "charming little company" of smartly gowned actresses and noted that they were "loudly cheered on their way, as the crowd recognised one after another footlight favorite."[38] Ashwell's recollections were distinctly more somber: "In the windows of the clubs and along the crowded streets were curious and contemptuous people. Well-dressed men with ridicule in their eyes and the smile of superiority on their sneering lips stared as we passed along."[39]

Nor was Ashwell's involvement in the suffrage campaign limited to parades: in late spring 1911 a delegation of suffragists called upon the Prime Minister, H. H. Asquith, to lobby in behalf of the compromise Conciliation Bill enfranchising women householders. Although the Bill enjoyed bipartisan sponsorship and support in Commons, Asquith and his Chancellor of the Exchequer, David Lloyd George, were suspicious of a measure that might enfranchise more Conservative than Liberal women. The delegation was broadly based and included militants such as Charlotte Despard, WFL leader, and Millicent Fawcett, head of the more moderate NUWSS. The AFL's delegates included Ashwell, Maud Arncliffe-Sennett, Winifred Mayo, and Eva Moore. "We were just a very little ordinary group of women," Ashwell wrote, "received by the flunkeys as if we had a strange odour and had been temporarily released from the zoo."[40]

Asquith listened politely to the women's arguments but was resolute in his opposition to the Conciliation Bill. Although he promised the delegates that he would try to "give you something better" at a future session of Parliament, Ashwell, who observed Asquith closely throughout the meeting, was skeptical: "His expression made me think of that iron curtain which descends in the theatre to ensure that the stage is completely shut off from the audience," she noted. He had "made up his mind" on the suffrage question, and temporize though he might for political purposes, he would never willingly yield.[41]

This insight did not discourage her from appealing directly to the Liberal Cabinet. Ashwell's financial problems as actress-manager of the Kingsway had given her experience of the discriminatory aspects of the Married Women's Property Tax. Because her husband had become acquainted with Lloyd George on the golf course, she was able to secure a personal hearing. With five other protesters she called upon Lloyd George to urge revision of the law: "I was the sole proprietor and licensee of the Kingsway Theatre; I engaged the company, the staff, the manager, the solicitor, and the chartered accountants. When the income tax returns were filled in by my accountants, with the help of my solicitor and business manager, I disappeared utterly from view because the paper had to be signed as correct in every detail by my husband who knew nothing about the theater or the work of the stage."[42] Again, as in their earlier encounter, Lloyd George was affable but unresponsive. The taxes collected under the terms of the Married Women's Property Act were needed by the government, he explained in somewhat patronizing fashion, and tinkering with the law was therefore inappropriate.[43]

The frustrations engendered by such encounters explain Ashwell's growing sympathies for the WSPU, despite the militants' potentially dangerous course. Attacks on property by WSPU members became more violent after the defeat of the Conciliation Bills. Wide-scale window smashing was a favorite technique, and arson became a regular weapon in 1913, as mail boxes, railway stations, timber yards, and even churches were set ablaze. Works of art including Velasquez's *Rokeby Venus* in the National Gallery were slashed, and golf courses were routinely damaged. Hunger and thirst strikes were countered by prison forced feedings of the militants.[44] Although these tactics did not sway the Cabinet, they outraged the public, and it became increasingly risky for well-known personalities such as actresses to identify themselves with the militants.

Although many women's organizations were divided over support for the militants, the AFL was virtually destroyed by the controversy. Initially the League had pledged neutrality "in regard to Suffrage tactics," a policy that had led to steady growth and a healthy treasury.[45] By 1913, however, it was impossible to avoid taking sides, especially after an April police raid on WSPU offices yielded evidence of a well-organized conspiracy to destroy public property and inflict bodily harm on political leaders.[46] A few days after the raid the League held a rally at Drury Lane Theatre to enlist support for the Dickinson Bill, which a private Member had introduced in Commons. The speakers, representing a broad cross-section of the suffrage movement, initially attempted to focus the crowd's attention on ends rather than means, emphasizing the need for women "to march side by side with men . . . unhandicapped by laws" as well as the obligations of well-to-do celebrities to less fortunate women.[47]

This was a theme close to Ashwell's heart. She had in the months before the rally increasingly participated at meetings in Workman's Hall, where exploitation of female labor had been protested by union leaders such as George Lansbury.[48] In an impassioned speech at Drury Lane, she denounced employers guilty of overworking and underpaying women workers, demanding greater solidarity between middle-class suffragists and their economically exploited sisters.[49]

Militancy could not be avoided, however, especially after fiery Maud Arncliffe-Sennett declared from the rostrum that "she dared not defend the militants but with Heaven's help she would never repudiate them." Immediately, there was a rejoinder from moderate Irene Vanbrugh, a prominent stage star: "She had no sympathy with militant methods and with the terrible disorder that they had brought about. There was a deplorable state of disorder. Disorder caused by the action of the militants."[50] Vanbrugh records in her memoirs that she was shattered not only by the storm provoked in the audience but by Lena Ashwell's rejoinder that it was not possible for any feminist organization in 1913 to disassociate itself from those women who had put themselves at risk in England's prisons. Ashwell was not alone in her defense of the radicals, but her words were the signal for the "constitutionalists" to march off the stage in high dudgeon and shortly after to tender their resignations from the AFL.[51]

Although courageous for a major star such as Ashwell to defend publicly the WSPU's unpopular methods, it was politically unwise, especially since the resulting controversy destroyed the League's effectiveness. Moreover, as the militants accelerated their campaign in late 1913, like other defenders, Lena Ashwell began to withdraw support while remaining committed to the cause of women's rights. In February 1914 together with Lillah McCarthy, Nina Boucicault, and Ellen Terry, Ashwell joined a public protest against forced feeding, calling upon the Government to withdraw its infamous "Cat and Mouse Act." Significantly, the sponsor of the petition, Lady Maud Parry of the NUWSS, designated the petition a "constitutional" attempt to end "the deplorable conditions that prevail."[52] In April she made a personal appearance along with Ellen Terry, Lydia Yavroska, and Irene Vanbrugh at the Women's Kingdom exhibition at the Olympia, under the aegis of the NUWSS.[53] Notwithstanding such ongoing efforts, most would have agreed with Winifred Mayo, the League's executive secretary, who in late spring 1914 declared that "everyone is dead or asleep."[54]

That sleep was to be shattered in August 1914 with Britain's entrance into World War I. In a matter of days Ashwell and the Moore sisters, acting as AFL representatives, met with members of other feminist organizations to establish the Women's Emergency Corps.[55] There followed six months of efforts to persuade the government that entertainers had much to contribute. "One never-to-be forgotten day, when I had quite lost hope of the drama and music of the country being regarded as anything but useless," Ashwell later wrote, "Lady Rodney called on behalf of the YMCA . . . to ask if it was possible for a concert party to go to Havre."[56]

This call inaugurated for Ashwell a period of frenetic activity into which she threw the energy previously reserved for the suffrage campaign. At first the YMCA was tentative in its new association with theatrical people—"the Nonconformist Conscience suddenly confronted with the scarlet Woman."[57] However, British armies needed recreation, especially as the war ground on and shell shock victims proliferated. This need grew desperate enough to allay the YMCA's fears of "peroxide hair and flamboyant manners."[58] Ashwell took the lead in recruiting actors, musicians, and singers and in raising funds in London to sustain the entire enterprise. Thousands of concerts and shows were performed for troops in hospitals and in camps scattered throughout Britain and the continent. Writers, including such veterans of the suffrage campaign as Cicely Hamilton and Gertrude Jennings, were recruited by Ashwell to turn out scripts for the entertainers.

Ashwell, although burdened with enormous administrative responsibilities, was eager to perform for men in the field. By mid-March 1915 she was in the Harfleur Valley entertaining troops in huts and tents and traveling the hospital circuit, diverting the wounded with her recitations of Elizabethan love lyrics. By the war's end "Lena Ashwell Parties," as these traveling performing troupes were known, were appearing in Malta, Egypt, and Palestine—wherever British troops were found. Ashwell alternated between fundraising matinees at the Kingsway in London and performing near the front in France. On more than one occasion her recitation was punctuated by German shells dropped from airplanes circling overhead. "At Acheux, a mile and a half from the Line," she wrote, "the concussion of the guns was so great that one could not hear oneself speak."[59] She was in France when the Armistice came, and she has left an unforgettable description of the ruins which the great guns left in their wake:

> My last journey from Lille, through Armentieres, Bailleul, Locre, Dickiebusch, Ypres, Fuenes, Nieueport, La Panne, Pervyse filled me with indescribable nausea. The blackened, tortured fields, the horrible stagnant water, the poisoned earth, the ghastly remains of tortured trees, the skeletons of houses, the disused factories, the silence haunted with black fear—even Dante in his Inferno did not draw a picture of desolate misery equal to this.[60]

The year 1918 brought with it not only the Armistice but long-sought legislation enfranchising women over thirty. The victory was, however, accompanied by apparent exhaustion of that social conscience that had so strongly typified the actress of the pre-war era. There were no attempts to revive the AFL, as women disappeared again from the workplace and feminism itself appeared to be in retreat. To be sure, a campaign for equal citizenship was launched that resulted a decade later in better pensions for widows and improved maternity services for pregnant women. However, the Labour movement was chiefly responsible for these reforms rather than any revival of women's organizations.[61]

Although activism had waned among performers, there were a few exceptions. Maud Arncliffe-Sennett devoted herself to the anti-vivisection campaign almost to the day of her death. Lena Ashwell's urge to do good also remained alive; the habit of seeking a large cause in which to submerge herself had become an integral part of her character. Fortuitously, her wartime experience pointed the way to the future. Ashwell notes in her memoirs that she was continually amazed by the good taste and sensitivity of her soldier audiences as she toured camps and hospitals: "What they asked for was not current Jazz or rag-time . . . but the finest music and Shakespeare plays." She herself had recited Elizabethan sonnets and speeches from Shakespeare and had been "very much astonished at the deep interest and very real response the men made."[62]

When the war ended, Ashwell's work in organizing the "Concerts at the Front" parties was recognized by the award of the Order of the British Empire. She was fifty and the wife of a prominent physician. A graceful retirement might well have beckoned. However, she was convinced that what had been accomplished in war might be continued in peace by "introducing good drama and music to the home population."[63] Thus, when a group of Labour Party mayors approached her to organize a series of performances in town halls throughout the various boroughs of Greater London, she sensed an opportunity at hand. Assembling a troupe of actors drawn largely from the ranks of the "Concerts at the Front" organization, Ashwell embarked upon an ambitious plan to bring the works of Barrie, Galsworthy, Shaw, Wilde, Pinero, Ibsen, Chekhov, Maeterlinck, Masefield, and Cicely Hamilton to the London boroughs at prices even the working poor could afford.[64] For ten years the Lena Ashwell Players performed a different play weekly in another part of London each night, from Battersea to Shoreditch and from Lewisham to Wandsworth. There were no dressing rooms, and frequently they performed without scenery or proper lighting. Community volunteers known as Friends of the Players seated the audience, distributed the programs, and conducted post-performance discussions of the more than two hundred and fifty plays Ashwell produced in ten years of touring working-class London.[65]

In the end, financial losses that nearly bankrupted Ashwell and her husband brought an end to the enterprise. However, the failed experiment convinced Ashwell of the "moral need" for a government-subsidized National Theatre "where the very best plays, the very best music, and the very best films" could be offered to assuage the "desperate hunger and thirst" of industrial workers and to break down class barriers.[66] Interestingly, she couched her advocacy of a National Theatre in idealistic terms reminiscent of the Fabian commitment of her youth. Idealism for Ashwell was an enduring faith and activism on behalf of worthy causes a life-long imperative, whether an end to censorship in the theater, the enfranchisement of women, or the establishment of a theater for the masses.

Although Lena Ashwell's acting career ended in 1926, she lived well into the age of Hitler, Mussolini, and Stalin. "It is an age of Producer-Directors," she wrote in 1936. "Stalin in Moscow, Mussolini in Rome, Hitler in Berlin conducting a mass-mind and using such instruments as death or ruin as penalties for independent thought or individual action."[67] Ashwell was destined to live through World War II and to see women once again on factory production lines, returning to a work force desperately in need of their services. Eventually the independent career-oriented heroine would reappear on the stage and in films. There again would come a time when the privileged few who enjoyed the prominence and independence associated with success in the performing arts would seek greater self-realization by lending themselves to ideological or reformist causes.

In so doing, they would reprise a historic role, one pioneered by an earlier generation of actresses for whom the wealth, social mobility, and personal autonomy provided by a successful theatrical career had not been enough. For Shaw's "best of actresses" self-fulfillment inevitably encompassed a need to escape the inbred theatrical world and the isolation of their profession. Lena Ashwell, Eva Moore, Elizabeth Robins, Lillah McCarthy, and others sought an identity not simply as actresses but as human beings participating on equal terms in the social and political life of Edwardian and Georgian England. In the end they demonstrated that the advantages conferred by celebrity can be used not only to achieve women's rights but in the service of an array of causes, some of which their spiritual descendants in the West End, Hollywood, and Broadway continue to champion today.

Notes

1. Ellen Terry, *The Story of My Life* (New York: McClure, 1908), 268–69.
2. Ibid.
3. John C. Trewin, *The Theatre Since 1900* (London: A. Dakers, 1951), 38–39.

4. *Votes for Women*, 21 July 1911.

5. *Morning Post*, 3 May 1913.

6. Lena Ashwell, *Myself A Player* (London: Michael Joseph, 1936), 23–48.

7. Ibid., 52.

8. Terry, *Story*, 269.

9. Ashwell, *Myself a Player*, 57–60.

10. Clement Scott, *The Drama of Yesterday and Today*, vol. 2 (London: Macmillan, 1899), 347.

11. Ashwell, *Myself a Player*, 83–84.

12. Ibid.

13. H. Barton Baker, *History of the London Stage and Its Famous Players* (London: G. Routledge, 1904), 510.

14. Ashwell, *Myself a Player*, 118.

15. Ibid., 122.

16. Ibid., 136–37. For Ashwell's stage technique, see Albert E. Wilson, *The Edwardian Theatre Since 1900* (London: Arthur Barker, 1951), 118–20.

17. Ashwell, *Myself a Player*, 137–38.

18. Wilson, *Edwardian Theatre*, 171–74.

19. Julie Holledge, *Innocent Flowers: Women in the Edwardian Theatre* (London: Virago, 1981), 25–29.

20. Elizabeth Robins, *Theatre and Friendship* (New York: G. P. Putnam, 1932), 33–34.

21. See especially Gay Cima, "Elizabeth Robins: The Genesis of an Independent Manageress," *Theatre Survey* 21 (November 1980): 145–63.

22. Lillah McCarthy, *Myself and My Friends* (New York: E. P. Dutton, 1933), 63–64. See also Karen Grief, "Lillah McCarthy: 1875–1960)," *Turn-Of-The-Century-Women* 3 (Winter 1986): 27–28.

23. McCarthy, "An Aside by Bernard Shaw," preface, 8.

24. Ashwell, *Myself a Player*, 80.

25. Ibid., 113–16.

26. Ibid., 171.

27. Ibid., 141.

28. Ibid., 145–46.

29. Trewin, *Theatre Since 1900*, 194–95.

30. Ashwell, *Myself a Player*, 110.

31. Elizabeth Robins, *Votes for Women* (London: Mills & Boon, 1923), 1. See also Max Beerbohm, *Around Theatres*, vol. 2 (New York: Knopf, 1930), 595.

32. Holledge, *Innocent Flowers*, 44–45.

33. A. J. R., ed., *The Suffrage Annual and Women's Who's Who* (London: Stanley Paul, 1913), 9–11. See also Holledge, *Innocent Flowers*, 49–72.

34. For a list of officers, see Actresses Franchise League, *Annual Report 1912–13*, 1–4.

35. Ashwell, *Myself a Player*, 164. For the unpopularity of the suffrage cause, see Peter Rowland, *The Last Liberal Government: Unfinished Business 1911–1914* (New York: St. Martin's 1971), 349–50.

36. *Daily News*, 16 April 1909. See also Ashwell, *Myself a Player*, 165–68.

37. Ashwell notes further that as the procession marched through Piccadilly, she heard an onlooker say to his neighbor: "You see 'er, that ther in black? That there is the bad girl of the family" (ibid., 168). See also Eva Moore, *Exits and Entrances* (London: Chapman and Hall, 1923), 94–95. For the procession itself, see "Great Procession of Women," papers of Maude Arncliffe-Sennett, British Museum, vol. 14, no. 55 (hereafter cited as Arncliffe-Sennett Papers).

38. *Pall Mall Gazette*, 19 June 1911.

39. Ashwell, *Myself a Player,* 168. She was more comfortable a few months later when she marched alongside Mrs. George Bernard Shaw in a suffrage parade in Boston, where she appeared on tour. In Boston the "tiny, well-ordered body" was hailed by a "polite and sympathetic crowd" and received at town hall by the mayor and the city council, ibid.

40. Ibid., 165. See also Sennett, *The Child* (London: C. V. Daniel, 1936), 61–63. For Asquith's policies, see Constance Rover, *Woman's Suffrage and Party Politics in Britain 1866–1914* (London: Routledge and Kegan Paul, 1967), 122–28; David Morgan, *Suffragists and Liberals* (Oxford: University Press, 1975), 156–57. For the militants' reactions, see Andrew Rosen, *Rise Up Women* (London: Routledge & Kegan Paul, 1974), 96–97. For the attitude of the "constitutional" suffragists, see Leslie Parker Hume, *The National Union of Women's Suffrage Societies* (New York: Garland, 1982), 117–18.

41. Ashwell, *Myself a Player,* 166.

42. Ibid., 166–67.

43. For Lloyd George's attitude on the suffrage issue, see Rover, *Woman's Suffrage,* 129–32.

44. Ibid., 80–86.

45. "We were all suffragettes in those days" (McCarthy, *Myself and My Friends,* 149).

46. Rosen, *Rise Up Women,* 191–95.

47. Actresses' Franchise League, *Programme,* 2 May 1913, Arncliffe-Sennett Papers, vol. 22, no. 18. For speeches, see *Morning Post,* 3 May 1913.

48. For Ashwell's views on the exploitation of labor, see Ashwell, *Myself a Player,* 171–72.

49. *Morning Post,* 3 May 1913. See also Holledge, *Innocent Flowers,* 54–55.

50. *Daily Chronicle,* 3 May 1913; *Morning Post,* 3 May 1913.

51. Irene Vanbrugh, *To Tell My Story* (London: Hutchinson, 1949), 83–84. For the general antipathy of constitutional suffragists to militant tactics, see Patricia Jalland, *Women, Marriage and Politics 1860–1914* (Oxford: University Press, 1986), 214–15.

52. Parry to Arncliffe-Sennett, London, 13 February 1914, Arncliffe-Sennett Papers, vol. 23, no. 98.

53. "Women's Kingdom," ibid., no. 94.

54. Mayo to Arncliffe-Sennett, London, 23 January 1914, ibid., no. 96.

55. Ashwell, *Myself a Player,* 183; Arncliffe-Sennett Papers, 67–68. See also Ethel B. Tweedie, *Women and Soldiers* (London: Beck & Inchbold, 1919), 129–39.

56. Lena Ashwell, *Modern Troubadours* (London: Gyldendal, 1922), 6.

57. Lena Ashwell, *The Stage* (London: Geoffrey Bles, 1929), 143.

58. Ibid., 144. For a full account of the activities of British entertainers during World War I, see Ashwell, *Troubadours.*

59. Ashwell, *Myself a Player,* 211.

60. Ibid., 218.

61. Holledge, *Innocent Players,* 100–1.

62. Ashwell, *Myself a Player,* 209; Ashwell, *Troubadours,* 15–16.

63. Ashwell, *Myself a Player,* 220.

64. Ibid., 237–38.

65. Ibid., 237–50. See also Ashwell, *The Stage,* 153–66.

66. Ashwell, *Myself a Player,* 258.

67. Ibid., 260.

"With Reluctant Feet": The Meeting of Childhood and Womanhood in Works by Women Artists

Mara R. Witzling

"Standing with reluctant feet
Where womanhood and childhood meet."[1]

This misquotation of Longfellow's words is particularly meaningful to me, because my mother repeated it often throughout my preteen and teenage years, with a rueful tone in her voice, usually when I had just done something that seemed particularly immature, something that showed that despite my developing body I was still a child at heart. They describe so well Gertrude Käsebier's photograph *Blessed Art Thou Among Women* (1902): a somewhat apprehensive young girl stands at a threshold, supported by her mother who seems to be encouraging her to cross it.[2] The photograph emphasizes the door motif—the doorframe "frames" the figures, convincing us that the girl's passage into the adjoining room will be a dramatic action. In contrast to the burst of light around her, her dark dress intensifies this sense of drama. The work's title enhances its meaning. While *Blessed Art Thou Among Women* refers specifically to the salutation of the Virgin Mary reiterated by the framed image over the girl's head (possibly a picture of the Virgin and hence a reference to the mother in the photograph), the work also communicates the sense that the young girl is about to take the step of being "among women," of acknowledging the fruitfulness of her own womb.

Käsebier's image is one of several early twentieth-century works that deal with the theme of a girl's oncoming sexual maturation from the girl's point of view. Hardly dominant in the western art historical tradition, this motif was newly conceptualized at the turn of the century. Significantly, most of the artists who use it are women. In this essay I will first present a series of images that relate to a young girl's coming awareness of her body in pre-adolescence and puberty. Then I will discuss how such images radically depart from stereotypical ways of envisioning women's sexuality. Finally, I will show how they thereby contribute to the reconstruction of the western visual tradition.

Mary Cassatt's painting *Mother and Child* (1905), like Käsebier's photograph, emphasizes the link between mother and daughter.[3] In this work a woman holds her naked daughter on her lap, showing her her face in a hand-held mirror. Both mother and daughter, situated on the right-hand side of the canvas, face left, staring into the mirror; the unit is reflected in a wall-length mirror on the canvas's left-hand side. Cassatt creates a tight structural unity in this work, which contributes to its meaning of how a woman teaches her daughter to be a woman. The woman and child are connected to each other and to the upheld mirror through the circular pattern created by their arms. The circle motif is further emphasized by the connections thus achieved between the round forms of the child and mother's heads and the same, round mirror. Another important circle is the giant sunflower on the mother's bodice that punctuates the movement from mother's head to daughter's. Although Cassatt probably did not intend that we ascribe overt symbolic meaning to this flower, it surely suggests epithetic connotations about youth and its flowering. The use of mirrors also is thematically suggestive here and connects this work to others that are "about" seeing and being seen. However, it differs from the usual conceptualization of this in that the viewer is not turned into a voyeur.[4]

Suzanne Valadon also dealt with the theme of a young girl confronting her reflected image, accompanied by an older woman, a guide. In *Little Girl at the Mirror* (1909), an older woman shows a girl her reflection in a hand mirror, in an "almost violent" gesture. Valadon elaborates this theme in *The Abandoned Doll* (1921), in which a mother tries to dry her pubescent daughter who twists away, gazing at her face in a hand-held mirror.[5] Both figures are seated on a bed, at whose side in the lower right-hand corner of the painting lies a doll, which appears to have been tossed carelessly on the floor. An analogy between the girl and doll is made by the pink bow each wears in her hair. Although the mother and daughter reflect each other in their poses, "the physical contact between them is broken by their separate glances."[6] Thus the image has an element of internal conflict. Not only does it reflect the conflict between mother and daughter; the work also appropriately expresses the inner tension of the girl who stands between childhood and womanhood.

Dorothea Tanning treats the subject of oncoming sexual maturity from a different perspective in her many works with pubescent girls as protagonists. Although Tanning, often associated with the Surrealist movement, "continues to regard these paintings as the carriers of emotions that cannot be specified as sexual," the erotic content in such works as *Guardian Angels, Palaestra, Children's Games, The Guest Room,* and *Eine Kleine Nachtmusik* appears unmistakable.[7] As in Käsebier's photograph, doors recur in most of these paintings, symbolic of the "passage" from childhood to womanhood. A somewhat menacing, even violent, atmosphere is created in most of these works: the hair that bursts into flames in *Children's Games,* the hooded seated figure in *The Guest Room,* and the chaotic, bloody brutality of *Guardian Angels.* In *Eine Kleine Nachtmusik,* Tanning explores the mysterious, hypnotizing, overpowering nature of the call to sexual awareness. In a corridor, light emanates from a slightly opened door to which one young woman seems drawn by a large, animate sunflower that she clutches in her hands. Like the sunflower in Cassatt's work cited above, the one here suggests female sexual "flowering." The girl's hair stands on end as if the flower were electrically alive. Another young woman leans against the wall, apparently exhausted, her clothes in disarray, clutching some petals from the same flower. The painting effectively communicates the charged atmosphere created by the sexual force during puberty. Often frightening, at times it seems to emanate from within, while at other times it feels like an external magnetic force.

Paula Modersohn-Becker depicted the mysterious, sacramental aspect of an adolescent girl's awareness of her impending entrance to womanhood. In *The Stork,* a young girl kneels on a white circle surrounded on each side by a round fruit, clasping a leafy branch with both hands. Her head and wrists are adorned with beads; a stork wades in the water to her right, its beak close to her face. The girl in *Young Girl Seated on Bed* holds a leaf in her hand and is similarly adorned with jewels. She is surrounded by several varieties of flowers.[8] The ceremonial aspect of these works is enhanced by the beads that adorn the girls' bodies, reminiscent of neolithic goddess-figures from both Vinca and Crete who are usually depicted wearing necklaces and bracelets.[9] Modersohn-Becker's paintings create the aura of a mysterious ritual, an initiation rite into the forces of sexuality and fertility, with their symbolic fruits, vegetation, and the stork itself. Some recent feminist art historians have described Modersohn-Becker's images as "failures," possibly because they seem to mirror the essentialist theories of such turn-of-the-century writers as Johannes Bachhofen.[10] I disagree with these criticisms. In these and other works in which she explores female reproductive strengths, Modersohn-Becker breaks western stereotypes in significant ways by creating what Lucy Lippard has called overlays, visual correspondences with art of other cultures.[11] In particular, she creates images in which the passage from childhood to womanhood is conceived as a solemn event, a life-crisis in which the young woman makes unconscious decisions about her female identity and the relation of her body to the world at large.[12] By rationalizing the sacred aspect of such transitions, our culture has suffered a psychological loss.

All the works discussed above disrupt traditional representations in which female sexuality has been conceived as passive, voyeuristic, and one-dimensional. From the Renaissance through the contemporary period, women have been depicted as sex objects, as objects for male enjoyment and pleasure. The content has changed somewhat over the centuries; whereas initially the objects had to be legitimized by mythology as Venus, or by history as raped Sabine women, or by the Bible as Susannah spied on by the Elders, during the twentieth century artists were free to explore the sexuality inherent to the artist-model relationship for itself.[13] John Berger, in *Ways of Seeing*, first suggested that in Western culture as well as in its art, men are the surveyors and women the surveyed, seeing themselves only through the male gaze.[14] Several critics have expanded the critique of the imbalance of power in the determining male gaze vis à vis the female object. For example, Lisa Tickner describes the female body as "occupied territory," and suggests that "the colonized territory must be reclaimed from masculine fantasy, the 'lost' aspects of female body experience authenticated and reintegrated in opposition to its more familiar and seductive artistic role as raw material for the men."[15]

Simply by not conforming to the representational norm—women on display for men—the artists of the works discussed here have begun the process of reclaiming the female body from its stereotyped use. Furthermore, the subject that they have chosen and their point of view toward it have a significant relationship to knowledge gained from their own female bodies. It could be said that they have created the visual equivalent of Hélène Cixous's dictum to "write in white ink," from "that good mother's milk."[16] Although it would be erroneous to assume that because of their female "nature" women artists "see differently" from their male contemporaries, "it can be argued that the particular force of [their] experience produced work that was differently placed within the dominant forms of representation of [their] periods."[17] That is, these artists drew upon their own biological and cultural experiences in choosing to depict the onset of puberty, a significant moment in a woman's life cycle, although it is invisible to (and feared by) men. In Stephanie Demetrakopoûlos's phrase, they "listened to their bodies."[18] In so doing they saw a subject where previously none was seen.

The internal drama of the process Penelope Washbourn describes as "becoming woman" has eluded male artists who see the female body from without, simply as a repository for their own feelings. When men have chosen to depict adolescence, they have done so from a perspective more consistent with the norm. This can be seen when one compares the images above to some by male artists that use similar motifs. Modersohn-Becker's *Seated Nude* bears a close resemblance to Edvard Munch's *Puberty*, an image of a girl seated on a bed, a haunted look on her face, a sinister black cloud encroaching on her left-hand side.[19] Despite the similar format of these works, their meanings are diametrically opposed. Munch viewed sexuality as a curse, which he saw misogynistically as emanating from women's unnatural desires. Thus he used the girl's apprehension to express his own haunted state of mind; rather than showing menarche as scary but sacred, he conceptualized female sexualization as an encounter with an evil, menacing force. When Tanning's images of nubile, sexualized young women are compared with works with similar subjects by male artists, their innovative nature is easily discerned. Two good examples of works by male artists that focus on female adolescents are Fragonard's late-eighteenth-century *Girl and Dog* and Balthus's mid-twentieth century *The Golden Days*.[20] While Tanning is interested in communicating the girls' complex experiences, Fragonard and Balthus create prurient images, seductive Lolita figures. In Fragonard's work the viewer is constructed as a voyeur, peeping in on this haughty, intimate moment of the boudoir. Balthus's girl, on the other hand, coyly invites the ravishing gaze of the viewer. Thus these works tell us more about the artist and the—presumed male—viewer's sexuality than that of the girls.

In this context of seeing and being seen, mirrors are imbued with a heightened importance. As the object of the male gaze, women have become sensitized to their own visual impact; by looking in a mirror one is able to see the image of one's self as it is presented to the world. Typical of the double bind of women under patriarchy, this self-reflective tendency has been described as "narcissicism," an unnatural and unproductive contemplation of one's own image. Even such an astute philosopher as Simone de Beauvoir frames the alleged preoccupation of women with their own images in negative terms. In the Western art historical tradition, women's identification with mirrors has also assumed a pejorative connotation.[21] Since the Renaissance, the image of Vanitas has often been represented by a young woman gazing at her reflection in a mirror. But as in the sixteenth-century painting of that theme by Hans Baldung Grien, her reflection is really an image of death, communicating the moralistic caveat that all is vanity and beauty will fade. In that context, when young women and old were shown together the negative aspects of the crone were stressed as a hostile warning that the beauty of youth would soon decay into the hideousness of old age.[22] Cassatt and Valadon's depictions of young and old together at a mirror are much kinder to both "ages of women." To these artists the process of becoming woman does not have negative significance, and self-contemplation is revealing, not destructive. Furthermore, the links between the generations are seen as constructive rather than competitive, because they are not based on perception of surface beauty, or its absence.

Dolls and games also have symbolic significance in images exploring a young woman's sexual maturation. For a young girl, playing with her dolls is something like looking in a mirror.[23] She measures her own image against theirs; through them she creates social scenarios that reflect those she has or will encounter in life. They are her alter-egos. But to a man the concept of a woman as a doll is something else again. "She's a doll," while seemingly a compliment, really contains dangerous misogynism; after all, a doll is not a real woman but a construct whose brittle beauty is never subject to change and who is totally passive, absolutely devoid of will or need. In Valadon's painting, the abandoned doll is the childish self that the girl must cast aside to move on to womanhood. Likewise, in Tanning's work *The Guest Room*, the doll clutched by the sleeping girl is her childish self to whom she clings, despite evidence of her sexual initiation, the broken eggshells, the faceless yet macho dwarf. But to Hans Bellmer, who also uses dolls as an artistic motif, dolls are things to be used, dismembered body parts subject to the male will.[24] His brutalized images are exaggerations of the "position" of the female body in Male Art, that is, the post-Renaissance tradition: prone, objectified, existing for men. Once again there is a disjunction between women's actual experience and its conceptualization by men.

Another way of describing the disruption created by women artists' images of female sexuality is to say that these works move into the public sphere that which has been relegated traditionally to the private sphere. They are revolutionary because they take household reality and make it public reality. One can interpret this quite literally: women and children contemplate their reflections at home, girls play with dolls at home; a painting makes these activities visible publicly.

There is also a more global interpretation. In western culture, women's experience of female sexuality has not been allowed to be voiced—or visualized—in the public sphere. Furthermore, female sexuality itself has been invalidated by the culture. Both the earlier view that women's sexuality is insatiable, as expressed in the late fifteenth-century *Malleus Maleficarum*, which said that "all witchcraft comes from carnal lust which is insatiable in women," and the nineteenth-century belief that women had no sexual needs, were inaccurate polarizations of women's sexual natures, derived from men's fears.[25] The actualities of women's sexual experiences were only mentioned in private. Women confided in their diaries, where, for example, the painter Marie Bashkirtseff described her various courtships and the thrill of being kissed by a lover.[26] They also talked among themselves about "women's problems." Mary Hallock Foote, for example, wrote about contraception to her friend Helena deKay Gilder, but she entreated her not to share with her husband her letter, which she described as "the cries that one woman utters to another."[27] When Hélène Cixous calls for writing that comes from the female body, she is calling for cultural validation of women's sexual realities; the private must be said in public in order to demarginalize it, to make it a valid part of the cultural norm.[28]

The works discussed in this essay do that, although it is unlikely that their artists were working from a polemical point of view. Rather, they were simply creating from their own experience and knowledge, an epistemological stance negated previously by patriarchal culture. In so doing they identified an aspect of women's experience, sexual awakening and passage into womanhood, that had been previously unspeakable in the public realm. Through their art they gave it body; they made it a visible participant in public discourse.

Notes

1. The correct quotation reads, "Standing with reluctant feet / Where the brook and river meet / Womanhood and childhood fleet," Henry Wadsworth Longfellow, "Maidenhood," stanza 3, 1842.

2. Käsebier's image was recently used as the cover for Cathy Davidson and E. M. Broner's, *The Lost Tradition* (New York: Crossroad/Continuum, 1986), a discussion of the relationship between mothers and daughters throughout history.

3. A black and white photograph of this image can be found in Adelyn Beeskin, *Mary Cassatt: A Catalogue Raisonné of the Oils, Pastels, watercolors and Drawings* (Washington, D.C.: Smithsonian Institute Press, 1970), 180. Another image on the same page, "Denise and Her Child Holding a Hand Mirror," seems to concern the same subject. Some viewers have suggested that in this work Cassatt is making a negative critique of the trappings of femininity that young girls need to assume.

4. Cassatt's work, "At the Opera" (1880), (ibid., 55), focuses on a young woman observing the opera while she, herself, is being observed by a man in a distant box through a pair of opera glasses. The concept of turning the viewer into a voyeur is deeply rooted in the history of western painting since the Renaissance. Themes such as Susannah spied on by the Elders have been exploited for this content.

5. The image is reproduced in Rosemary Betterton's analysis, "How Do Women Look? The Female Nude in the Work of Suzanne Valadon," in *Visibly Female*, ed. Hilary Robinson (New York: Universe Books, 1988), 259.

6. Ibid., 267.

7. See Whitney Chadwick, *Women Artists and the Surrealist Movement* (Boston: Little, Brown & Co., 1985), 135. Most of these images by Tanning are reproduced in Chadwick, *Women Artists, Guardian Angels* pl. XIV, *Palaestra*, p. 139, *The Guest Room*, p. 212, and *Eine Kleine Nachtmusik*, pl. XV.

8. Both works are reproduced as color plates in Gillian Perry, *Paula Modersohn-Becker* (London: The Women's Press, 1979), pls. XVII and XXII.

9. See Maria Gimbutas, *Goddesses and Gods of Old Europe* (Berkeley: University of California Press, 1982), esp. 201–5.

10. The term *failure* was used to describe Modersohn-Becker's "Self Portrait" (1906) by Griselda Pollock in "What's Wrong with 'Images of Women'?" in *Framing Feminism*, ed. Roszika Parker and Griselda Pollock (London and New York: Pandora Press, 1987), 138, who criticizes that work "because of the inseparability of the signifier and the signified." In her critical biography cited above, Perry discusses the relationship between Modersohn-Becker's images of mothers and late nineteenth-century conceptualizations of the "earth mother," 62–63.

11. See Lucy Lippard, *Overlay* (New York: Pantheon Books, 1983), esp. chap. 2, "Feminism and Prehistory," 41–76.

12. Penelope Washbourn, *Becoming Woman* (New York: Harper and Row, 1977), explores the spiritual questions implicit in the life crises of women. In her chapter on menstruation she discusses the psychological loss that accompanies the rationalization of the sacred aspect of menstruation in our culture (9–12). She provides a cogent response to those critics who suspect such a study of biologism: "To celebrate the particular potential of the female sexual structure does not imply identifying one's goal in life with the power of fertility. It means, rather, understanding that our bodies are to be owned as good" (17).

13. See *Gardner's Art Through the Ages*, 8th ed., ed. Horst de le Croix and

Richard G. Tansey (New York: Harcourt Brace Jovanovich, 1986) for Titian's *Venus of Urbino* (p. 648), Rubens's *The Rape of the Daughters of Leucippus* (p. 738), and Picasso's *Les Demoiselles D'Avignon* (p. 900) for just several such images.

14. John Berger, *Ways of Seeing* (London: Penguin Books, 1972), esp. chap. 3.

15. Lisa Tickner, "The Body Politic: Female Sexuality and Women Artists Since 1970," reprint in Parker and Pollock, *Framing Feminism*, 263–76, unfortunately without the notes. It appeared originally in *Art History* 1, no. 2 (June 1978): 236–49. This topic has also been discussed by Laura Mulvey, "Visual Pleasure and Narrative Cinema," *Screen* 16, no. 3 (1975), and from a different perspective by Margaret Miles, *Image as Insight* (Boston: Beacon Press, 1985).

16. Hélène Cixous, "The Laugh of the Medusa," *Signs* 1, no. 4 (1976): 881.

17. Betterton, *Visibly Female*, 258.

18. See Stephanie Demetrakopoulous, *Listening to Our Bodies* (Boston: Beacon Press, 1983). In this book Demetrakopolous explores how images that arise from "Knowledge from the bodies of women. . . . constellate powerful archetypes that could redeem humankind if allowed full manifestation" (133). In general she sees that women's physical fertility symbolizes psychic fertility.

19. See Thomas R. Messer, *Munch*, The Library of Great Painters (New York: Harry N. Abrams, 1970), pl. 15, p. 79.

20. For Balthus, see Sabine Rewald, *Balthus* (New York: Harry N. Abrams 1984), pl. 26, p. 110. Fragonard's *Girl and Dog* (no page reference is available) is exhibited in the Alte Pinakothek in Munich. In this work a young girl lies sprawled on a bed, holding a fluffy, white dog between her bare thighs. When I saw the work in 1984, I happened to be in the company of a group of adolescent boys who were not unmoved by its prurient interest.

21. Simone de Beauvoir, *The Second Sex*, trans. H. M. Parshley (New York: Alfred A. Knopf, 1953), has much to say about women's narcissism, which she refers to as the "cult of self" (342). She views this alleged narcissism as a detriment to women artists, for whom the "inability to forget themselves is a defect that will weigh more heavily upon them than upon women in any other career. . . ." As opposed to Cixous, de Beauvoir sees it as negative that "the woman writer will still be speaking of herself even when she is speaking about general topics," 706–7.

22. See James Snyder, *Northern Renaissance Art* (New York: Harry M. Abrams and Englewood Cliffs, N.J.: Prentice-Hall, 1985), 365, for a reproduction of Hans Baldung Grien's *Death and the Maiden*.

23. de Beauvoir, *The Second Sex*, 630–31.

24. See Chadwick, *Women Artists*, 120, for reproductions of Bellmer's dolls.

25. These words provide the preface to the *Malleus Maleficarum* ("Witches Hammer") originally written by two inquisitors, Heinrich Kraemer and Jackob Sprenger, in 1486, and translated by Montague Summers (London: Pushkin Press, 1948). See Carroll Smith-Rosenberg, *Disorderly Conduct* (New York: Oxford University Press, 1985), for discussions of conflicting aspects of female sexuality in the nineteenth and early twentieth centuries.

26. Marie Bashkirtseff, *The Journal of Maire Bashkirtseff*, trans. Mathilde Blind, intro. Rozsika Parker and Griselda Pollock (London: Virago Press, 1985), 104–5.

27. Cited by Melody Graulich in "The Cries That One Woman Utters to Another" (Paper delivered at the Western American Literature Conference, Durango, Colorado, October 1986).

28. Cixous, *Signs*, 1, no. 4 (1976): 881; see also "Castration or Decapitation?" *Signs* 7, no. 1 (1981): 41–55.

The Womanly Art of Breastfeeding: Art and Discourse in Nineteenth-Century Britain

Leslie Williams

B reast-feeding in nineteenth-century Britain was by no means the universal rule. There was, in fact, a considerable discourse on the subject in medical texts, household books, poetry, and art. Although breast-feeding would seem to be the only sensible method available for feeding infants, the use of artificial foods even for very young infants seems to have been widespread and was probably one of the major contributors to the period's relatively high infant mortality rate. Many newborns were cared for initially by midwives rather than their mothers, breast-fed by hired nurses, and weaned to solid foods at an early age. These practices raise the question of infant-maternal bonding in Victorian life. A close examination of paintings from the period reveals, quite incidently and unself-consciously, attitudes and practices in Victorian childrearing.

Two views of breast-feeding from the reign of William IV, just before Victoria took the throne, can be seen in *Maternal Affection* by Sir George Patten (1834) and *A Highland Breakfast* by Sir Edward Landseer. Patten's work derives from the Grand Manner. The boy turns in a Michelangelesque contraposto as he toys with his mother's breast. She lowers her eyes demurely and, in fact, does not touch the child. The composition is rather baroque and the figures classically idealized. (Patten was later portraitist to Prince Albert.) The title of the work probably refers to Plutarch's *Moralia* in which the sage advocates breast-feeding by the mother to stimulate maternal affection.[1] This painting is obviously aimed at an educated elite, a group nursing their own children less and less as can be inferred from the number of wet nurse advertisements in the London *Times* for this decade. For the aristocracy, nursing was a paid-for service of a temporary nature.

George Patten. *Maternal Affection*. 1834. Courtesy of the Walker Art Gallery, Liverpool.

Landseer's work, although its subject is a poor Scottish Highland cottage interior, also is intended for the elite art market. It
derives from a series of mothers—horse, collie, deer, human—he
did for Georgiana, Duchess of Bedford. The painting draws a
parallel between the poor rural mother nursing her baby and the
terrier in the foreground of the painting who nurses her pups as
she laps her own breakfast from a low wooden tub. The animals,
the crowded cottage, even the rough, low chair in which the
woman sits cumulatively represent nursing as natural, albeit
lower class, and her Highland costume suggests that it is slightly
foreign or exotic activity. The title with its implied parallel between the humans and the dogs is both humorous and slightly
denigrating.

These opposite poles of idealization and condescension, of
looking up to or down on nursing, suggest that nursing was not a
perfectly commonplace activity for the class who patronized art.
The upper-class avoidance of maternal duties in terms of nursing
is commented on by the poet Robert Montgomery:

"On the Neglect of Maternal Duties in High Life":
A mother's love—restless speaks that claim,

Edwin Landseer. *A Highland Breakfast.* **1834. Courtesy of the Victoria and
Albert Museum, London.**

When first the cherub lists her gentle name!
And, looking up, it moves its little tongue
In passive dalliance to her bosom clung.
'Tis sweet to view the sinless baby rest
To drink its life-spring from her nursing breast
And mark the smiling mother's mantling eyes,
While, hushed beneath, the helpless infant lies.
How fondly pure that unobtruding prayer,
Breath'd gently o'er the listless sleeper there.
'Tis Nature thus!—the forest breast can hug
And cubs are nestled 'neath its milky dug;
But FASHION petrifies the HUMAN heart,
Scar'd at her nod, see ev'ry love depart.
In Rome's majestic days long fleeted by
Did not her mighty dames sing lullaby?
. . . But England's mighty dame is too GENTEEL
To nurse and guard, and like a mother feel.

Here Montgomery suggests economic reasons—a class-biased desire for fashion and gentility—for lack of mother-care among the "mighty." This view is supported by the physician Pye Henry Chavasse.[2] It was Chavasse's medical belief that a mother's milk is the best food for an infant. However academic the execution, it is the nursing of a child that Patten took as his symbol for *Maternal Affection.* Thus by 1839 we have a confluence of three kinds of male discourse—artistic, poetic, and medical—all dealing with the vexing question of how best to persuade fashionable, literate, presumably upper-class women to breast-feed. The desirability of maternal nursing was clearly recognized; the means of appeal differ. Patten's work has obvious erotic overtones in the sensuality of the boy's rosebud mouth on the nipple. Landseer shows the emotional satisfaction of *en face* presentation in which the mother looks directly into the nursing baby's eyes. While Patten's is an abstracted, idealized work, Landseer's is really reportorial as well as humorous and entertaining.

The discourse on infant feeding and childrearing generally may be said to mark the end of Romanticism in regard to the child and the beginning of a more pragmatic and gradually professionalized approach to childrearing. Children were becoming the center of a new adult male interest. No longer a topic confined to a private, spoken concern of wives and mothers, childrearing was becoming a matter of male, that is, public and published concern. Writings on pediatric topics began in the middle of the eighteenth century with William Cardigan. His successor William Buchan in 1809 urged the "fond mother to give her child freely what nature freely

Charles West Cope. *The Young Mother.* 1845. Courtesy of the Victoria and Albert Museum, London.

produces" and lamented that "Infants are commonly deprived of the breast too soon."[3] That permissive attitude gave way to Chavasse's insistence that "Mothers generally suckle their infants too often" and that overfeeding was a major cause of distress for infants. Chavasse recommended scheduled feedings for babies: every hour and a half during the first month, every two hours for the second month and then every three or four hours, rather than "having them almost constantly at the beast."[4] One could interpret this shift from feeding on demand to scheduled feeding as a sort of industrialization of infancy, and the establishment at the earliest age of time-frame controls.

Masculine propaganda from artist, poet, and doctor in favor of breast-feeding seems to have met real physical resistance from the cultural milieu which insisted that the breast should be covered rather than displayed, encased rather than used. While Patten and Landseer (and later Ford Maddox Brown) show breast-feeding as a matter of easy accessibility, Charles West Cope is the only artist who, in *The Young Mother* (1845) portraying his wife nursing his daughter, gives an accurate description of the difficulty of breast-feeding in Victorian dresses. Access to the breast for the middle-class child was no longer a matter of simply dropping further an already low neckline, as in Patten's picture, or as in Ford Maddox Brown's *Young Mother* (1852), which shows a woman dressed in the low-cut bodice of an eighteenth-century gown. By 1845 Cope's fashionable mother with her high-necked Victorian dress required partial undressing to be able to nurse.

The Young Mother pose could be described in modern psychological terms as a well-bonded middle-class mother and child dyad. The mother holds the infant on her left arm, her right hand gently enclosing the child, pressing it to her. The child's head is held high, close to her own face in an *en face* gaze, like Landseer's Highlander, a position in which the mother seeks direct eye contact with the child by turning her head "so that her eyes and that of the infant meet fully in the same vertical plane of rotation."[5] This painting was exhibited in the 1844 Royal Academy exhibition. In the same exhibition Patten showed *Maternal Affection*, which in 1834 had won a prize in Liverpool. His idealization was decried as a misnomer in the Art Union's review:

A mother and her two children, both boys, one of whom, while she caresses the other, has much the appearance of being about to fall head foremost to the ground. . . . A loving mother would be more careful of her child.[6]

The reviewer also noticed and approved of Cope's young mother: "She is seated nursing her child, a simple subject which is treated with infinite sweetness."[7] Obviously, by 1844, realism was more appealing than the idealizations of the Grand Manner.

Not only does the mother's dress have a buttoned front which she must undo to nurse; the child as well is dressed elaborately in the long skirts of contemporary infant fashion. The freedom of movement for Patten's naked boy is gone. This is a middle-class madonna without the least lingering of Patten's or Montgomery's references to Rousseau or the classics. Her face is in a *profile perdu* pose, her exposed breast scarcely discernible. This pose indicates the intimacy of the scene, not to be intruded upon by the viewer. But the baby, nursing at the breast, is fully secure in his mother's arms. The painting seems to exemplify Eric Erikson's description of nursing as:

> mutual regulation with a mother who will permit him [to get] as she gives. There is a high premium of libidinal pleasure on this coordination. . . . The mouth and the nipple seem to be the mere centers of a general aura of warmth and mutuality which are enjoyed and responded to with relaxation not only by these focal organs, but by both total organisms.[8]

The importance of this loving, involved maternal care is underlined by the high infant mortality of this era.

Although an ideal of mothers working in the home or fields with their nurslings nearby is shown in a number of paintings (for example, Margaret Carpenter's *The Lacemaker* [1849], her brother-in-law William Collins's *In a Kentish Hop Garden* [1829], John Linnell's harvest scenes), factory situations unfortunately were not conducive to breast-feeding. Eyre Crowe's *The Dinner Hour at Wigan* (1874) shows only one mother, at the extreme far right, with her baby on her lap at noon. Pictures of women breast-feeding in the fields or at the factory are apparently nonexistent, although we know from sources such as Henry Mayhew that infants were brought to the factories to nurse by the young girls who minded them.

The fact that infant mortality declined in the Lancashire factory districts during the "cotton famine" is a statistical confirmation of how important mother care was. In a period when general mortality rose because of illness and starvation, infant mortality declined because there was no work for the mothers in the factories when the cotton supplies dried up during the American Civil War. Presumably, mothers, who commonly returned to the facto-

Thomas Faed. *Highland Mother.* 1870. Courtesy of the Tate Gallery, London.

ries a week to ten days after giving birth and left their infants in the care of childminders, stayed home instead, nursed their babies themselves, and thereby noticeably improved the infants' chances for survival.[9]

Although rural mothers might have had more opportunity to nurse their children and peasant costumes provided easy accessibility, the closeness and affection of Cope's middle-class urban mother or Landseer's cottager is not seen in Thomas Faed's *Highland Mother* (1870) at the Tate Gallery. Here the mother is presented frontally with her unfashionable peasant dress slipped down to accommodate her child. She holds the child securely in both arms, but her eyes are lowered or, perhaps closed, as she drowses, and her face is at a ninety-degree angle to the baby's. The child is held low on the lap, its head almost horizontal.

This inattentive pose may show the effect on maternal bonding of the traditional British practice of not putting the baby to the breast until the mother's milk came in. Traditional practice was to wait up to three days, the colostrum period, before nursing the child.[10] Some modern research has shown that this delay interferes with bonding. Mothers who have immediate post-birth contact with their children tend to behave in ways distinctly different from those whose first contact with their infants is delayed. Interestingly, Faed's *Highland Mother* closely resembles the pose of late-contact mothers.

Nursing was recommended in child care manuals including those by Dr. William Buchan, Dr. Chavasse, and Mrs. Beeton. Chavasse insists that even delicate women can nurse and that nursing is one of the most healthful periods of a woman's life. The question, nonetheless, remained as to whether nursing was something a delicate or genteel woman would wish to do. Generally, the art market seems to have agreed that nursing was a lower-class activity. Mrs. Beeton's advice on nursing in 1861 stressed that "the nine or twelve months a woman usually suckles must be, to some extent, to most mothers, a period of privation and penance. . . ."[11] She repeats this gloomy view two pages later, referring to suckling again as "a season of penance," which certainly appears to be the case in Faed's *Highland Mother*. Still, any woman who was "strong enough" could be expected to nurse. Physical strength, however, was not a quality cultivated by ladies. Delicacy, on the other hand, was a near virtue, and hypochondria was not unknown. Mrs. Beeton's view that nursing was a penance may have reflected as well as influenced the opinions of her middle-class readers.

Mrs. Beeton felt that "the infant can hardly be too soon made independent of the mother."[12] All three authors, immediately after praising the nursing mother, give advice on hand-rearing with gruel or pap (a mixture of bread, sugar, and water). For many mothers there was no economic choice. Although some had their babies brought to them at work for feeding, malnutrition and exhaustion may have made it difficult or impossible for poor mothers to nurse. Such may be the case in Ford Maddox Brown's *Work* (1852–65) which shows, to quote the artist's description, "A young shoeless Irishman with his wife, feeding their firstborn with cold pap. . . ."[13] The mother holds the child on her lap as the father wields the spoon from behind the child's head. Obviously, feeding a baby on pap meant that the father could be involved in direct nurture of his child. William Mulready's *Father and Child* or *Rustic Happiness* (1825–30), shows a bowl and spoon quite prominently in the foreground, but feeding time is past, and the baby is seated on its father's lap looking at a book with pictures, while its mother turns her back. This may to some extent reflect Mulready's disaffection from his wife and the interest he himself took in raising his four sons. In Frederick Daniel Hardy's *Expectation* (1854), a little sister holds the bowl of pap for the mother who has the infant on her lap. The spoon is actually in the baby's mouth. The *Art Journal* reviewer called it a work of "unimpeachable exactitude." In Thomas Faed's painting *Time About Is Fair Play* (National Gallery of Scotland Photo Archive), the young child seated on his mother's lap lets his dog lick the spoon as his mother looks on. (There was, of course, no germ theory to distract mothers at this point.)

Buchan considered the use of "spoon meat" to be "improper," although he recognized that it was "a common practice, not only with hired nurses, but even with affectionate mothers, from a foolish though prevalent idea of lessening the demands on the breast, or of strengthening the child with additional nourishment." Chavasse complained, "We frequently hear of infants having no notion of sucking. This 'no notion' may generally be traced to bad management, to stuffing children with food, and thus giving them a disinclination to take the nipple at all." Mrs. Beeton, on the other hand, while recommending nursing "where the mother had the strength to suckle her child . . . would insist on making it a rule to accustom the child as early as possible to the use of an artificial diet, not only that it may acquire more vigour to help it over the ills of childhood, but that, in the absence of the mother, it might not miss the maternal sustenance."[14]

The actual nutritional quality of pap depended on the quality and quantity of cow's milk or sugar available to make it. Even then, it was a rather poor substitute for mother's milk, and its preparation was quite casual and often unhygenic. As Sylvia McCurdy recalled of her own early childhood in a house on the south side of Russell Square:

> . . . we were all born in a house into the windows of which no glint of sun had ever penetrated. As we were probably fed on nothing but pap made by soaking bread baked in the oven in milk, for several months, we were, I imagine, then pale little specimens.[15]

Children reared on pap did survive. Pip in Charles Dickens' *Great Expectations* was "brought up by hand." Pip was an orphan, but many children were apparently reared on pap, even in the well-to-do households of Russell Square.

Spoonfeeding was not the only unhygienic practice likely to lead to intestinal infections. Rather than using a spoon, Mrs. Beeton recommended the bottle. These came in various guises, but a clear example of a boat-shaped porcelain bottle such as is preserved in the collection at Bethnal Green can be seen in use in John D. Watson's drawing of *The Grandmother* (n.d., Sotheby's). Chavasse recommended, "A bottle, not only as it is a more natural

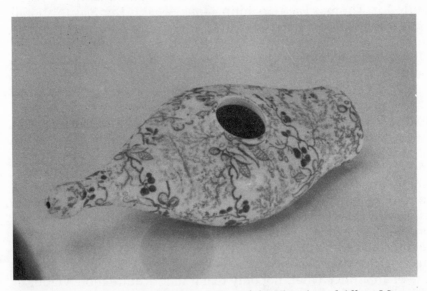

Porcelain baby's bottle. Ca. 1850. Courtesy of the Victoria and Albert Museum, London.

way of feeding an infant than any other, but . . . it seems to satisfy the child [more than spoonfeeding]. . . . The neck of the bottle should be covered with a prepared calf's teat, which, when not in use, should be kept in weak gin and water."[16] Mrs. Beeton's instructions for caring for the teat appear to be absolutely pathological by present-day standards: "When once properly adjusted, the nipple need never be removed till replaced by a new one [the opening for food being in the center of the boat-shaped bottle], which will hardly be necessary oftener than once a fortnight, though with care one will last for several weeks."[17]

"Poor food" was acknowledged as a cause of babies' deaths. Gastroenteritis and diarrhea were probable causes for much of the infant mortality, as they are today in Third World countries. While modern evidence suggests that breast-feeding could have prevented such illnesses, cures were attempted using various preparations, one recommended by Dr. Buchan being "syrup of poppies." The recurrent figure of a child sleeping limply on its

John Henry Henshall. *Behind the Bar.* 1882. Courtesy of the Museum of London.

mother's lap, untouched, simply balanced there, suggests that an infant or young child's exceptionally deep, perhaps drugged, sleep was a customary sight as exemplified in Ford Maddox Brown's *Waiting* or *an English Fireside, 1854*.

Chavasse and Beeton both strongly denounced the use of narcotics, but it is reported that in Manchester large quantities of "Godfrey's Cordial" and other opium-laced sedatives were sold as pacifying drugs. Indeed, the problem was sufficiently widespread to elicit a rather serious page-long commentary in *Punch* in 1846 in which "Baby Bib" is gradually introduced to a whole list of preparations, including "Eden Liquor, Bliss, Mother's Helper." Baby Bib ends, *Punch* says, by being a drunkard [addict] before his first birthday.[18] To this effect, *Punch* published a scene in a bar in which a mother doses her infant with gin while a small boy and girl share a jug of beer. In 1882 in his watercolor *Behind the Bar,* John Henry Henshall also depicts a mother dosing her child with gin in a public bar while a very small child proffers a bottle to the bar man to be refilled. Alcohol and narcotics were both available to children in over-the-counter sales until quite late in the queen's reign. Although the intent in administering laudanum-based syrups may have been to soothe and quiet babies who suffered from a lack of breast milk and mother care, the indirect effect may have

William Collins. *The Reluctant Departure.* **1815. Courtesy of the Birmingham Art Gallery.**

been to slow the passage of poorly digested food through the alimentary canal and to reduce dehydration in cases of chronic or acute diarrhea. "Godfrey's" was not a treatment of choice, but it may have had some beneficial side effects.

According to contemporary practice, those who were nursed may have been weaned rather early and sometimes rather drastically. *The Reluctant Departure* by William Collins (1815) shows a mother leaving her child, but because the child she kisses is wearing shoes, it is unlikely to be a baby left to a country nurse, but may instead be one who is being left to be weaned at a servant's home by his fashionably dressed mother in her great hat and embroidery-edged shawl. Chavasse recommends that the mother leave home for a few days, after gradually weaning her child, and the diary of a Welsh coffinmaker documents just such a leave-taking when his fifteen-month-old son was sent away from home to be weaned.[19] Walter Williamson in *Diseases of Infants and Children* (1857) opposed sending the child away or leaving it to wean it:

> Nothing ought to induce a mother, except in case of sickness, to give her infant into the hands of another person . . . for the purpose of weaning. Neither should a mother absent herself from home during the trying period. . . . it is grieved at her absence, besides losing its favorite nourishment, and then is doomed to disappointment on her return, which is almost as painful as the first privation.[20]

Weaning under such circumstances might produce a permanent sense of deprivation. Erickson suggests what the long-term effect of abrupt weaning could be:

> A drastic loss of accustomed mother love without proper substitution at this time can lead (under otherwise aggravating conditions) to acute infantile depression or to a mild but chronic state of mourning which may give a depressive undertone to the whole remainder of life. But even under the most favorable circumstances, this stage leaves a residue of a primary sense of evil and doom and of a universal nostalgia for a lost paradise.[21]

An alternative technique in weaning among working mothers, in which the succor of the breast was removed abruptly, was to paint the nipples black, a shocking sight to the nursling. Alice Foley recalled in *A Bolton Childhood*: "Poor mothers daubed their breasts with soot to discourage suckling, and dim memories remain of spasmodic howls of rage produced by the offer of those coal-black nipples."[22]

Overall, then, paintings of breast-feeding and its alternatives seemingly show evidence of late contact rather than immediate bonding between mother and infant, hand-rearing by spoon or bottle feeding, and the custom of abrupt separation at the time of weaning. The combination of these experiences in infancy suggests a lack of oral satisfaction for many young Britons.

Evidence of this lack may be seen in the numerous pictures beginning with Sir David Wilkie's *Rent Day* (1807), which shows a man comically sucking on his cane head, a figure eventually immortalized in literature by Charles Dickens, possible referring to figures drawn by George Cruikshank. Oral gratification is seen as light comedy in all these incidents. The humor is based on this infantile urge emerging in grown men when they are under certain kinds of pressure or simply showing off. Thomas Faed uses the same motif in *Faults on Both Sides;* George Cruikshank uses it in *Family and its Shoes.* A pretty girl inspires cane sucking in William Maw Egley's *Omnibus Life* and in John Pettie's *Two Strings to Her Bow* (1887).

Such pictures as these where the theme dwells on orality would

George Cruikshank. *A Frightful Narrative* **(detail). Ca. 1844.**

seem to be related to a lack of active oral satisfaction in infancy not only among the poor where hand-rearing was often made necessary by economic exigencies, but among the middle-class and well-to-do when even "affectionate mothers" turned to the cup and spoon. The sense of trust, which Eric Erikson considers to be the preferred outcome for this period of development, seems replaced, in these paintings, with a comic anxiety.

Notes

1. Lawrence Stone, *The Family, Sex and Marriage in England, 1500–1800* (New York: Harper & Row, 1977), 431.

2. Chavasse quotes this poem in his *Advice to Mothers on the Management of Their Offspring* (New York: Appleton & Co., 1844), 20–21.

3. William Buchan, *Domestic Medicine* (Philadelphia: Thomas Dobson, 1809).

4. Chavasse, *Advice to Mothers*, 32–33.

5. Kennell, Voos and Klaus, "Parent-Infant Bonding", *Handbook of Infant Development*, ed. Joy D. Osofsky (New York: Wiley, 1979), 787.

6. *Art Union*, VI [1844], 278.

7. Ibid., 174.

8. Eric Erikson, *Childhood and Society* (New York: Norton, 1963), 75.

9. Margret Hewitt, *Wives and Mothers in Victorian Industry*, (London: Rockliff, 1958), 117–22.

10. Chavasse, *Advice to Mothers*, 21.

11. Elizabeth Beeton, *Book of Household Management* (London: S.O. Beeton, 1869 reprint), 1034.

12. Ibid., 1038.

13. Ford Maddox Brown, *The Exhibition of Work, and Other Paintings* (London: McCorquedale & Co., 1865), 3.

14. Beeton, *Household Management*, 1039.

15. Sylvia McCurdy, *Sylvia: A Victorian Childhood* (Laverham: Eastland Press, 1972), 9–10.

16. Chavasse, *Advice to Mothers*, 36.

17. Beeton, *Household Management*, 1042.

18. "Mrs. Bib's Baby," *Punch* x [1846], 122.

19. Thomas Jenkins, *Diary of Thos. Jenkins of Llandeilo* (August 1860), 120.

20. Walter Williamson, *Diseases of Infants and Children*, revised by G. N. Epps (London: 1857), n.p.

21. Erikson, *Childhood and Society*, 80.

22. Alice Foley, *A Bolton Childhood* (Manchester: Manchester Extra Mural Department, 1973), 4.

Housewives and Their Maids in Dutch Seventeenth-Century Art

Wayne Franits

The theme of the housewife supervising her maids was frequently depicted in seventeenth-century Dutch genre painting. As is the case with all other domestic themes in art, these paintings must be interpreted in the context of the contemporary familial ideal. Because this ideal was largely fostered by and reflected in contemporary literature, sixteenth- and seventeenth-century books pertaining to women and the family are the most revealing sources for understanding these works of art. Contemporary literature affords ample insights into ideas that underlie painted representations of the mistress's supervisory role. However, the relationship between literature and art in these cases is not one of direct influence but of parallel expression of ideals concerning housewifely tasks and obligations.

The housewife's duty to oversee her servants was discussed ad infinitum in domestic conduct books, enormous treatises of household government popular at this time, and in other related works.[1] For example, in his *Mirrhor mete for all mothers . . . of* 1579, Thomas Salter states that when a woman married she must,

> . . . knowe the office and duetie of householde servauntes, lette her note, and look how aptly and cleanly thei keepe the Chambers, and other like places . . . and lette her be present at every thing that longeth to housholde affaires . . .[2]

The close ties between the depiction of housewives supervising their servants in art and the description of this duty in literature are perhaps best demonstrated by the little frontispiece inserted before the introduction to the chapter, "Vrouwe," in the fourth edition of the most popular family book published in the seventeenth century, Jacob Cats's *Houwelyck* (1632).[3] The print, by Cornelis Kittensteyn, shows a virtuous family in an interior. The housewife has had her sewing interrupted by a maid holding a shopping pail. This scene is strikingly similar to those portrayed in a number of paintings of mistresses who are about to send their maids off on shopping trips for the family. All of these paintings postdate the book illustration, and it is possible that they were influenced by it, especially because Cats's book was so widely known. However, the possibility that they may have originated independently cannot be ruled out.

A related group of paintings represent maids who have returned from shopping, displaying their purchases to their ever-watchful mistresses.[4] Related as well are the seemingly countless renditions of maids showing housewives food offered for sale by travelling vendors. In a picture by Quiringh van Brekelenkam, a maid shows a tray of meat to her mistress while the vendor waits at the door. The mistress has been sewing and her shoe lies on the floor in front of her, both motifs symbolizing her virtue as a housewife. A large painting of a shepherdess in a landscape hangs on the wall behind her.[5] In view of the housewife's manifold domestic duties, it can be assumed that this picture refers to her guidance and maintenance of the household and its goods:

Cornelis Kittensteyn. Illustration from J. Cats, *Houwelyck*, 4th ed., The Hague 1632, Amsterdam, Universiteits-Bibliotheek.

Pieter de Hooch. *Woman giving money to a servant*. Los Angeles, Los Angeles County Museum of Art, Mr. and Mrs. Allan C. Balch Collection (Photo: Museum).

Quiringh van Brekelenkam. *Maid showing fish to her mistress. Present location unknown* (Photo: © Christie's).

Quiringh Brekelenkam. *Mistress with a servant.* Manchester, Manchester City Art Gallery (Photo: Museum).

Pieter de Hooch. *Mother and child*. Philadelphia, Philadelphia Museum of Art, John G. Johnson Collection.

just as the shepherdess must care for her flock, so must the mistress tend to the needs of her family.[6]

A similar scene is depicted in a painting by Pieter de Hooch in Philadelphia, in which a mother has paused from feeding her child to inspect a large flatfish held by her maid. The vendor, a fishwife, waits in the background by the dwelling's entrance. In a recent book, Mary Frances Durantini interpreted a version of this painting in Copenhagen as an image replete with sexual overtones. In her opinion, the purchase of fish was often associated at this time with the purchase of flesh.[7] The cornerstone of this rather surprising analysis is an article published in 1973 by Jan Emmens that examined sixteenth-century paintings of market scenes with episodes from the Bible depicted in their backgrounds.[8] Emmens, however, discussed works of art with entirely different visual contexts than that of the painting by de Hooch. In de Hooch's picture the motif of the fish is not an erotic metaphor—it is simply used to demonstrate the woman's virtue as a circumspect housewife who chooses the "best buys" for her family. Moreover, the fact that the maid shows the fish to her mistress

Hendrick Sorgh. *The kitchen.* **Manchester, Manchester City Art Gallery (Photo: Museum).**

Egbert van Heemskerck. *Housewife and servants*. Present location unknown.

illustrates what the artist's contemporaries would have perceived
as their proper working relationship.

The theme of housewives supervising their servants included
other subjects besides the inspection of food for purchase. Mistresses and maids are also depicted cooking and, in what is likely
a portrait attributed to Egbert van Heemskerck, a housewife over-
sees her servants as they perform several tasks, among them
ironing. In *The Linen Chest* by Pieter de Hooch, signed and dated
1663, a housewife helps her maid place linens for storage into a
large chest.[9] The identities of the figures are clarified by their
dress. The woman to the left wearing a black jacket and an apron
is a servant. She takes linens from the pile held by her mistress,
who is more elegantly attired. De Hooch's use of dress to indicate
the social positions of the housewife and her maid would have
certainly met with the approval of contemporary moralists; as
William Gouge states in his domestic conduct book of 1622:

Pieter de Hooch. *The linen chest.* Amsterdan, Rijksmuseum (Photo: Museum).

". . . apparell is one of those outward signes whereby the wisdome of masters and mistresses in well governing their servants is manifested to the world".[10] Contemporary moralists also would have been pleased that the artist has shown the housewife actively assisting her maid. According to the authors of domestic conduct books, the mistress was not to supervise her servants by delegating every task to them; on the contrary, she was to work alongside them.[11] For example, William Gouge interprets Proverbs 31:15, which states that the good housewife "gives a portion" to her maids, as a sign that "shee is with them her selfe; shee worketh willingly with her hands".[12]

Recently, the motif of women storing linens was interpreted as a reference to the futility of vain, greedy hoarding. An emblem by Jan Luiken was cited in this context because its *pictura* shows figures performing the very same task as an illustration of miserliness and vanity.[13] This interpretation is misleading because it relies on Luiken's emblem as a *clavis interpretandi*, an emblem not published until 1711. Luiken, whose work is often quoted, discusses the symbolic significance of nearly every conceivable object. Yet this very fact serves as a warning against applying his emblems indiscriminately. Many of his emblems' subjects—and this is especially true of one cited here—were of his own invention. Because they had not been published previously, they could not have been known by artists of an earlier generation.

There is no evidence that the women in de Hooch's painting are guilty of greedy hoarding. On the contrary, their activity of putting linens into a chest actually illustrates the housewife's duty to supervise her maids by working alongside them. Art historians have long noted that these women are working in a sumptuously and elegantly ornamented room, one characteristic of de Hooch's interiors at this stage in his stylistic development.[14] Because the housewife and her maid are virtuously at work, it is possible that these rich surroundings were intended to allude, among other things, to the material benefits and blessings of diligent labor. In essence, the painting can be viewed as a celebration of the assiduous performance of divinely ordained labor and its material benefits.

Housewives were also expected to be continually vigilant for lapses in their servants' behavior. Quoting once again from a seventeenth-century domestic treatise:

> She [the mistress] must have a diligent eye to the behavior of her servants, what meetings and greetings, what tickings and toyings,

Nicholaes Maes. *A sleeping maid and her mistress*. London, The National Gallery (Reproduced by courtesy of the Trustees, The National Gallery of London).

and what words and countenances there be betweene men and maides, lest such matters being neglected, there follow wantonnesse, yea folly, within their houses, which is a great blemish to the governours.[15]

Contemporary moralists repeatedly claimed that idleness was one of the sins that servants committed most frequently. Consequently, mistresses were advised to be watchful for its slightest trace among their maids,[16] a housewifely duty illustrated in a painting by Nicolaes Maes, appropriately entitled *The Idle Servant*. Here, a woman wearing a jacket trimmed with ermine—its richness indicating that she is a housewife—looks at the viewer while gesturing toward her maid, who is fast asleep.[17] Various cooking pots and other utensils are strewn about the floor, and a cat has seized a cooked bird from a platter directly behind the slumbering maid's head. The ultimate consequence of her idle sleep can be deduced from the scene in the back room: several figures are seated at a table, evidently waiting in vain for their dinner.

Earlier studies of this painting have linked the maid's somnolent state and pose—her head supporting her hand—to traditional images of sloth.[18] The dishes and utensils strewn about the foreground, some of them overturned, can therefore be understood as the aftermath of this slothful maid's neglect of duty.[19] The motif of the cat stealing the bird, depicted directly above the sleeping maid's head, should also be interpreted along these lines.[20] A proverb by Johan de Brune is quite fitting in this context: "A kitchenmaid must have one eye on the pan and the other on the cat."[21] De Brune's observation that maids must be vigilant when working in the kitchen is reminiscent of William Gouge's censure of indolent servants who allow food to be stolen by cats and dogs.[22]

In the painting by Maes the mistress's gaze and rhetorical gesture help to edify and admonish the viewer by demonstrating her vigilance and by exposing the maid's sloth. This picture is one of several that depict the vices of servants.[23] However, representations of servants who behave poorly are far outnumbered by those depicting servants who behave virtuously. The virtuous conduct of servants in so many paintings is mirrored by descriptions in contemporary literature of the ideal master/servant relationship. In these books, masters and mistresses are repeatedly enjoined to maintain authority through strict discipline over their hired help. However, the potential for severity is assuaged by the

advice that they treat servants as members of the family, instruct-
ing them in the Christian faith, and even caring for them when
they become ill.[24] Servants, for their part, were obliged to serve
their masters faithfully, diligently working "as unto the Lord."
Moreover, they were even enjoined to pray for their masters'
prosperity.[25]

Clearly, the relationship described in contemporary literature is
an archetypal one. The influence of these literary ideals has been
persistent over the centuries and actually misled social historians
of the nineteenth century who wrote about Dutch culture during
the Golden Age.[26] These historians mistook the ideals expounded
in literature for the actual situation at that time. For instance, G. D.
J. Schotel, in his Het Oud-Hollandsch huisgezin der zeventiende eeuw
(published in 1867–1868), maintained that during the seventeenth
century, maids were treated as full family members. Their privileges were said to extend to eating at the same table with the
family, even in the presence of guests.[27]

Modern-day social historians have only recently begun to re-
examine the nature of master/servant relationships in earlier
epochs. Their findings confirm that the writings of Cats, Wittewrongel, and their contemporaries on this subject present an
ideal vision generally nonexistent in daily life at that time. Far
from being "members of the family" who were loyal and trustwor-
thy, seventeenth-century servants were contractually hired for
only several months at a time in only a small percentage of
households. Moreover, disputes over wages seem to have been
the norm. Lastly, servants form one of the largest groups recorded
in the criminal records of seventeenth-century Amsterdam.[28]
Contemporary servant ordinances only confirm this view. These
municipal laws concerning master/servant hiring procedures and
relationships were used by the authorities to control the market
for servants and equally important, to control their behavior. The
ordinances included lengthy enumerations of both virtuous and
unseemly servant behavior. From her study of such seventeenth-
and eighteenth-century ordinances, Marlies Jongejan concluded
that, "The ideal servant was obedient and served his or her master
for many years to come in 'all diligence and faithfulness.' The
extensive legislation makes one suspect that practice was not in
agreement with this ideal."[29]

These findings offer compelling evidence that the world of the
housewife and maid as it appears in Dutch art is fictitious. More
and more, art historians are using social history to uncover the
daily reality of seventeenth-century life that is thought to underlie

contemporary paintings. However, this is one instance in which findings in that field do not enable us to understand Dutch art as a reflection of the "actual situation" at that time. Far from objectively confronting the viewer with this actual situation, the paintings represent a plausible reality, a re-creation of it in the interests of artistic verisimilitude and of symbolism. Reality has been re-created as the paintings function as propagandistic topoi expressing, like the literature they mirror, an exemplary and theoretically imitable vision of the roles and conduct of housewives and maids.[30] As such, both art works and literature played important roles in espousing and maintaining the male-dominated, male-oriented status quo and thus shed further light on the subordinate position of women in seventeenth-century Dutch society.

Notes

1. For domestic conduct books, see Chilton L. Powell, *English Domestic Relations, 1487–1653*, 3d ed. (New York: 1972), 101–46; Louis B. Wright, *Middle-Class Culture in Elizabethan England*, reprint. (New York: 1980), 201–27; Julius Hoffmann, *Die 'Hausväterliteratur' und die 'Predigten über den christlichen Hausstand.' Lehre vom Hause und Bildung für das häusliche Leben im 16. 17. und 18. Jahrhundert* (Weinheim/Berlin: 1959); Suzanne W. Hull, *Chaste Silent & Obedient; English Books for Women 1475–1640* (San Marino: 1982), 31–70, 144ff; L. F. Groenendijk, *De nadere reformatie van het gezin; de visie van Petrus Wittewrongel op de Christelijke huishouding* (Dordrecht: 1984).

2. Thomas Salter, *A mirrhor mete for all mothers, matrones, and maidens, intituled the mirrhor of modesty* (London: 1579), sig. C8^v. Salter's book is a close translation, without acknowledgment, of the then-famous work by Giovanni Bruto, *La institutione di una fanciulla nata nobilmente* (Antwerp: 1555); see Ruth Kelso, *Doctrine for the Lady of the Renaissance* (Urbana: 1956), 344 no. 161. For the housewife's duty to oversee the servants, see also Juan Vives, . . . *the instruction of a Christen woman* . . . , trans. R. Hyrde (London: 1547), sig. 107^v; William Perkins, *Christian oeconomie*, trans. T. Pickering, *The workes*. . . , vol. 3 (London: 1613), 700; William Gouge, *Of domesticall duties* . . . (London: 1622), 682–83; Jacob Cats, *Houwelyck. Dat is de gansche gelegentheyt des echten staets*, (Middelburg: 1625), chap. 4, sigs. 101^v–07^v, esp. sigs. 106–06. English, mostly Puritan writings on the subject of marriage and the family, will be cited extensively in this study. These works were highly influential in The Netherlands, not the least of reasons being that many were translated into Dutch, in some cases almost immediately after their initial publication in English. For example, a Dutch edition of Perkins's *Christian oeconomie*, vol. 3, was published in 1614. Perkins's writings were well known in The Netherlands; see the bibliography in William Perkins, *The Work of William Perkins*, ed. I. Breward (Appleford: 1970), 612–32. For a bibliography of English works translated into Dutch at this time, see J. van der Haar, *From Abbadie to Young: a Bibliography of English, Most Puritan [sic] works, translated i/t Dutch language* (Veenendaal: 1980). See also the important study by Cornelis W. Schoneveld, *Intertraffic of the Mind: Studies in Seventeenth-Century Anglo-Dutch Translation with a Check List of Books Translated from English into Dutch, 1600–1700*

(Leiden: 1983). Even English works that remained untranslated found their way into the margins of similar books by Dutch authors. Jacob Cats was familiar with such English works: to cite one of many examples, in the second edition of *Houwelyck* (1628), he quotes Gouge, (*Of domesticall duties* . . .); see Alice Clare Carter, "Marriage counselling in the early seventeenth century: England and The Netherlands compared," in *Ten Studies in Anglo-Dutch Relations,* ed. J. van Dorsten (London/Leiden: 1974), 97 n. 9, 105 n. 33.

3. This frontispiece is cited and reproduced by Peter C. Sutton, *Pieter de Hooch* (Ithaca: 1980), 47, fig. 47, where it is incorrectly said to have come from the second edition of *Houwelyck.* The second edition had already been published in 1628.

4. One of the earliest depictions of a housewife inspecting the purchases of her maid is found in a print by Jan Saenredam after Hendrick Goltzius of *Midday* from the series *The Four Times of Day;* reproduced in F. W. H. Hollstein, *Dutch and Flemish Etchings, Engravings and Woodcuts ca. 1450–1700,* vol. 23 (Amsterdam: n.d.), 74, no. 99.

5. This background picture appears in reverse in another painting by van Brekelenkam showing a housewife inspecting provisions offered for sale by a street vendor. This painting is now in Leipzig and is reproduced in *Katalog der Gemälde* (Leipzig [Museum der bildenden Künste]: 1979), 296, fig. 992.

6. This idea is inferred from several contemporary references that describe parents as shepherds of their families; see Cornelius Hazart, *Het gheluckich ende deughdelyck houwelyck* . . . (Antwerp: 1678), 243–44. Hazart's book was addressed to Catholics, but many of his ideas about marriage and family life were shared by Protestants. See also Petrus Wittewrongel, *Oeconomia Christiana ofte Christelicke huys-houdinghe,* 3d enlarged ed., vol. 1 (Amsterdam: 1661), 235, who calls the good ruler of a republic (and by extension of a family) a shepherd. For shepherds and shepherdesses in Dutch art—motifs often replete with amorous associations—see Alison McNeil Kettering, *The Dutch Arcadia: Pastoral Art and Its Audience During the Golden Age* (Montclair: 1983).

7. Mary Frances Durantini, *The Child in Seventeenth-Century Dutch Painting* (Ann Arbor: 1983), 43. See Wayne Franits, "Review of Mary Frances Durantini, *The Child in Seventeenth-Century Dutch Painting,*" *The Art Bulletin* 67 (1985): 698. For the two versions of the painting, see Sutton, *Pieter de Hooch,* cat. nos. 112A, 112B.

8. J. A. Emmens, " 'Eins aber ist nötig'—zu Inhalt und Bedeutung von Markt—und Küchenstücken des 16. Jahrhunderts," *Album Amicorum J. G. van Gelder* (Utrecht: 1973), 93–101.

9. For this painting see Leonard J. Slatkes, *Vermeer and His Contemporaries* (New York: 1981), 126–27; Durantini, *Seventeenth-Century Dutch Painting,* 215–17; Wayne Franits, " 'Domesticity is a woman's crowning ornament': Women at Work in Dutch Genre Painting," *Images of the World: Dutch Genre Painting in Its Historical Context,* ed. C. Brown and M. Stevens (forthcoming). Behind these women to the right, a child plays colf, a popular amusement and ancestor of modern golf. For the history of golf and the older games from which it evolved, see the exhibition catalogue *Colf. kolf. golf; van middeleeuws volkspel tot moderne sport* (Amersfoort [Museum Flehite]: 1982). The possible significance of this motif is explained in Franits, "Domesticity."

10. Gouge, *Of domesticall duties* . . ., 670. See also Wittewrongel, *Oeconomia Christiana,* vol. 1, 210. Durantini (*Seventeenth-Century Dutch Painting,* 354, n. 117)

argues that the relationship between the women is unclear. If the plainly dressed woman is the servant, Durantini wonders why the mistress would allow her to put the "valuables" away. In my opinion the servant is simply helping her mistress. Mistresses were exhorted to work alongside their servants; see the literature cited in note 11 below.

11. See Gouge, *Of domesticall duties . . .*, 682–83; Wittewrongel, *Oeconomia Christiana*, vol. 2, 723–24.

12. Gouge, *Of domesticall duties . . .*, 682. Curiously, the words "gives a portion" in this verse actually refer to the virtuous housewife who feeds her family and servants: see the print in the series of Dirch Volkertsz. Coornhert after Maarten van Heemskerck, illustrating this verse, discussed and reproduced in Ilja M. Veldman, "Lessons for Ladies: A Selection of Sixteenth and Seventeenth-Century Dutch Prints," *Simiolus* 16 (1986): 115–16, fig. 4. Proverbs 31 was used to justify the mistress's duty to supervise her servants, but verse 27, "she looketh well into the ways of her household," was *usually* cited; see, for example, Wittewrongel, *Oeconomia Christiana*, vol. 2, 724.

13. Durantini, *Seventeenth-Century Dutch Painting*, 215–17. The emblem in question can be found in Jan Luiken, *Het leerzaam huisraad*(Amsterdam: 1711), 22–5 nr. 7. Slatkes *Vermeer,* 126, cites the Luiken emblem but does not believe that its meaning can be applied to the painting.

14. Slatkes, *Vermeer,* 126. For de Hooch's stylistic development at this time, see Sutton, *Pieter de Hooch,* 28–34.

15. John Dod and Robert Cleaver, *A godly forme of houshold government . . .*, 5th ed. (London: 1612), sigs. F5–F5ᵛ.

16. See, for example, Gouge, *Of domesticall duties . . .*, 620, 624; Thomas Carter, *Carters Christian commonwealth; or domesticall dutyes deciphered* (London: 1627), 230; J[ohanes] C[olerus], *De verstandige huys-houder . . .* , 2d enlarged ed. (Amsterdam: 1663), 9. Colerus's book, originally published in German in six parts between 1591 and 1605, was one of the most popular family books during the seventeenth century.

17. For this painting, see exhibition catalogue *Tot lering en vermaak; betekenissen van Hollandse genrevoorstellingen uit de zeventiende eeuw,* Amsterdam (Rijksmuseum) 1976, cat. no. 33; Slatkes, *Vermeer,* 120; Nanette Salomon, *Dozing and Dozers: Aspects of Sleep in Dutch Art* (Diss., Institute of Fine Arts, New York University, 1984), 191–97.

18. *Tot lering en vermaak,* 145; Slatkes, *Vermeer,* 120; Salomon, *Dozing,* 191.

19. A similar idea is expressed by the objects strewn on the ground around the personification of negligence in a print by Crispijn van der Passe I; see Hollstein, *Dutch and Flemish Etchings,* vol. 15, 183, no. 453. Salomon, *Dozing,* 196, states that the painting "is best understood as a moralistic statement about the consequences of being 'asleep on the job'."

20. Slatkes, *Vermeer,* 120, links the motif of the cat stealing the bird to a contemporary English emblem of this very same subject. Slatkes quotes its *subscriptio,* but the relationship between this emblem and the motif in the painting remains unclear.

21. Johan de Brune, *Bankket-werk van goede gedagten,* 2d ed., vol. 2 (Middelburg: 1660), 386, no. 620, "een keucken-meyt moet d'eene ooghe, naer de panne, en d'ander naer de katte hebben." This passage is quoted in *Tot lering en vermaak,* 146. There and in Salomon, *Dozing,* 195, it is argued that the motif of the cat stealing the chicken can probably be interpreted as a sexual metaphor in this

picture. Despite this animal's longstanding association with lust, there seems to be no visual evidence in the painting for interpreting it in this manner. In Maes's *Eavesdropper* in Dordrecht, the cat is definitely meant as an erotic metaphor, because it steals a bird in the vicinity of a maid embraced by her lover. For this painting, which seems to be more iconographically complex than *The Idle Servant*, see Eddy de Jongh, "Realisme en schijnrealisme in de Hollandse schilderkunst van de zeventiende eeuw," in exhibition catalogue *Rembrandt en zijn tijd* (Brussels [Paleis voor Schone Kunsten]: 1971, 180–83; *Tot lering en vermaak*, cat. no. 34; Slatkes, *Vermeer*, 122; exhibition catalogue *Masters of Seventeenth-Century Dutch Genre Painting* (Philadelphia [Philadelphia Museum of Art]: 1984, cat. no. 67.

22. Gouge, *Of domesticall duties* . . . , 624.

23. See, for example, *The Idle Servant* by Esaias Bourse, cited by Salomon, *Dozing*, 192, fig. 170; *The Eavesdropper* by Nicolaes Maes, cited in note 22 above.

24. See, for example Gouge, *Of domesticall duties* . . . , 646ff; Perkins, *Christian Oeconomie*, 696–97; Carter, *Carter's Christian*, 205ff; Wittewrongel, *Oeconomia Christiana*, vol. 1, 220ff. See also Groenendijk, *De nadere reformatie*, 174–75.

25. See, for example, Gouge, *Of domesticall duties* . . . , 589ff; Perkins, *Christian Oeconomie*, 697–98; Carter, *Carter's Christian*, 240ff; Willem Teellinck, *Sleutel der devotie ons opende de deure des hemels* in *Alle de wercken* . . . , vol. 3, pt. 1 (Amsterdam: 1664), 412; Wittewrongel, *Oeconomia Christiana*, vol. 1, 207ff. See also Groenendijk, *De nadere reformatie*, 173–74.

26. See Rudolf M. Dekker, "Masters and servants in the Dutch republic: an uneasy relationship," *Images of the World: Dutch Genre Painting in Its Historical Context*, ed. C. Brown and M. Stevens (London: forthcoming).

27. G. D. J. Schotel, *Het Oud-Hollandsch huisgezin der zeventiende eeuw* (Haarlem: 1867–1868), 321. This passage is cited by Dekker, who also discusses the erroneous ideas of other social historians working during the nineteenth and early twentieth centuries. Their ideas continue to influence our modern-day conceptions about life in Holland during the seventeenth century. For example, Schotel's specious assumption that servants ate together with family members is repeated by Deric Regin, *Traders, Artists, Burghers: A Cultural History of Amsterdam in the 17th Century* (Assen/Amsterdam: 1976), 142 and n. 102, and following Regin, by Salomon, *Dozing*, 193.

28. See A. M. van der Woude, "Variations in the Size and Structure of the Household in the United Provinces of The Netherlands in the Seventeenth and Eighteenth Centuries," in *Household and Family in Past Time*, ed. P. Laslett and R. Wall (Cambridge: 1972), 314; Donald Haks, *Huwelijk en gezin in de 17de en 18de eeuw* (Assen: 1982), 164–74. These works are cited by Dekker, who also concludes from studies of contemporary diaries that servants were treated rather roughly. See also Marlies Jongejan, "Dienstboden in de Zeeuwse steden 1650–1800," *Spiegel historiael* 19 (1984): 214–21; Simon Schama, *The Embarrassment of Riches; An Interpretation of Dutch Culture in the Golden Age* (New York: 1987), 455ff. Naturally, there were exceptions; see Alan Macfarlane, *The Family Life of Ralph Josselin, A Seventeenth-Century Clergyman* (Cambridge: 1970), 147. Schama, *Embarrassment* (456) observes that because servants sometimes appear in family portraits, it gives the strongest possible sign of their integration within the family circle.

29. Jongejan, "Dienstboden," 216, "De ideale dienstbode was gehoorzaam en diende zijn of haar meester tot in lengte van jaren in 'alle neerstigheyt en getrouwigheyt.' De uitgebreide wetgeving doet vermoeden dat de praktijk niet

in over eenstemming was met dit ideaal." See also Haks, *Huwelijk*, 168–70; the ordinances published in Purmerend in 1696 that are reprinted in Wantje Fritschy, ed., *Fragmenten vrouwengeschiedenis*, vol. 2 (The Hague: 1980), 75–80.

30. The evidence presented here would seem to contradict the statement by Schama, *Embarrassment* (456), that there was no art that featured the exemplary servant.

Austen's Shackles and Feminine Filiation

Chiara Briganti

"If *Pride and Prejudice* is light and bright and sparkling, *Sense and Sensibility* is bleak and nasty."[1] Thus John Halperin summarizes his critical account of Austen's first published novel, attributing its "nastiness" to Austen's "foul mood" during its composition. Halperin claims, in fact, that the book is prevented from being a masterpiece "by the author's ill-temper and impatience with her own characters" and concludes that "perhaps its chief interest is the glimpse it gives us into the dark side of the novelist's personality."[2] Of course Halperin speaks as a psychobiographer constructing the writer's portrait; my interest is on the text as intersubjective process, but I agree with Halperin's sense of darkness. *Sense and Sensibility* certainly is a dark novel, preoccupied with money and arrayed with disagreeable characters, made even darker by the shadow cast by its ambiguous and disturbing ending. Critics have been unanimous in faulting the ending, attesting to this novel's problematic character rather than its failure as a text. To use Roland Barthes's distinction, *Sense and Sensibility* is certainly not a "text of pleasure," one which "contents, fills, grants euphoria; the text that comes from culture and does not break with it [and] is linked to a *comfortable* practice of reading." It is rather what Barthes would call a "text of bliss: the text that imposes a state of loss, the text that discomforts . . . unsettles the reader's historical, cultural, psychological assumptions."[3]

An unwillingness to relinquish expectations created by Austen's later novels has caused *Sense and Sensibility*'s dismissal as a work marked by flaws typical of many first novels. Douglas Bush, for instance, observes that "whereas the other novels open with arresting and more or less ironical animation, this one begins with a rather flat account of the recently widowed Mrs. Dashwood and her daughters."[4] Biased by a desire to judge *Sense and Sensibility* against the rest of Austen's production, Bush fails to notice that the novel's opening is concerned only marginally with Mrs. Dashwood. Its claim is much more ambitious: by blurring the content of individual lives, the compression in time shifts the emphasis to the patriarchal frame in which they are inscribed. Compressing several years in half a chapter, the novel opens with characters unable to control the eddies of time and brings forth the patrilinear sequence that establishes the heroines' future. The chapter is dominated by a dislocation Edward W. Said defines as nineteenth-century fiction's "imagery of succession, of paternity, of hierarchy."[5] Here, too, as in most nineteenth-century novels, the genealogicial premise is central. However, signs of a crisis soon become apparent: the two *patres familias* are quickly disposed of, although not quickly enough to avoid revealing their failure as figures of authority—the whimsical uncle through his lack of judgment, the well-meaning weakling Henry Dashwood through his financial powerlessness and blind trust. The father's place is taken by the son from a previous marriage, and a break in the narrative sequence anticipates that "collapse of the genealogical line," which according to Said happened in fiction at the beginning of the twentieth century and resulted in the disruption of linear narrative and the abolition of character. The dispossession of the Dashwood women becomes a paradigm for that "tentative discomfort with linear dominance"[6] that Patricia Tobin has described in the nineteenth-century novel, a discomfort that later writers reflect in the abolition of well-constructed narrative, and that in Austen results in a proliferation of characters and stories. So, while a linear narrative shaped by the succession principle dominates the nineteenth-century novel, Austen flouts this principle at *Sense and Sensibility*'s beginning, replacing it with principles typical of much later fiction—"adjacency . . . parallelism and . . . complementarity"[7]—almost in an attempt to disengage the novel's heritage from the father, to expose temporal anteriority as a principle inadequate to guarantee meaning.

Opening with the history of a family rather than of an individual tends to root the narrative in the solid, secure ground of a respectable past. Solidity and security are emphasized further by the novel's language: the Dashwoods have been "long settled in Sussex," living "for many generations" in a "large estate" in a "respectable manner." However, this sense of security soon appears to be an empty shell. To start with, the late owner of Norland is not a patriarch with a large family but a bachelor with a sister for companion and housekeeper. He has no direct descendants: to replace the loss of his sister he invites his nephew's family to come to live with him. His nephew, in turn, has married twice, and it is not to himself but to his son's son that the property will be bequeathed by the uncle, who has been conquered "by such attractions as are by no means unusual in children of two or three years old," attractions that "outweigh all the value of all the attention which, for years, he had received from his niece and her daughters."[8] This surrogate father figure represents the first of a series of examples in the novel of paternal failure, parallel to, and indeed a cause of, Henry Dashwood's ineffectuality and failure to provide for his daughters. The seemingly solid world of Norland Park crumbles quickly in the narrative's compressed time, and degradation becomes more than a possibility while family affection, respectability, and security are prey to the avarice and petty prudence of "halfblood" relations. Soon we are aware of the dispossession and disinheritance that connects the loss of the estate and the failure of parental authority.

Austen shows patriarchal hierarchy's inadequacy and fantasizes a purely feminine filiation. In the first chapter she introduces a whimsical surrogate father, an impotent father unsuccessful in occupying his legitimate place and still subject to a higher authority; and an avaricious and calculating son. Father and son are duplicates insofar as they are failures, sharing their inadequacy to fill the place of authority, but otherwise different from each other. Then, almost as if to suggest that the father is dispensable after all, she concludes the chapter by sketching a matrilinear succession: we are told that "the resemblance between [Marianne] and her mother was strikingly great." Both are women of romantic generosity, "eager in everything," "amiable, interesting," "everything but prudent," given to encouraging "the violence of their affliction" and to give "themselves up wholly to their sorrow." As Barthes has observed, storytelling is a way of searching for one's origins, and Austen searches for hers in a matrilinear succession: the patrilinear sequence, seeming to have formed the narrative's frame, collapses through exposure of its representative's inadequacy. In its place emerges a lineage of women, while the monological narrative branches out to create two heroines, two stories, two subplots, and a proliferation of sets of characters.

Doubling is everywhere, inscribed in the text both spatially and temporally.[9] Sets, or pairs, abound in this novel—the most obvious being Marianne and Elinor, Lucy and Nancy Steele, Lady

Middleton and Mrs. Parker, Lady Middleton and Mrs. John Dashwood, Mrs. John Dashwood and her husband (of whom she is a
caricature), and Robert and Edward Ferrars. Then there are Mrs.
Ferrars and Mrs. Jennings, the former with a propensity to es-
trange her children, the latter with a tendency to adopt impoverished young women; Marianne and her mother, sharing
romantic taste and lack of prudence; Marianne and the two Elizas,
protagonists of the double subplot; Lady Middleton and Sir John
Middleton; Nancy Steele and Marianne; and Lucy Steele and
Elinor.

Pairing allows the narrator to create a multifaceted surface while
dispensing with direct commentary. But the function of pairs is
multifold: they echo each other, throw light on each other, call
attention to hidden possiblities in similarities and differences. The
most disquieting doubles are the self's extreme distortions, presenting threatening possibilities. Thus the precarious financial
situation functions as a first connection between the Dashwood
and Steele sisters, reinforced by further similarities: both Marianne and Nancy Steele have a tendency to say too much at the
wrong time, and behind Marianne's lack of sense looms Nancy
Steele's utter silliness. Lucy's avarice and manipulative character
casts a shadow over Elinor's prudence and compliance to social
rules.

As Otto Rank has noted, not only the "shadow" but also the
brother (and sister) are common forms of double. The self represses its unacceptable instincts and desires and personifies
them in the double, where they can be vicariously gratified and
punished. The ego loves the double, seeing in it its own copy and
hating the difference, attempting to protect itself by killing the
double, only to find out that it is "really a suicidal act."[10] In Elinor
and Marianne's "subtle, undeclared rivalry . . . in romantic endeavors"[11] we perceive intimations of this troubled relationship,
intimations that climax during Marianne's illness. We should recall that beneath surface differences, Elinor and Marianne's lives
have been proceeding along very similar paths. Although Elinor
has forced herself to remain civil, her misfortunes in love have not
been less serious than Marianne's.

After much talk of Elinor's civil behavior under the strain of
Lucy's shattering revelation (which has not prevented her from
keeping a constant watch on her sister), we receive the first
intimations of Marianne's illness, voiced simultaneously with
Elinor's unconcerned reaction. We learn that Marianne is ill by
Colonel Brandon's "looks of anxious solicitude," which Elinor

promptly dismisses as "the quick feelings and needless alarm of a lover" (245). Elinor's ill-grounded lack of concern is indeed strange for such an alert and watchful observer, and Colonel Brandon is justly astonished at her composure. Whereas Miss Jennings is inclined from the first to think Marianne's complaint is serious, Elinor continues staunchly optimistic, trusting "to the certainty and efficacy of sleep" and feeling "no real alarm" (246). Whereas the apothecary's report worries Mrs. Jennings, "Mrs. Dashwood was . . . sanguine." When Marianne has a sudden relapse, Elinor, "still sanguine [and] willing to attribute the change to nothing more than the fatigue of having sat up," finally "saw her with satisfaction sink at last into a slumber from which she expected the most beneficial effects" (248). At this point the language's sinister quality is corroborated by Elinor's rapid change from optimistic composure to a vision of Marianne's certain death. Marianne's slumber, into which Elinor happily sees her sink, seems perilously close to death. From feeling confident that there is nothing seriously wrong with Marianne, Elinor fancies "that all relief might soon be in vain," and she pictures to herself "her suffering mother arriving too late to see this darling child" (250). To conjure up such a scene when no change in Marianne's condition has occurred is, so to speak, to invoke it.

In Marianne's death Elinor envisions a possible solution to the subversive impulses of her double, impulses threatening to disrupt her painfully achieved balance by reaffirming the priority of desire over self-restraint, pleasure over duty. Significantly, Marianne's illness and her confinement allow Elinor to have her first and only full-length conversation with Willoughby. Far from leaving her disgusted by a man who offers only a lame excuse for abandoning the woman he has seduced and made pregnant, who explains his breach with Marianne only by his dread of poverty and his notion of what "common prudence" is, and who does not hesitate to lay the blame for his behavior on everybody around him, this conversation produces quite the opposite result: Willoughby, whom until that moment "she had abhorred as the most worthless of men" (267), now receives her commiseration. A strange anxiety over the absence of men pervades much of the novel: it structures Nancy's pathetic speeches, silences Marianne, engages Elinor and Lucy in protracted double-talk, and results in Elinor's strange vulnerability to Willoughby's charm. In her conversation with Willoughby she acknowledges this vulnerability, realizing the extent of her erotic investment: "She felt that his influence over her mind was heightened by circumstances which ought not in reason to have weight: by that person of uncommon attraction, that open, affectionate, and lively manner which it was no merit to possess; and by that still ardent love for Marianne, which it was not even innocent to indulge" (268). From now on "'poor Willoughby'" will be "constantly in her thoughts" (269). The erotic tension of this scene is Elinor's production as much as Willoughby's. Peter Brooks, drawing on Roman Jakobson's notion of the "phatic" and "conative" functions of language, observes how in embedded tales, "where the storyteller speaks to someone who listens," what is at stake "is perhaps less than the 'message' of the story than its reception . . . how, and by what means, the message is received . . . how, and by what means, the message is received, and with what results." And, he concludes, "the tale told may represent an attempt at seduction."[12] This is certainly true of Willoughby's confession to Elinor.

Doubling is not only spatial in this novel but also temporal, not limited to the splitting and twinning of characters but constituting the narrative's shaping principle. Judged against the Aristotelian principle that "it is necessary for the well-constructed plot to have a single rather than a double construction,"[13] *Sense and Sensibility*, despite its brevity, with its two heroines, its double plot, its two subplots, and the mirroring and splitting of characters, fits well Henry James's definition of a "loose baggy monster" or Peter Garrett's more recent Bakhtinian description of the multiplot novel shaped by a dialogical structure (6).[14] The dialogical structure adds to the complexity of the novel and is also a means to explore the antinomy between 'sense' and 'sensibility' set forth in the title and developed into a range of nuances rather than rigidified into a schematic opposition. Austen starts from the eighteenth-century opposition between sense and sensibility and revises it to develop a complex web of various possibilities. As Elinor and Marianne do not embody the opposition between sense and sensibility but rather partake of both in varying degrees, so other characters are reduced to mere caricatures by total commitment to sense or a complete lack of it.

However, Garrett's notion of the dialogical as opposed to monological novel, although helpful to explain the relationship between Elinor's and Marianne's stories, does not account for the insertion of the episodes of the two Elizas. Neither "regrettable lapse into threadbare melodrama"[15] or a "wretched episode,"[16] these two subplots are important for the novel's structure and force us to ask crucial questions. What is their function in the novel? Why does Colonel Brandon tell Elinor? Why couldn't Austen content herself with one story? Why is young Eliza's story a replica of her mother's? Why are a mother and a daughter doomed to being seduced and bearing children out of wedlock? And what is the relationship between their lives and Marianne's? The repetition of the seduction story in *Sense and Sensibility* implies both resemblance and difference, those two formal categories in whose tension, according to Todorov, narrative is constituted.[17] The narrative plot (Todorov's *récit*) stands in metaphorical relation to the story (Todorov's *histoire*). It is this relationship that Austen seems to be asking us to consider: not only should we notice the similarities between Marianne and the two Elizas that Brandon points out; perhaps we should also consider the stories' differences, that is, the difference in the transformation of the *histoire* into the three *récits*.

The first major difference concerns the story's author; the two Elizas exist outside the space of Austen's representations and are created by Colonel Brandon, at once the father/author of their narratives and a lover/brother/father figure. The second difference concerns the women's ultimate fate: whereas the two Elizas bear illegitimate children and either die or live in isolation, Marianne is timely saved from seduction and will, at least apparently, rejoin the community. Let us start with the first Eliza, whose "strong resemblance" to Marianne—"the same warmth of heart, the same eagerness of fancy and spirits" ostensibly prompts Colonel Brandon to relate her life to Elinor. She is one of his "nearest relations, an orphan" placed under his father's guardianship. They grow up as playfellows and friends, almost as brother and sister, but Colonel Brandon cannot remember a time when he did not love her. Their plan to elope together unfortunately falls through, and she is married off to Colonel Brandon's older brother. Colonel Brandon is prevented from acting because of his patrilineal position: as a younger son, he has no more privileges than a daughter. Banished, he comes back from abroad years later, only to find an "altered," "faded" Eliza, a "melancholy and sickly figure." All he can do is to place her "in comfortable lodgings and under proper attendants" (166) and wait for her death. Brandon is convinced that "a firmer mind or a happier marriage," that is, the guidance of a wise and loving husband could have prevented Eliza's disgrace. Until very recently, novels have shown how women's sexual indulgence inevitably leads to madness or illness; thus, it is only appropriate that Eliza should pay for her own excesses by becoming ill. The account of her illness, related with much insistence on her loss of beauty and bloom, on her isolation and exile from the social community, casts the shadow of death on Marianne's illness, an illness also accompanied by loss of beauty and estrangement from the community, and invokes another similarity: for both women disease provides a way out of an uncongenial plot—be it a marriage scheme or a narrative plot. "Narrating is never innocent," Peter Brooks has said, "and the narrative that frames another allows the writer to dramatize the results of the telling."[18] As Willoughby's embedded narrative makes Elinor the object of a seduction, the embedded tales of the two Elizas become the means through which Colonel Brandon offers his services. After bringing up the similarities, Brandon is the first to call attention to the differences between Eliza and Marianne. Eliza fell because she had no friend to advise or restrain her, and, significantly, according to Brandon, such a friend could have been found in her guardian, had he lived, notwithstanding the fact that that person was the cause of her wretched marriage and consequent disgrace. He proceeds to assure Elinor that "their fates, their fortunes, cannot be the same." However, his assurance is offered conditionally: Marianne will avoid Eliza's fate provided she accepts a husband's gentle supervision, a paternal figure who can channel her desire. His assurance actually camouflages a marriage offer that in turn disguises an offer of paternal tutelage invested with incestuous desire. Colonel Brandon, who as a son had been banished, has returned to affirm himself as father and the figure of authority, and to alienate Marianne into the mansion of civilized language.

Now let us turn to the younger Eliza's story. Colonel Brandon, suspected to be her natural father, has adopted her and failed to prevent tragedy—Eliza's elopement with Willoughby is facilitated by the insufficient supervision of a "well-meaning but not quick-sighted" father. Once again, after calling attention to the similarities between this other Eliza's story and Marianne's, Colonel Brandon stresses differences: he lingers on "the self-reproach which must attend [Eliza] through life," furthering that accumulation of guilt of which Eliza is herself an offspring, while Marianne will at least be able to draw consolation from the knowledge that her sufferings "proceed from no misconduct and can bring no disgrace" (169). And while Marianne, waiting to be removed to Barton, is resting on the comforting knowledge of her virtuous behavior, where is Eliza? Of course Colonel Brandon has "removed her and her child into the country, and there she remains" (170).

Colonel Brandon tells his tale of seduction, desire, and death with many hesitations. He approaches it very early in the novel, when he observes to Elinor, "I once knew a lady who in temper and mind greatly resembled your sister, who thought and judged like her, but who from an enforced change—from a series of unfortunate stances—." But here he has to stop. His tale cannot be handled lightly, nor can it be narrated until he is sure that Elinor is ready to receive it. He broaches it again when later he appears "on the point either of disclosing or of inquiring something particular about her" (138), but once more he stops. Finally he will return to it, and the story will get to be told, although with many hesitations. For he, no less than Austen, is aware that "a subject such as this—untouched for fourteen years—it is dangerous to handle it all!" (167), but he also feels threatened by the tale's unconscious fantasy of feminine filiation. In Colonel Brandon's hands Eliza's story becomes a warning, repeated twice, preventing any further illusion about Willoughby that Marianne still may have nourished. It is a tale of sameness, paralysis, illegitimacy, and subversive desire. This man, who has been a lover to the first victim and an adoptive father to the second, now unites his two roles in his offer of tutelage of Marianne. Thus the unconscious discourse is an effect of Colonel Brandon's desire, that desire which is the "motor of the narrative,"[19] and which insists to be heard. And, in turn, the story is the unconscious discourse of Austen's narrative. Her story of Marianne is a repetition in difference of Colonel Brandon's Eliza tale. The conspicuous repetition in the spatial and temporal doubling—the expression of a compulsion that, according to Freud, overrides the pleasure principle—reveals Austen's efforts to master the trauma of the seduction story that is the masterplot of a male "author" such as Brandon, her attempts to rebel against it, and to go from passivity to authority. Both Brandon and Austen use their stories to validate themselves, to silence all other voices, and to appropriate the authority of the father and master of the text. And if Brandon occupies the place of the father by virtue of temporal anteriority, Austen disclaims him as author by pointing to the spuriousness of his function—by showing how all along Brandon, son/father, is also father/lover and rescuer/seducer, as his becoming a double of Willoughby reveals.

There is an almost diametrical opposition between Colonel Brandon and Willoughby, emphasized by their introduction in two contiguous chapters. Although the only connection between them seems to be their rivalry over Marianne, we soon discover that their bond is tighter: where one is Eliza's seducer, the other is her rescuer; further, in a sense, both Willoughby's role as seducer and Colonel Brandon's ineffectuality as rescuer are determined by their temporary occupation of the locus of femininity, making them subject to representatives of patriarchal authority.[20] Colonel Brandon and Willoughby also share the incestuous aspect of their relationship to Marianne. I have already spoken of Colonel Brandon's incestuous desire for Marianne. Let me now turn to Marianne's relationship to Willoughby. More than a real individual, he is the hero of a favorite story, her creation, the image she sees in the mirror. Both Marianne and Willoughby are described in the same chapter with the same language: they both have spirit, eagerness, frankness, and vivacity; they show neither shyness nor reserve. Their tastes are "strikingly alike": they are passionately fond of music and dancing; they idolize "the same books, the same passages." In short, Willoughby,

> a young man of good abilities, quick imagination, lively spirits, and open, affectionate manners . . . was exactly formed to engage Marianne's heart, for with all this, he joined not only a captivating person, but a natural ardour of mind which was now roused and increased by the example of her own, and which recommended him to her affection beyond everything else. . . . Willoughby was all that her fancy had delineated in that unhappy hour (41–42).

The encounter with Willoughby functions as a belated mirror stage for Marianne—that moment, indispensable and misleading, because it is based on a misrecognition, which for Lacan constitutes the first step in the self's construction, the first of a series of fictional images of unity. He is her totalizing image, the first identification, which threatens to be the last. He is the expression of her narcissism, which John Irwin has described as an "attempt to return to a state in which subject and object did not yet exist . . . in short, to return to the womb."[21] But, as Irwin tells us, the desire to return to the womb is the desire for incest, a thread that also runs in *Mansfield Park*, but is never as compelling as in this novel. Incest is an Imaginary transaction and like narcissism, to which it is related, is essentially regressive. To give way to Marianne's incestuous desire would be to give way to her death-wish—her death-wish proper after the breach with Willoughby, and the death-wish that is implicit in her choice of a sister-soul, which leads her back to the Imaginary order and which is also the death-wish of the narrative, the desire for the end, "the collapse [of the beginning into the end], of life into immediate death."[22] As

Marianne herself acknowledges, the Willoughby she had fallen for is an Imaginary characterization, the pursuit of which "would have been self destruction" (278).

But Willoughby is also Marianne's fiction, her revision of Edward, and her creation of the ideal lover. Marianne in fact revises Edward as lover and creates Willoughby, much as Austen, by pointing to paternal failure and substituting her fantasy of a purely feminine filiation for patriarchal genealogy, revises the patriarchal novel she has inherited. Marianne's and Austen's revisions raise the question of feminine subjectivity and of whether the feminine subject can speak or write, for there is no doubt that Jane Austen was well aware of the power implicit in the use of language and of the traditional exclusion of women from it. Like Anne Elliott, she is painfully aware that "Men have had every advantage of us in telling their own story. . . . The pen has been in their hands!" Sandra Gilbert and Susan Gubar have noticed how in all of her novels Austen projects onto her female characters her attempt at establishing herself as author, a process which always involves "the initiation into conscious acceptance of powerlessness" together with "the fall from authority into the acceptance of one's status as mere character."[23] For Gilbert and Gubar it is Emma who is the avatar of the artist, while Marianne, fanciful and imaginative, is the paradigm of the Romantic heroine. I believe, instead, that in Emma Austen asks us to consider the improvement in her ability to read, while the insistence on the importance of language and Marianne's commitment to it point to her role as the alter-ego of the author.

> Les trous entre les besoins apaisés de la survie et entre les mots étoffés de la communication, ces trous parlent aussi, ou crient silencieusement. (Bellemin-Noel, *Vers l'inconscient du texte*)

Marianne's fastidiousness about language, her abhorrence of clichés, her horrified reaction to John Middleton's fondness for phrases such as "making a conquest," "setting one's cap at a man," certainly reflect Jane Austen's preoccupation with the degradation of language as reflection of ethical and intellectual deterioration. There is no doubt that she would have agreed with Marianne that the tendency of clichés "is gross and illiberal; if their construction could ever be deemed clever, time has long ago destroyed all its ingenuity" (39). Such preoccupation with the ethical consequences of slack language, which characterizes Marianne, is often expressed in Austen's letters and is also found in the narrator's comments on Lady Middleton calling Elinor and Marianne satirical because they are fond of reading, on the insistence on Mrs. Parker's inconsequential talk, and on Lucy's disregard of grammar.

However, what demands special attention is language both as a means of revealing Marianne's kind of sensibility—her love for the picturesque and poetry, her romantic taste—and of showing her refusal to play by social rules. Marianne's investment in language is enormous and is linked with her position in the civilized and discontented world of the novel, in which social decorum frowns upon the unrestrained expression of real feeling and demands that it be domesticated and made safe. Marianne's solution is silence: "sometimes I have kept my feelings to myself because I could find no language to describe them in but what was worn and hackneyed out of all sense and meaning" (80). Not only does silence become for her a viable alternative to the degradation of language; more important, by refusing to speak at certain crucial moments Marianne establishes herself as a rebel against the restraints imposed by the social code so willingly adopted by Elinor. To social decorum requiring polite lies Marianne opposes her utter commitment to sincerity, for "to say what she did not believe was impossible," even when at stake is the risk of wounding her sister's feelings.

Whereas for Elinor language functions as a cover allowing her to engage in protracted double-talk with her rival in love, for Marianne language *is* reality and the means of authenticating the self. Thus Marianne is finally convinced of Willoughby's disaffection by the language of his letter, which proves him neither the sister-soul she had seen in him nor the incarnation of her dreams, but in fact, a projection of herself, an imago, "equal to what her fancy had ever drawn for the hero of a favorite story," but rather to belong to another, because the language of the letter does in fact belong to another. It is significant, too, that through Willoughby's language—that is, when Willoughby is allowed to speak—their romance loses its uniqueness and becomes just another affair to be described through stale metaphors involving "thunderbolts and daggers."

If an uncompromising seriousness about language sets Marianne apart from the other characters and makes her the alter-ego of the author, her choice of silence, paralleled as it is by Austen's reticences and evasions, haunts the novel. As Angela Leighton has observed, "to recover the Sense of Jane Austen's Silences . . . is to hear the voices which her notoriously conservative and limiting language would conceal: the voice, in particular, of her younger, Romantic heroine, Marianne."[24] Marianne's journey to silence concludes with her acceptance of the language of politeness—the only one to which she is permitted access and the language that continues to be heard in the novel, together with the empty prattle of Nancy Steele and the vicious and ungrammatical ravings of Lucy. Even after she has recovered from her illness, and by her own admission has reacquired the ability to talk on the subject of Willoughby, "a thousand inquiries sprang up from her heart, but she dared not urge one" (279). Although the text insists that Elinor's silence and secretiveness are proof of her self-denying nature and strength of character, Marianne's silence does not bespeak heroism but unfettered imagination and madness. Thus, as Edward Said has said of madness, it must be *"incorporated, covered* and *articulated* in the discourse of reason."[25] However, Marianne's silence can still make itself audible by coinciding with her illness, the very center of the novel. By virtue of her withdrawal, Marianne becomes the text's "reserve of silence,"[26] the silence that supports and underlies the text, the silence *out of which* it speaks.

Many critics have noticed Austen's ambivalence toward Marianne's sincerity and spontaneity. Her plots have been viewed by some as acts of bad faith, timid disavowals of her early recognition of society's ineffectuality and supportive of the hypocrisies imposed by decorum. The defenders of Austen's "conventionality," on the other hand, have emphasized how individualism during Austen's time had different connotations from our own time. Further, they have pointed to Jane Austen's awareness of the dangers of unlimited imaginative freedom in authors as in heroines, so that for Austen "to withdraw from society and place faith in a passionate relationship, as Marianne does with Willoughby, is to take a direction to be censored even as its appeal is admitted."[27] Freud has said that the poet's daydreams all share "a hero[ine] who is the center of interest, for whom the author tries to win our sympathy by every possible means, and whom he places under the protection of a special providence."[28] Although Austen, in her attempt to win our sympathies for her most romantic heroine, may be more temperate than the romancers considered by Freud, her attraction to Marianne is palpable. She makes Marianne's individualism appealing not only by contrasting it with the petty prudence of disagreeable characters, but also with Elinor's propriety. We are ready to admit with Colonel Brandon the appeal of her "romantic refinements" and to appreciate the artistic talent she lavishes on the invention of her object of love. Although on the surface the novel seems to support the bildungsroman frame toward comic resolution, Austen pits her own language against this interpretation, a language refusing to subscribe to a desirable comic ending, and Marianne pits a silence that demands to be heard. Marianne becomes the gap in the text, the hole, the absence, the desire muffled and repressed in "silent agony," that calls the comic ending into question. Her silence casts doubts on the judgments the novel seems to make. At the end the tension becomes palpable between the ethical construct that the novel asks us to accept and the daemonic, destructive, and erotic element demanding to be heard through the repetition compulsion of the narrative and Marianne's silence.

> Which of us has his desire? or, having it, is satisfied?—come, children, let us shut up the box and the puppets, for our play is played out. (W. Thackeray, *Vanity Fair*)

The ending of *Sense and Sensibility* is obviously problematic and hurried. One gets a sense of the author being in a sudden flurry to impose closure on the novel, to resolve its tensions, to get all the strands neatly tucked in, and to shut all the puppets into the box. Marianne, we are told, has learned a new language that will enable her to partake of the customs and rules by which the community operates. Now she can look into the mirror and see the mirror itself instead of those imagos that were an expression of her narcissistic nature. And yet, despite the claims made by a number of critics on the ostensible direction toward which Austen's fiction moves, on her unquestioning support of the social code, the language ("with such a confederacy against her . . . what could she do" but submit to Colonel Brandon's "fond attachment"?) betrays such assumed compliance. Thus the ending seems to be not only a question of closure but also of enclosure; not only of marriage but of death, the end of the story and the end of life.[29] The first Eliza is "placed in comfortable lodgings and under proper attendants," and there she will die. Younger Eliza is removed together with her child into the country, "and there she remains." Marianne, too, is removed. From now on she will inhabit a house in the village with a butcher hard by, "a nice old-fashioned place, full of comforts and conveniences; quite shut in with great garden walls . . . close to the church and only a quarter of a mile from the turnpike road, so 'tis never dull, for if you only go and sit up in an old yew arbour behind the house, you may see all the carriages that pass along" (158). Marianne has become a spectator, for as an actor she was too dangerous. Excluded from action, she stares out into the world, refusing even to voice her awareness of being a prisoner, as Maria Bertram will do in *Mansfield Park*. She is no Maria Bertram, nor is she a puppet that can be shut snugly into a box and forgotten; she is more like the madman staring out of the window of David Copperfield's room. And, like the madman who haunts David's imagination, she becomes herself an image of demonism,[30] significantly related to the repetition compulsion in the narrative, which induces Austen to repeat the seduction story but with a difference: in this novel, the metaphorical marriage of father and daughter (Colonel Brandon's marriage to Marianne) becomes the means—the only means—of halting the succession of illegitimate children. As Colonel Brandon most efficiently suggested to Elinor, lack of paternal tutelage, which he offers to Marianne through marriage, may well result in a replica of the fate of the two Elizas. But such a marriage points to its own illegitimacy as a solution and to the spuriousness and inadequacy of the father as authority figure, as author, *auctor*, begetter of all the stories, or as agent of closure, enclosure, marriage and death.

Moi, Pierre Rivière, ayant égorgé ma mère, ma soeur et mon frère. . . .
(Michel Foucault)

I murdered my Father at a very early period of my life, I have since murdered my Mother, and I am now going to murder my sister. (Jane Austen, *Minor Works*)

In an essay on Austen's accommodation of femininity and authority in *Sense and Sensibility*, Deborah Kaplan argues that while Austen's first published novel "shows metaphors of masculine authority to be socially sanctioned and metaphors of feminine authority to be illegitimate." *Sense and Sensibility* ultimately "registers disapproval not just of feminine authority but of all its human forms however conventional."[31] Anglicanism, according to Kaplan, equips Austen with the means of questioning the legitimacy of patriarchal authority. Although I agree that Austen deconstructs male authority, I do not believe that she does so by judging it "against the standard of spiritual paternity." Invoking divine authority as the only one sanctioned by Austen does not enrich the texture of *Sense and Sensibility*, nor does it provide answers as to the "oddities of the novel." I am convinced instead that the question of authority ties up with Austen's rebellion against the patriarchal genealogy and family and is intimately related to the question of authorship: by confronting one, Austen could not avoid confronting the other. In her attempt to establish herself as the parent of her own story, she must confront the metaphor of paternity. Fatherhood in this novel does not belong solely to the representational level but to the metafictional as well: Brandon is a father figure in the novel but also the author of tales of seduction and the representative of the Law that Austen must confront to make her fantasy of agency come true. As a woman writer, Austen is caught in the paradoxical situation of revealing through the very creation of a male author—Brandon—the alienation and madness that are consequences of transgressive gestures of trespassing—Marianne's walks, "not merely on the dry gravel of the shrubbery but all over the grounds, and especially in the most distant parts of them where there was something more of wildness than in the rest" (245). Austen reveals her alienation through her own splitting and consequent creation of a teller of seduction tales who will proceed to silence the feminine in her fiction and provide the binding promoted by the Symbolic. This will assure a linear and coherent narrative, a domesticated and safe life, and the repression and articulation of desire in the discourse of reason, the alternative to which "is the spectre of the unchecked death wish in the ultimate merger of subject and object, desire and law, self and the natural world."[32] Caught in the dilemma, on the one hand, between compromise with male authority figures in order to negotiate her access in language and self-exclusion from patriarchal discourse on the other, Austen will discover that no one can claim ownership of a text after all. As Mary Jacobus has observed in a discussion on femininity and language,

> the prison of sensibility is created by patriarchy to contain women; thus they experience desire without Law, language without power. Marginalised, the language of feeling can only ally itself with insanity—an insanity which, displaced into writing, produces a moment of imaginative and linguistic excess over-brimming the container of fiction, and swamping the distinction between author and character.[33]

This is particularly true of a novel like *Sense and Sensibility*, in which Marianne's "language of feeling" is equated with insanity and therefore must be silenced. But it is also true that if Marianne's language can be silenced, her silence continues to "speak" and while undermining the finality of the comic ending, continues to produce meaning and refuses to be appropriated by the discourse of reason. Her silence, that is, insists to be heard, becoming the unconscious of the text, the "discourse of the Other," the novel's "censored chapter." Thus it dissolves the very notion of an exclusive, appropriating narrative, and questions the legitimacy of authorship itself.

> "What does it matter who is speaking," someone said, "what does it matter who is speaking."
>
> (Beckett, *The Trilogy*)

We have moved far indeed from the perspective of the psychobiographer with which this essay opened. Whereas Halperin reads *Sense and Sensibility* to construct the portrait of a woman of foul moods and to gain a glimpse "into the dark role of the novelist's personality," I have avoided curiosity for the woman in the work and have attempted to reveal the text's obsessions and evasions without recourse to the writer's personality. Furthermore, I am proposing that Austen, too, had a sense of her own powerlessness and dispensability vis à vis the text. *Sense and Sensibility* is in many respects the most daring of Austen's novels, the work running the greatest risks and revealing most painfully in its silences and discontinuities and doubling her attempts to counteract a pressing fragmentation and to reacquire *auctoritas*. Of course, Austen was writing within a tradition organized around the author, and no one would expect to find in her works a full-fledged elaboration of the problematic relationship between author and text and its philosophical implications. This does not imply, however, that one should ignore the artistic tension present in all her novels, a tension particularly acute in the ruptures and evasions, in the insistence on secrecy and secretiveness, of *Sense and Sensibility*. Such tension can be explained, at least partly, by the implications of the critical question that psychoanalytic, marxist, and post-structuralist critics alike have come to address as the "death of the author."

Jacques Lacan's theory of the unconscious as "the discourse of the Other" has exploded the illusion of the wholeness of the psyche, while introducing into it an element of irreducible otherness and unknowability and consequently exploding the illusory wholeness of the author figure. If neither subject nor text possesses integrity, and if author and text are both structured by language, it becomes clear that they cease to be separate entities governed by a relationship of filiation; rather, they participate in an intersubjective dialectic that invalidates the notion of the author as father of the narrative. As Foucault has observed in "What is an Author?", *auctor,* begetter, father, the author becomes the means to ensure that no one will enter the order of discourse if he or she does not satisfy certain requirements, and also the means to ensure protection against the discourse of folly. The "author's" function, in short, is an essentially repressive function assuming on itself the task of censorship. The father, the author, is dead, while what speaks is fiction itself.

> Et la fiction littéraire, elle, que raconte-t-elle? Elle parle de soi. Elle ne dit rien de plus de son auteur qui l'a portée et mise au monde, que le discours de ma vie n'en dit de celle qui m'a porté et mis au monde. (Jean Bellemin-Noel, *Vers l'inconscient du texte*)

Austen deconstructs male authority by pointing to Brandon's spuriousness as father figure; by presenting female characters who occupy the place of authority (namely Mrs. Ferrars and Mrs. Smith) and male characters such as Colonel Brandon, Edward Ferrars, and Willoughby who temporarily occupy the site of femininity and are prevented from being the originators of action by their exclusion from the patriarchal lineage; and, finally, by counteracting Brandon's fantasy of seduction with her own fantasy of feminine filiation. Austen's gesture is naturally fraught with risks. In her search for authority she will finally discover that, far from being subversive, her function is ultimately repressive, that her fantasy of agency finally coincides with Colonel Brandon's fantasy of seduction—for both strive to erase Marianne's difference, to reduce her to mere textual product, and to censor her efforts as textual producer. Austen will discover that she must leave it to the fiction to tell itself, for only surreptitiously can she articulate and incorporate the discourse of folly and untrammeled desire. Although as a writer she has been committed to domesticating the discourse of madness, she is powerless to silence it effectively.

Marianne has been tamed; she has been transformed into her acceptable double and is determined to let religion and reason become her guides. But then, why does she still remind us of the "Young Lady" of Austen's *Juvenilia* "whose feelings being so strong for her judgement led her into the commission of Errors which her Heart disapproved"?[34] What induced Austen to retain certain details of her extraordinary early account of a woman's folly? The Young Lady's interlocutor is called Ellinor; her suitor is a Colonel—like Colonel Brandon, the second son of a man "who died immensely rich" and bequeathed only a small portion of his wealth to his younger children while leaving the bulk to the eldest. The Young Lady, who confesses to a certain Ellinor that she has murdered her father at a very early period of her life, has since murdered her mother, served as false witness to a dispossessed Colonel, thus enabling him to receive his inheritance, and received from him a marriage proposal as a token of his gratitude. After this appalling account, she concludes her letter to Ellinor—who might in fact be her sister—by stating that she is now going to murder her sister. The link with Marianne is perhaps tenuous, yet not so tenuous as to let the similarities go unnoticed or be ranked as mere coincidences. It becomes tempting, in fact, to perceive Marianne as the result of a process of gradual silencing and taming of the subversive impulses that threatened Austen's early fiction—a process that will continue in her later works. The Elizabeths, Fannys, Annes, and Emmas of the later novels will lead a life contained within proper boundaries because women such as the mad Young Lady and maddened Marianne can no longer roam freely, but have been safely secured in the attic of Austen's fiction. Yet the Young Lady's murderous ravings and Marianne's "screams of agony" soon to be choked by grief haunt Austen's journey to silence and become the "unsaid" of the narrative, that "reserve of silence" that cannot be articulated in the discourse of reason and which constitutes literariness itself.

Notes

1. John Halperin, *The Life of Jane Austen* (Baltimore: The Johns Hopkins University Press, 1984), 84.

2. Ibid., 94.

3. Roland Barthes, *The Pleasure of the Text*, trans. Richard Miller (New York: Hill & Wang, 1985), 14.

4. Douglas Bush, *Jane Austen* (New York: MacMillan, 1975), 78.

5. Edward W. Said, *Beginnings: Intention and Method* (New York: Basic Books, 1975), 161.

6. Patricia Drechsel Tobin, *Time and the Novel: The Genealogical Imperative* (Princeton: Princeton University Press, 1978), 29.

7. Said, *Beginnings*, 16.

8. Jane Austen, *Sense and Sensibility* (New York: New American Library, 1961), 6. All subsequent citations in the essay are to this edition.

9. For the definitions of spatial doubling and temporal doubling, see John T. Irwin, *Doubling and Incest/Repetition and Revenge: A Speculative Reading of Faulkner* (Baltimore: The Johns Hopkins University Press, 1975), 55.

10. Otto Rank, *The Double: A Psychoanalytic Study,* trans. and ed. Harry Tucker, Jr. (Chapel Hill: University of North Carolina Press, 1971), 79.

11. Halperin, *Life of Jane Austen*, 94.

12. Peter Brooks, "The Tale vs. the Novel" (Paper read at The Novel Conference, Providence, R.I., April 1987), 2. I thank Professor Brooks for sending me a copy of his unpublished paper.

13. Aristotle, *Poetics*, trans. Leon Golden (Englewood Cliffs, N.J.: Prentice-Hall, 1968), 22.

14. Peter Garrett, "Double Plots and Dialogical Form in Victorian Fiction," *Nineteenth-Century Fiction* 32 (1977), 1–17.

15. Bush, *Jane Austen*, 80.

16. Alistair M. Duckworth, *The Improvement of the Estate: A Study of Jane Austen's Novels* (Baltimore: The Johns Hopkins University Press, 1971), 103.

17. Tzvetan Todorov, *The Poetics of Prose*, trans. Richard Howard (Ithaca: Cornell University Press, 1977), 233.

18. Brooks, "The Tale vs. the Novel," 2.

19. Peter Brooks, *Reading for the Plot: Design and Intention in Narrative* (New York: Knopf, 1984), xx.

20. It is worth noticing that through an interesting reversal Austen makes a woman, Mrs. Smith, the authority figure who can decide Willoughby's destiny.

21. Irwin, *Doubling*, 43.

22. Peter Brooks, "Freud's Masterplot: Questions of Narrative," *Yale French Studies* 55/56 (1977): 292.

23. Sandra Gilbert and Susan Gubar, *The Madwoman in the Attic: The Woman Writer and the Nineteenth-Century Literary Imagination* (New Haven: Yale University Press, 1979), 161.

24. Angela Leighton, "Sense and Silences: Reading Jane Austen Again," in *Jane Austen: New Perspectives* (Woman and Literature 3, new series), ed. Janet Todd (New York and London: Holmes & Meier, 1983), 130.

25. Said, *Beginnings*, 301.

26. Shoshana Felman, "Turning the Screw of Interpretation," *Yale French Studies* 55/56 (1977), 193.

27. Duckworth, 82.

28. Sigmund Freud, "The Relation of the Poet to Day-Dreaming," in *Collected Papers*, trans. under the supervision of Joan Rivière (New York: Basic Books, 1959), 179.

29. It is worth noting in this context that in *Emma* marriage and death will be explicitly equated.

30. Sandra Gilbert has observed, "Freud confided to Fliess in 1897 that he saw connections between his 'hysterical' patients and the possessed, diabolical women described in the fifteenth-century *Malleus Maleficarum*." "Introduction: A Tarantella of Theory," in Hélène Cixous and Catherine Clément, *The Newly Born Woman*, trans. Betsy Wing (Minneapolis: University of Minnesota Press, 1986), xii.

31. Deborah Kaplan, "Achieving Authority: Jane Austen's First Published Novel," *Nineteenth-Century Fiction* 37 (1983): 537.

32. Robert Con Davis, "Epilogue: The Discourse of Jacques Lacan," in *The Fictional Father: Lacanian Readings of the Text*, ed. Robert Con Davis (Amherst: University of Massachusetts Press, 1981), 188.

33. Mary Jacobus, "The Difference of View," in *Women Writing and Writing About Women* (London: Croom Helm; New York: Harper & Row, 1979), 15.

34. Jane Austen, *Minor Works*, ed. R. W. Chapman, vol. 6 (London: Oxford University Press, 1963), 175.

The Gender of American Individualism: Fanny Fern, the Novel, and the American Dream

Joyce W. Warren

Mid-nineteenth-century America was characterized by a strident individualism. Yet the cry for self-reliance and the belief in the American Dream were seen wholly as male phenomena. Emerson, Thoreau, and Whitman preached to and for male Americans; the Jacksonian democratic man was by definition a man. In 1833 Emerson declared, "I am thankful that I am an American as I am thankful that I am a man."[1] And in the dominant American culture, the two seemed to be synonymous.

In the "classic" American novel this masculine bias is most obviously reflected in the heroes created by James Fenimore Cooper, Herman Melville, and Mark Twain. Individualists like Leatherstocking, Captain Ahab, and Huckleberry Finn have no female counterparts in the novels by these authors; women in the novels tend to be passive, selfless, or nonexistent. Nathaniel Hawthorne, who did not create individualists among his male protagonists, did not create female individualists either; Hawthorne frowned upon self-assertion in both men and women.

In the popular novel the male individualist assumed one of two forms: the poor boy whose skill and self-reliance enabled him to fulfill the American success myth, or the adventurer whose skill and self-reliance enabled him to master the wilderness. In either case, the protagonist succeeded because of his independence, his self-reliance, and his self-assertion. And the protagonist was always male. In Horatio Alger's *Ragged Dick* (1866), Dick is "manly and self-reliant." Alger writes of his hero: "He knew that he had only himself to depend on, and he determined to make the most of himself,—a resolution which is the secret of success in nine cases out of ten."[2]

If nineteenth-century American male novelists did not provide us with a female individualist, what about the period's women writers? There were a few works by women that portrayed a strong, self-reliant heroine. E. D. E. N. Southworth's *The Hidden Hand* (1859) is an example of one. Capitola Le Noir, the novel's lively heroine, as a child earns her own living disguised as a boy on the streets of New York. Later, when she is rescued from the streets, she remains independent and unsentimental. She fights a duel, rescues a maiden in distress, captures an outlaw, and engineers a jail break. However, she no longer is required to earn her own living, and, at the end of the novel she marries, as would any conventional heroine.

Another independent heroine is Louisa May Alcott's Jean Muir in the novella *Behind a Mask,* which was published anonymously in 1861. In this work Alcott's heroine is not kind or likable like Jo March; instead she is manipulative and self-assertive. Behind the mask of a conventional governess, she controls the actions of all of the book's other characters. Her triumph at the end is a mixed triumph, however, and although the author sympathizes with her situation, she does not condone her methods. Moreover, although Jean Muir gains wealth and power at the novel's end, she does not succeed independently but, like the conventional heroine, gains her money through an advantageous marriage.

The majority of mid-nineteenth-century American women novelists accepted the same image of women as male novelists. Their novels differed in that their protagonists were always female. However, these female protagonists cannot be called individualists. In fact, the first lesson these young women have to learn is, not to *express* the self, but to *repress* the self. The mother of Ellen Montgomery in Susan Warner's *Wide, Wide World* (1850) urges her daughter to submit: "though we *must* sorrow, we must not rebel."[3] Gerty in Maria Cummins's *The Lamplighter* (1854) struggles hard to attain perfect "self-control."[4] And Edna Earl in Augusta Evans Wilson's *St. Elmo* (1866) urges woman to be content with her "divinely limited sphere. . . . her own quiet hearthstone."[5]

This double standard—assertive men in the marketplace and docile women in the home—was accepted by both men and women, the novelist and the reader. The success that Alger is talking about in his novels is, of course, monetary success. That he is not directing his advice to young girls as well as to young boys would have been understood by all of his readers. Not only are the self-reliant protagonists not female, but the public knew that their maleness was made essential within the construct of the novel—to the extent that women writers found it almost impossible to envision the female protagonist as the same self-reliant hero. Few writers questioned this double standard. The female protagonist's selflessness was balanced by the male protagonist's self-assertion, and whereas he sought to make a name for himself in the world, her world was circumscribed by the home. If a female protagonist was even able to earn her own living, the phenomenon was seen as a temporary measure, until she fulfilled what she, the author, and society regarded as her true vocation: a selfless marriage. As Edna's fiance in *St. Elmo* says to her before their marriage:

> To-day I snap the fetters of your literary bondage. There shall be no more books written! No more study, no more toil, no more anxiety, no more heart-aches! . . . You belong solely to me now.[6]

It was within this context that Fanny Fern wrote her novel *Ruth Hall*. Fern, who lived from 1811 to 1872, was the first American woman newspaper columnist and the most highly paid American newspaper writer of her day, man or woman. Her real name was Sara Willis Parton, but she wrote under the pseudonym of Fanny Fern, and in fact went to court in 1856 to gain legal rights to the exclusive use of the name. She was the originator of the now-famous saying, "the way to a man's heart is through his stomach."

Ruth Hall, published in December 1854, is a fictionalized account of Fern's struggle for economic independence. The autobiographical novel created a sensation when it was published because of its satirical portrayal of Fern's relatives, primarily her brother N. P. Willis, who had refused to help her when she was left a widow with two children to support nine years before. *Ruth Hall* tells the story of a woman who, without the help of the men in her life (father, brother, father-in-law, and cousin), and in spite of their hindrances, steps out of the home sphere and seeks what Fern calls her "port of independence."[7] Demonstrating all the qualities of the male individualist, Ruth shows self-reliance, self-assertion, and independence as she climbs the ladder of success to fulfill the American Dream. And, at the end of the novel, instead of acquiring a husband, she acquires ten thousand dollars in bank stock and sets out to conquer new worlds.

Unlike the male individualists, however, Ruth Hall and her creator, Fanny Fern, who succeeded in the same way, receive not praise and encouragement, but blame and criticism for their "unfeminine," "unwomanly," and "vulgar" success. Ruth's relatives offer no assistance, and, in fact, attempt to impede her progress. Her father, father-in-law, and cousin, all of whom are prominent citizens, not only will not help her financially, but they will not even use their influence or recommendation to help her obtain a teaching position. Her brother, Hyacinth Ellet, a successful New York editor, refuses to help her find a market for her newspaper articles when she begins to write, and when he discovers that she is succeeding without his assistance, he tries to stop her from writing.[8] The editors for whom she writes exploit her because she is a woman, and when she asks for more money, they use her status as a woman to denigrate her. "Just like a woman," they say; "women are never satisfied."[9]

Commenting on this double standard, Fern wrote in *The New York Ledger* in 1861:

> As a general thing there are few people who speak approbatively of a woman who has a smart business talent or capability. No matter how isolated or destitute her condition, the majority would consider it more "feminine" would she unobtrusively gather up her thimble, and, retiring into some out-of-the-way place, gradually scoop out her coffin with it, than to develop that smart turn for business which would lift her at once out of her troubles; and which, in a man so situated, would be applauded as exceedingly praiseworthy.[10]

In her struggle to attain and portray female success, Fanny Fern was herself subjected to this kind of gender-specific criticism. When *Ruth Hall* was published, reviewers focused on the author rather than on the book: she was "unfeminine," "vulgar," "indelicate," and "irreverent," and she did not show the proper filial piety. *Putnam's Monthly* described *Ruth Hall* as a book "overflowing with unfemininely bitter wrath and spite."[11] The *Protestant Episcopal Quarterly Review* condemned Fanny Fern for attacking the "ever-sacred associations of home," and condemned her for not being "decorous and womanly."[12] And the *New York Times* warned girls against breaking the fifth commandment like Ruth Hall.[13]

In all of this criticism, however, not one conventional reviewer praised *Ruth Hall* or Fanny Fern for the phenomenon contained in the novel that made it unique: its triumphant portrayal of female success. Despite the fact that novels about self-made men were commonly viewed as expressions of the promise of the American dream, critics did not recognize this same message in *Ruth Hall*. Because the person who succeeded in the novel was a woman, critics found it impossible to place the novel in the tradition of the American success story. Consequently, American reviewers focused on the author and not the book, criticizing her use of autobiographical materials and her satirical treatment of her male relatives. The British reviewers were better able to understand her satire, and without criticizing Fern any more than they would a male writer, pointed out that if people were able to recognize themselves in the satirical portraits in Fern's novel, they must deserve the censure. As the reviewer for *Tait's Magazine* noted, if *Ruth Hall* is Fanny Fern's revenge, "a revenge *is* a revenge, after all, i.e., injury given for *injury.*"[14] American reviewers, however, focused on the "unfeminine" character of such revenge. The *New York Times* explicitly stated that if the book had been written by a man, it would have been "natural and excusable"; but it was not proper for a "delicate, suffering woman" to write such a book.[15]

Not only did reviewers fail to look at *Ruth Hall* in the context of the American success story commonly associated with men, they criticized Fanny Fern for her positive portrayal of her heroine, maintaining that because the novel was based on the author's own life, she was being egotistical in portraying her heroine positively. Criticism of Fanny Fern for seeming to portray herself positively in her heroine is particularly significant when we consider the self-exaltation of many of the male writers of the period. "I celebrate myself," wrote Walt Whitman in *Leaves of Grass.*[16] Henry David Thoreau declared that he had the highest mission in life— the development of himself—and wrote in 1841 that he kept a journal because he would "live in it for the gods."[17] And Ralph Waldo Emerson described himself as "an astronomer royal whose duty it is to make faithful minutes . . . for the ages."[18] Alongside such grandiose proclamations about the self, Fern's portrayal of Ruth Hall's struggle based on her own experience seems tame. Yet the critics found it reprehensible in a woman. The *Knickerbocker Magazine* complained that Fern praised her heroine too much.[19] The *National Era* said that she was "in love with her heroine."[20] Other papers criticized Fern for her "strong self-love," her "self-exaltation," and a self-esteem that indicated that she was "swallowed up in vanity and egotism."[21] Clearly the pride of accomplishment that was a given in any man's chronicle of his triumph over American economic adversity was not expected or condoned in a woman; women were expected to be self*less* not self-assertive; passive, not aggressive; and deferential to—not critical of—men.

The only American review of *Ruth Hall* that I have been able to find that recognized and praised the novel as a female success story is Elizabeth Cady Stanton's review in the suffragette paper, *The Una*. Stanton writes: "The great lesson taught in *Ruth Hall* is that God has given to woman sufficient brain and muscle to work out her own destiny unaided and alone."[22] Stanton also decries the critics who focused on Fern's satire, noting, like the British reviewer for *Tait's Magazine*, that "if her pictures are not pleasing ones, it seems to me the censure more justly belongs to the living subjects."[23] To emphasize her meaning, Stanton points out that no one accuses a mulatto slave of "filial irreverence" if he or she tells of the cruelty and injustice of his or her white father or brother—thus indicating that, unlike the male reviewers, Stanton does not find it irreverent for Fern to criticize male relatives who deserve censure. In fact, Stanton is impatient with the reviewers whose focus on this ostensibly "unfeminine" characteristic of the author has caused them to miss the more important point of the book: the female success story.

The male reviewers—and the conventional female reviewers—were unable to see the significance of Fern's novel within the context of American individualism because they did not associate women with individualism. *Harper's New Monthly Magazine* expressed a common feeling in its complaint that the novel lacked significance because, unlike other private histories, it contained no "universal meaning" in its story.[24]

Because the "universal" in American individualism was essentially male, American critics could see in *Ruth Hall* only the *particular*: the story of one woman and the character of the author of the book. This focus on the particular resulted in an obsession with the personality of the author and the extent to which she had deviated from the conventional feminine role. The other result of this focus on the particular was that the critics were unable to see the story's significance. The *Southern Quarterly* complained of the novel's "littleness," for example, maintaining that there was no interest in "conversations between mothers and children, and enemies and patrons, such as you cannot escape in a morning's business and an evening's visit." The reviewer also found little of interest in the literary career of a woman: "she is nothing but a woman who has perpetrated a book; as if that astonishing merit, like the birth of a child, was the crowning feat of her existence."[25] Because the self-made American was perceived as inherently male both in American culture and American fiction, critics were unable to place Fern's novel in that tradition and consequently missed the point of the novel.

That it was not so difficult for critics to see the message of American individualism in a book that told the story of a man's success in America is apparent in a notice of a book that ironically was published in the same month and by the same publisher as Fern's *Ruth Hall*, and was written by the man who within a year was to become Fern's husband. In December 1854 James Parton published his first biography, *The Life of Horace Greeley*. The book was well reviewed, and although it was not as successful commercially as Fern's novel, it marked the beginning of Parton's distinguished career as a biographer. In reviewing the book, the reviewer for *Peterson's Magazine* wrote in February 1855:

> The chief purpose of the narrative is to prove, by a well known example, that perseverance and talent is sure of its reward, at least in America. The work will do good. [26]

There is a certain irony contained in the fact that this comment could so easily apply also to *Ruth Hall*, whose author, like Horace Greeley, was born in 1811, and whose career also was in journalism. It might have been said of Fanny Fern and Horace Greeley that *both* proved that perseverance and talent are sure of their reward, at least in America. Although the critics of the time could easily see Greeley's life as exemplary of the American success myth, they could not see the same pattern in *Ruth Hall*, which chronicled a woman's rise to prominence.

Moreover, except for Elizabeth Cady Stanton, who was writing in a magazine whose stated goal was "the elevation of women," the critics could not say of *Ruth Hall*, as *Peterson's Magazine* could say of the Greeley biography, "The work will do good." Instead, they castigated the author for being "unfeminine." Yet Fanny Fern herself hoped that her novel would "do good." She hoped that it would help to give women the courage to depend on themselves. As she wrote in the preface to her novel, "I cherish the hope that . . . it may fan into flame, in some tried heart, the fading embers of hope, well-nigh extinguished by wintry fortune and summer friends." It was her hope that women as well as men could profit from her chronicle of one woman's struggle against and triumph over adversity. And, as she wrote elsewhere, she believed that women would never be truly independent until they were economically independent. "I want all women to render themselves independent of marriage as a mere means of support," she wrote in 1869. [27]

The American myth of the individual—a belief in the attainment of the American dream through self-reliance and hard work—was a male myth. Reflected in the title of the Horatio Alger novel, *Strive and Succeed*, the myth offered hope to [white] male

Americans that they could gain wealth and power through their own efforts.[28] But it so obdurately excluded women that American reviewers could not even recognize it when it appeared in the form of a novel in which the American individualist was a woman.

Notes

1. *The Letters of Ralph Waldo Emerson*, ed. Ralph L. Rusk, 6 vols. (New York: Columbia University Press, 1939), 3:253.

2. Horatio Alger, *Ragged Dick* (New York: Macmillan, 1962), 43–44, 167.

3. Susan Warner. *The Wide, Wide World* (New York: Feminist Press, 1987), 12.

4. Maria Cummins, *The Lamplighter* (Boston: Houghton, Mifflin, 1902), 83–84.

5. Augusta Evans Wilson, *St. Elmo* (New York: Cooperative Publication Society, 1986), 465–66, 522.

6. Ibid., 562.

7. Fanny Fern, *Ruth Hall and Other Writings*, ed. Joyce W. Warren (New Brunswick: Rutgers University Press, 1986), 133.

8. Ibid., 134.

9. Ibid., 131, 147.

10. *New York Ledger*, 6 June 1861.

11. *Putnam's Monthly* 5 (February 1855): 216.

12. *Protestant Episcopal Quarterly Review* 2 (April 1855), 301.

13. *New York Times* 4 (20 December 1854): 2.

14. *Tait's Magazine*, cited in *The Eclectic Magazine of Foreign Literature, Science, and Art* 35 (June 1855): 197.

15. *New York Times* 4 (20 December 1854): 2.

16. Walt Whitman, *Leaves of Grass*, ed. Malcolm Cowley (New York: Viking Press, 1959), 25.

17. *The Journal of Henry David Thoreau*, vols. 7–20 of *The Writings of Henry David Thoreau*, Walden Edition (1906, reprint, New York: AMS Press, 1968), 1:206–7.

18. Emerson, *Letters*, 4:32.

19. *Knickerbocker* 45 (January 1855), 84–86.

20. *National Era* 9 (5 April 1855), 55.

21. See, e.g., *Dansville* [*New York*] *Republican*, 1855; *Olive Branch* 19 (30 December 1854), 2; *True Flag* (13 January 1955), 3.

22. Elizabeth Cady Stanton, review of *Ruth Hall*, *The Una* (February 1855): 29.

23. Ibid.

24. *Harper's New Monthly Magazine* (March 1855): 551.

25. *Southern Quarterly* 27 (April 1855); 443, 449–50.

26. *Peterson's Magazine* 27 (February 1855); 179.

27. Fanny Fern, "Wanted—A Definition," *New York Ledger* (26 June 1869). See also, *New York Ledger*, 16 July 1870; 18 September 1869.

28. For a discussion of the masculine identity of American individualism, see Joyce W. Warren, *The American Narcissus: Individualism and Women in Nineteenth-Century American Fiction* (New Brunswick: Rutgers University Press, 1984).

The Thwarting of the Artist As a Young Working Class Woman: Gender and Class Acts in Eudora Welty's *The Golden Apples*

Leslie K. Hankins

Rewriting the *Künstlerroman* genre by challenging its margins and omissions, Eudora Welty in *The Golden Apples* uses various strategies to engage and refute the *Künstlerroman* tradition with which the text grapples. Using the critical strategy of examining margins and silences, we may read Welty's text as a methodological field for both a close reading and a metacommentary on the *Künstlerroman* genre itself. Between the lines of the genre we find the repressed *non-Künstlerroman*, the female *Künstlerromane*, the interface between the male-defined genre and that which it represses. *The Golden Apples* can be examined successfully as the conscious and unconscious workings of genre in complex relations of repression, distortion, and imitation.

What are the essential criteria of the traditional *Künstlerroman?* The Artist. Development. The Art Product. The genre traces the development of the artist and (usually) *his* achievement. The quest and development of the artist figure through an obstacle course to creation, the central plot of the *Künstlerroman,* is paralleled by the central movement of *Künstlerroman* genre theory: as the artist seeks artistic identity and creation, the critic seeks the artist figure and artifact. The artist's signature is the bottom line of the *Künstlerroman.* However, the elaborate game of pin-the-tale-on-the-artist is perhaps missing the point; stepping back from the tangle, we may situate the problem in the *Künstlerroman* genre itself. Privileging the artist and the work of art are essential to the genre, but these suggest the commodity fetish and the bourgeois subject and can be historicized and questioned.

The critical constructs traditionally used to define and examine the *Künstlerroman* display ethnocentrism, androcentrism, and class bias in their "universal" norms. The unexamined prescriptions for the figure of the artist include the formulas that the artist is born and not made, and that there is a magical childhood full of "markings" or signs. Critics frequently chart and discuss the "journey" or the "quest" of the artist, the "evolution" or development of the artist, and the "rites of passage" as if there were an inevitable sacred progression. Critics study the "portrait" of the artist, as he or she is foregrounded as a static figure against an environment considered simply backdrop. Such metaphors and clichés are not neutral, but ideologically loaded, as they emphasize the artist as the producer of a commodity, the linear development of the artist plot, and the monologic voice. They presuppose the bourgeois subjective individualism of the artist-function, as they suggest the magic figure of the artist-genius against an ahistorical backdrop, rather than situating the artist within a complex apparatus of economic, political, and cultural forces. The overlap between the genres of the *Bildungsroman* and the *Künstlerroman* is not accidental, but reflects the preoccupation of bourgeois art with the subject, for art from this perspective is primarily the development of the individual artist.

Such unexamined presuppositions, the genre's framework, must be explored and made problematic. This examination is of particular interest to feminist literary theory, as the issue of gender in the fit of the male *Künstlerroman* to the female form raises questions.[1] Does the traditional *Künstlerroman* reflect the struggles of the artist figure regardless of gender, or are the conventions principally reflections of male-gendered experience? Is the generic "he" gendered here? At times the disjunction between the prescriptions of the male *Künstlerroman* tradition and the female forms has been presented as the failure of the female *Künstlerromane* to measure up, to complete itself. Even Carolyn Heilbrun fell into this trap when in "The Failure of Imagination" she faulted women writers because "with remarkably few exceptions, women writers do not imagine women characters with even the autonomy they themselves have achieved."[2] We could, however, also read this lack or failure as a scathing critique of the social system which the male *Künstlerroman* inscribes and of women's exclusion from that system. Such "failures" then indict the *Künstlerroman* tradition as a class and gender-marked lie or myth.

The text of *The Golden Apples* foregrounds the social and economic ideologies that inscribe the narrative of Virgie Rainey. Defined by the modes of social control of which she is often oblivious, Virgie does not operate in a vacuum or in an autonomous space: she is fenced, bordered, and limited by the economic, social, and cultural networks which hem her in. Miss Eckhart, like the critic, like the reader, filtering experience through Romantic presuppositions, wishes to assign to Virgie the role of the artist, the genius, to turn the text of Virgie into a *Künstlerroman* in the traditional style. She lends Virgie books, gives her free lessons, gives her *the* Beethoven and love. But Welty's text ruthlessly undercuts this Romantic conception of the artist:

> Virgie would be heard from in the world, playing that, Miss Eckhart said, revealing to children with one ardent cry her lack of knowledge of the world. How could Virgie be heard from in the world? And "the world"! Where did Miss Eckhart think she was now? Virgie Rainey, she repeated over and over, had a gift, and she must go away from Morgana. From them all. From her studio. In the world, she must study and practice her music for the rest of her life. In repeating all this, Miss Eckhart suffered. (60)[3]

Virgie's life belies the Romantic narrative, for it is placed in a social context and the social apparatus is clearly delineated. The economic narrative of *The Golden Apples* might be titled "the thwarting of the artist as a young working class woman":

> Cassie herself was well applauded when she played a piece. The recital audience always clapped more loudly for her than they did for Virgie; but then they clapped more loudly still for little Jinny Love Stark. It was Cassie who was awarded the Presbyterian Church's music scholarship that year to go to college—not Virgie. It made Cassie feel "natural"; winning the scholarship over Virgie did not surprise her too much. The only reason for that which she put into words, to be self-effacing, was that the Raineys were Methodists; and yet she did not, basically, understand a slight. (64)

The "natural" feeling Cassie has about the social class distinctions is akin to cultural critics' analyses of the "natural" way we translate ideology into myth. Because social codes and forces control the placement of the individual, Virgie's failure to incarnate the Romantic artist-function is not simply a private failure, but the inevitable outcome of the social and cultural context. The awarding of the music scholarship is a class act, and Miss Eckhart's consolation prize to Virgie of the butterfly pin with a clasp that isn't functional indicates the ineffectuality of the Romantic Artist master narrative when confronted with the economic master narrative of the social system and culture industry.

Virgie's efforts to break through the barriers that define and control her are doomed, as her childish rebellion illustrates:

> School did not lessen Virgie's vitality; once on a rainy day when recess was held in the basement she said she was going to butt her brains out against the wall, and the teacher, old Mrs. McGillicuddy, had said, "Beat them out, then," and she had really tried. The rest of the fourth grade stood around expectant and admiring, the smell of open thermos bottles sweetly heavy in the close air. (43)

Virgie's rebellion is apparent in her fighting with the boys and her "airs of wildness," but she never seems to locate effectively the target for her energy and anger, never locating the cage that bars her way. Her sexual acting out and other gestures that turn her passion into a self-destructive force misplace the site of struggle. Even in her forties she milks the cows passionately:

> . . . as if she would hunt, hunt daily for the blindness that lay inside the beast, inside where she could have a real and living wall for beating on, a solid prison to get out of, the most real stupidity of the flesh, a mindless and careless and calling body, to respond flesh for flesh, anguish for anguish. (226)

Virgie's repressed struggle with the codes of the world around her is presented in the text not through intense subjective narration, but in many understated ways, as when her mother observes, "There's nothing Virgie Rainey loves better than struggling against a real hard plaid" (234).

Reading *The Golden Apples* as an anti-*Künstlerroman*, we may trace the reversal of the traditional genre in the silencing of Virgie Rainey, in the suppression of her art as Welty displays the *unmaking* of the artist. Virgie's identity as the non-artist may be traced in the omissions and in the absences. Virgie is defined by the presence of absence; she has no hymen, no spouse, and finally, no family. Her life is traced by the absences—her absence from Morgana, the loss of her brother, the loss of her mother, the loss of the music scholarship, the giving up of music, and the silence. Virgie is the "woman with a past," and although that past is a gap in the text that is never filled, a blank page, it resonates through the text as an enigma never revealed but tantalizingly displayed. Gossip and innuendo trace some site of pain and repression, but do not bare it:

> Virgie had felt a moment in life after which nobody could see through her—felt it young. (264)

"Juba, when I was in my worst trouble, I scared everybody off, did you know that? Now I'm not scared any more." (269)

The text's silence on the subject of Virgie's past, her subjective experience, is compelling. Although Virgie dominates *The Golden Apples*, she remains enigmatic, never articulating her narrative. Virgie seems always to be spilling over with energy, on the verge of life, but she is never given a voice, never allowed to tell her story. Her narrative is one of interruption and repression, and the text conspires to keep her in her subliminal status.

The textual strategy of describing Virgie from outside effectively barricades off her thoughts in "June Recital"; by omitting her reactions to key events such as the pigs' destruction of the piano, the awarding of the scholarship to Cassie, Victor's death, and Virgie's absence from Morgana, the text highlights those reactions. In "June Recital" Virgie's silencing is strategically reinforced by Cassie's use of indirect speech to report Virgie's words and by Cassie's presentation of this vignette:

Virgie told on Mr. Voight too, but she had nobody to believe her, and so Miss Eckhart did not lose any pupils by that. Virgie did not know how to tell anything. (49)

Virgie's silence is again emphasized in the line ". . . but that didn't make Virgie say she loved Miss Eckhart . . ." (64), and in Cassie's description of the encounter between Virgie and Miss Eckhart:

They were deliberately terrible. They looked at each other and neither wished to speak. They did not even horrify each other. No one could touch them now, either. (96)

It is in the silence and the act and process of silencing that Virgie's story is re-inscribed. Like the dying notes of the trace of her "Für Elise" signature, the absence of her narrative resonates.

The Golden Apples can be read as the silencing of the artist as a young woman, as Virgie's artistic energy is warped into self-destructive sexual energy and denial. Susan Gubar's essay, " 'The Blank Page' and the Issues of Female Creativity" is useful for reading the silence in *The Golden Apples* and for examining the reversal of the *Künstlerroman* plot, because Virgie's story involves the aborting of her musical gift. The recital on the threshold of puberty reflects Gubar's point about female anatomy and female creativity: "one of the primary and most resonant metaphors provided by the female body is blood, and cultural forms of creativity are often experienced as a painful wounding."[4] In "June Recital" this is enacted:

> But recital night was Virgie's night, whatever else it was. The time Virgie Rainey was most wonderful in her life, to Cassie, was when she came out—her turn was just before the quartet—wearing a Christmas-red satin band in her hair with rosettes over the ears, held on by a new elastic across the back; she had a red sash drawn around under the arms of a starched white swiss dress. She was thirteen. She played the *Fantasia on Beethoven's Ruins of Athens,* and when she finished and got up and made her bow, the red of the sash was all over the front of her waist, she was wet and stained as if she had been stabbed in the heart, and a delicious and enviable sweat ran down from her forehead and cheeks and she licked it in with her tongue. (73–74)

The image of Virgie, sweaty and bloodstained, suggests female creativity in the union of the body and art. The mystery surrounding Virgie's abandonment of music and initiation into sexual behavior may be illuminated by Gubar's claim:

> . . . if artistic creativity is linked to biological creativity, the terror of inspiration for women is experienced quite literally as the terror of being entered, deflowered, possessed, taken, broken, ravished—all words which illustrate the pain of the passive self whose boundaries are being violated.[5]

We never know Virgie's narrative, but the text suggests its outline through gaps, ruptures, interruptions, and silence. Between the lines, in an echo, Virgie's buried life waits, like Miss Eckhart's, for a sudden storm and a captive audience:

> Coming from Miss Eckhart, the music made all the pupils uneasy, almost alarmed; something had burst out, unwanted, exciting, from the wrong person's life. This was some brilliant thing too splendid for Miss Eckhart, piercing and striking the air around her the way a Christmas firework might almost jump out of the hand that was, each year, inexperienced anew.
> It was when Miss Eckhart was young that she had learned this piece, Cassie divined. Then she had almost forgotten it. But it took only a summer rain to start it again; she had been picked and the music came like the red blood under the scab of a forgotten fall. (57)

If Virgie's art or story are repressed, the text makes clear the social and cultural forces that are active agents of repression. As the spokesperson for those forces, or the witness to their power, it is Cassie who sees art as fearful and wounding, describing Virgie as bloodstained and sweaty after her recital performance. As the spectator or witness, Cassie reveals the fate of the woman artist figure most clearly, and what she learns from her spectator status is fear. These fears entrap her and shape her response to art, as she shifts her attention from the passionate music played by Miss Eckhart to the punishments for women who do not limit their activities to the patriarchal system's rigid code of female behavior. In a telling free-association, Cassie moves from thoughts of artistic wounding to dwell on rape: "She [Miss Eckhart] had been walking by herself after dark; nobody had told her any better" (57). Cassie's linking of women's art with punishment and fear tie her to the patriarchal system; she dreads being swept outside the barriers she experiences as protective, as her fantasies reveal:

> Cassie saw herself without even facing the mirror, for her small, solemn, unprotected figure was emerging, staring clear inside her mind. There she was now, standing scared at the window . . . she stood there pathetic—homeless looking—horrible. Like a wave, the gathering past came right up to her. Next time it would be too high. (37)

The Golden Apples can be read as a tragic anti-*Künstlerroman*, a tale of the ways class and gender conspire in the erasure of the female artist, as Cassie Morrison is paralysed into fearful conformity, Miss Eckhart is driven out of town and out of her mind, and Virgie Rainey is left poised on a threshold, a silenced spectator. At the end, poised on the stile, Virgie occupies an interesting and problematic boundary site:

> Then she and the old beggar woman, the old black thief, were there alone and together in the shelter of the big public tree, listening to the magical percussion, the world beating in their ears. They heard through falling rain the running of the horse and bear, the stroke of the leopard, the dragon's crusty slither, and the glimmer and the trumpet of the swan. (277)

Reading the text as the knotted underside of the fabric of the *Künstlerroman* poses interesting readings of this end. Is this story a carefully coded protest against the patriarchal system?[6] What does it mean at the end when the black woman and the unbridled white woman sit on the stile under the big public tree and witness patriarchal art's hit parade? At the end are Virgie and the black woman only spectators of the male symbolic order from which they are excluded? Are they eavesdroppers of the male artistic performance? Are they limited finally to marginal and spectator status? Poised on the question of stile, of style, the text leaves the reader on the threshold.

Is *The Golden Apples* a cautionary tale, or one to incite the woman artist to struggle? That is, of course, somewhat up to the reader. Certainly, the text bares the lies and omissions of the *Künstlerroman* tradition, giving an uncompromising *exposé* of the gender and class acts that make the traditional *Künstlerroman* a fairy tale preserve of male and class privilege. In her text Welty radically re-constructs the submerged, repressed, anti-*Künstlerromane* of the working-class woman, whose artistic destiny is silent survival.

Notes

1. Feminist critics interrogating the *Künstlerroman/e* tradition include, among others, Rachel Blau Du Plessis, "To 'bear my mother's name'; *Künstlerromane* by Women Writers," *Writing Beyond the Ending* (Bloomington: Indiana University Press, 1985); Hélène Cixous, "Reaching the Point of Wheat, or A Portrait of the Artist as a Maturing Woman," *New Literary History: A Journal of Theory & Interpretation* 19, no. 1 (Autumn 1987); Carolyn Heilbrun, *Reinventing Womanhood* (New York: W. W. Norton, 1979); and Grace Stewart, *A New Mythos: The Novel of the Artist as Heroine* (Vermont and Canada: Eden Press Women's Publications, 1979).

2. Heilbrun, *Reinventing Womanhood*, 71.

3. Eudora Welty, *The Golden Apples* (New York and London: Harvest/Harcourt Brace Jovanovich, 1977).

4. Susan Gubar, " 'The Blank Page' and Issues of Female Creativity," *Critical Inquiry* 8 (Winter 1981): 248.

5. Ibid., 256.

6. Patricia Yaeger effectively argues for Welty's appropriation of the patriarchal poetic order through the revisionist use of Yeats's poetry. See " 'Because a Fire was in my Head': Eudora Welty and the Dialogic Imagination," *Publications of the Modern Language Association*, 99, no. 5 (1984).

The Historical Dimensions of Mary Lee Settle's *The Scapegoat:* Appalachia, Labor, and Mother Jones

Joyce Dyer

At the end of Mary Lee Settle's novel *The Scapegoat*, an Italian immigrant is dragged out of his tent at gunpoint by Baldwin Feltz detective Goujot, forced to climb a fence to place him on company property, accused of trespassing in a language he does not understand, and shot in the back. Carlo Michele, "just a moving target, like a deer, crumpled, only a white spot in the leaves."[1] The detectives proceed to surround the body and fire volley after volley of shot into it. Only a flick of white undershirt is left when two women arrive to take Carlo Michele home. Everything else, including the mast he lies in, is bright red.

This atrocity is historical: it is the first murder that occurred during the very violent Paint Creek Strike in 1912–13 in West Virginia coal country.[2] But there were even more violent and dramatic episodes during the course of the Paint Creek Strike: the firing into the Holly Grove tent colony by guards on the Bull Moose armored train, the battles at Mucklow, the arrest and trial of Mother Jones. Violent episodes occurred for over a year, until Governor Hatfield dictated the terms of peace and forced both labor and management to accept them in June 1913, terms that included modest improvement for miners: two and one-half cents a ton increase in wages, recognition of the Cabin Creek union, employment of both operator and miner check-weighmen, and temporary respite from the prior rule that goods could be purchased only in the company store.[3]

Settle permits her character Mary Rose Lacey, daughter of Beverley and Ann Eldridge, to tell us why the book concentrates on events from 7 June 1912, at 3:00 P.M. to 8 June 1912, at 8:00 A.M., rather than the more dramatic events of fall 1912 or February 1913. Occasionally, characters narrate from times before or after this period, including Mary Rose at the book's start. But they always return to these hours, to this moment in history.

At the book's start Mary Rose is thinking about the Senate Investigation of conditions in the strike district being conducted by Senator Borah of Idaho. A subcommittee of the Committee on Education and Labor arrived in West Virginia to hold hearings on 10 June 1913, and published their report in 1914,[4] so Mary Rose is looking back from a time during the investigation. She is wishing, dreaming, that she might be called, that her opinion might be sought. She would tell them, "It didn't start with the big battles and the National Guard" (4). "They don't ask how it all began, oh no, not with that bunch of lawyers acting like they've got springs on their bottoms" (3), Mary Rose sneers.

But Settle does ask. She wants to find out how the atrocity committed against Carlo Michele could ever have occurred down this beautiful creek named "Paint." By trying to understand one small, preliminary episode in the strike's history, Settle really explains the causes of every other incident that would follow. And, in the process of looking hard at Paint Creek, Settle also pushes us toward a painful and complicated understanding of America and American character.

Mary Lee Settle's research for *The Scapegoat*, like that for each of her other novels in *The Beulah Quintet* (her history of West Virginia from its ancestral roots in England of 1640 to the present), is careful and exhaustive. She takes history itself, not only Appalachian mining history, seriously. As Roger Shattuck explains in his introduction to *The Beulah Quintet*, she is a meticulous and devoted researcher. He says, "Much of the striking detail in the writing comes from the relentless instinct for concreteness that has closeted Miss Settle at frequent intervals for solid months of reading in the British Museum and in libraries and archives throughout Virginia."[5]

In a 1980 interview Shattuck alludes to, Settle spoke about her efforts to research the Paint Creek strike. She read 5,000 pages of records from the Senate investigation and recorded fourteen hours of key testimony into a tape recorder. But she didn't stop there. "Right at the end I found stenographic transcriptions of three of [Mother Jones's] speeches to the miners. A court reporter made them for Brown, Jackson, and Knight, the coal owners' law firm."[6] Even before Philip S. Foner and Edward M. Steel began to locate and collect primary source material on labor organizer

Mother Jones,[7] Settle knew about the existence of three of Mother Jones's August and September speeches to the miners at Charleston and Montgomery, and had read them.

Settle's understanding of violence in the Appalachian coal fields is based largely on her analysis of these, and probably other, primary source documents about the strike.[8] She never read secondary material before writing her novels, as we know from her comments about *The Scapegoat* and *Prisons*.[9] It should not be surprising that a person with Settle's historical commitment should reach some of the conclusions of historical interpreters. Like fellow historians, she places much of the responsibility for Carlo Michele's death on greedy Northern capitalists, the company town, the forced evictions into tent colonies, and the guard system.

Settle, for example, concurs completely with historians of Applachia who name Northern industrialists as the main villains in the demise of Appalachia's agrarian economy. Ronald D. Eller describes pre-industrial 1880 Appalachia as a region where the average farm contained 187 acres, with twenty-five percent cultivated, twenty percent cleared for pasture, and the rest hillside woods for grazing of hogs and cattle.[10] During the 1880s and 1890s, however, Northern capitalists discovered the mineral and timber wealth in the Southern highlands, sent the C & O Railroad down spurs in every rich hollow, and bought up land for amounts that ranged "from twenty-five cents to three dollars per acre."[11] By 1906, Eller reports, "all but two of the coal companies on Paint Creek were purchased by Scranton, Pennsylvania, capitalists and reorganized as the Paint Creek Collieries Company"[12] (what Settle would call "Imperial Collieries").

Eller paradoxically describes Appalachia as "a rich land inhabited by a poor people."[13] John Gaventa recently spoke of it in Albert Romasco's terms as "the poverty of abundance."[14] After this time, as James Still records in his lyrical novel *The River of Earth*, few families could exist without supplemental income from work in the coal mines, from work in those "darksome holes."[15]

The story of land acquisition in Settle's Lacey Creek resembles the story Eller tells. The major families of the area—the Laceys, the Neills, and the Catletts—have all suffered severe land losses at the hands of devious companies. Grandfather Lacey had sold five miles of up-creek land outright to Mr. Pratt of the Imperial Land Company in 1907 for $250,000. Grandfather had kept his own mine, Seven Stars Colliery. A second mine he had turned over to Godley, who soon leased it to Imperial. As Settle's novel begins,

Beverley Lacey's Seven Stars is the only independent mine remaining in the area. All others belong to Imperial.

Dan Neill, captain of the Baldwin Feltz detectives on Lacey Creek, has also suffered from his family's coal deals. His senile grandfather, a senator, had been involved in a disastrous deal with the Tennessee Coal and Land Company in 1907 and lost his fortune. Lewis Catlett, father of union organizer Jake Catlett, had sold his mineral rights to the hill farm he owned at Beulah, "for next to nothing" (46). All that remains to Jake is the overburden, although at least that provides him with some private property on which he can erect a tent colony for miners evicted on yellow-dog contracts and then conduct union business.

Like social historians, Settle is severe in her criticism of huge corporate coal owners, finding them obscenely comic when they actually appear on Lacey Creek to see Beverley. She registers compassion for all other groups, but not for the rich Northerners who would become the hill's uncaring absentee landlords. Early in the novel seven executives alight from a train in Lacey Creek and proceed to Beverley Lacey's house to convince him to bring in "transportation" (a common euphemism for "strikebreakers") and sell his land. All seven have gone to fat: "There were seven of them, giants in the earth, and they *all* had stomachs and skinny legs." Mary Rose explains, "Maybe you will get the full import of the trainload of gentlemen if I call them Imperial Mining Company, Pratt Land Company, Chesapeake & Ohio, Peabody Sand and Gravel, Standard Oil, and a Philadelphia lawyer!" (16).

They are rare Settle stereotypes, and her strokes are vicious. The inside of their train sports turkey carpet, leather chairs that seem money-lined, and red velvet drapes. The men pray in the morning, following their prayers with a champagne breakfast. Mary Rose wonders why roast beef is being prepared in the dining car for the men on Thursday. "That's for Sunday" (19), she thinks. When Beverley proposes more humane bargaining methods ("you must realize that my people are *not* transportation. They've lived here many years"), the men recite, "Mr. Uh, that's an admirable but dated concept" (23).

Settle, however, also insists on looking at specific, direct causes of violence bred within the new community created by the coal companies' arrival. Along with many historians, she deplores the conditions of company towns, where residents lived in company houses, bought food from company stores, and worshiped a company Jesus in company churches. In an insightful study of West Virginia history, John Alexander Williams blames much of

Paint Creek's tension on the "isolated and autocratic character of the mining towns."[16] Eller exhibits outrage in his depiction of the unsanitary company towns that housed almost four-fifths (78.8 percent) of southern West Virginia miners during the coal boom.[17] Philip Foner introduces the segment of Mother Jones's writings and speeches that he groups under the heading "Barbarous West Virginia" by citing this 1913 line about company towns from the conservative *New York Tribune:* "It is a species of industrial feudalism to which he is subjected."[18]

Settle's coal town consists of creek houses that stand like "gray bones in the summer sun, a plague of empty shells" (32). The store and the Club House are "big solid wood buildings with stone foundations." But the houses of the miners are feeble skeletons. A few, Settle tells us, are "streaked with old whitewash, but the rest had never seen a paintbrush; dirt-colored Jenny Lind board-and-batten shacks, sprung-doored privies, bone-hard yards" (65). The company houses in Settle's novel are even uglier, somehow, than the Detroit dwellings Harriette Arnow's Kentucky outmigrants must occupy.[19]

In her speech to the mountain women and the Italian women in Jake Catlett's barn, Mother Jones provides a fiery list of grievances against the company town: "Nevermore will you be married by a company preacher, owned by a company store, put in a company house that ain't fit for nuthin' but a hawg, ready to fall in on your head, berried on company land your loved ones can't even put flowers on your grave if there's a strike" (197). Such grievances lead, in part, to Jake's permitting miners like Samuel Tremble to shoot warning shots at the guards (which proves disastrous), and to the "prayer meeting" the women hold early the morning of 8 June to prevent strikebreakers from entering the mouth of Godley. These actions, in turn, intensify the guards' hate and rage, rage that eventually causes them to hunt down Carlo Michele.

The eviction Settle records, the eviction of the Paganos from their house in Italian Hollow after the chance wounding of guard Mooney McKarkle by Samuel Tremble (the guards wrongly identify the shot as having come from the direction of Italian Hollow), further identifies the terrible sorrow and emerging anger of Lacey Creek's coal miners and the fury of the guards. The guards toss the family's possessions from doors and windows without care, without memory; they throw objects off the porch and press garden corn and tomatoes flat and hard. Ironically, it is Carlo Michele who watches it all from the safe distance Annunziata Pagano has insisted on: "the wooden rawboned toy house vomited from its toy windows and its broken front door, blankets, quilts, clothes, furniture turning in the air and falling, tearing, breaking into trash slowly, deliberately. A tiny stove was hauled out to the back door, dragged across the porch and let go at the top of the back steps" (112).

Eduardo Pagano, son of Annunziata and maimed Francesco (he had lost a leg when a saw used for undercutting came to rest on his leg instead of the coal-face), pathetically searches through the debris after his family has moved to Jake Catlett's, on their way to the tent colony. He spends time rounding up eight chickens and putting them into the orange crate his sister, Maria, had lined with red silk for her comb and brush. He places his parents' mattress back on their bed, "[t]he mattress stained with old love, old childbirth and children's night-wetting" (134). The evictions, their shame and humiliation, bring the women in the tent colony close, increasing their power and posing a threat to the guardians of law and order. The Italian women, for example, offer extravagant kindnesses to Annunziata, even though she had formerly bragged "that nobody can move [the Paganos] like they are a sack of potatoes." "They treat her gently because she has been fooled, and they respect the humiliation of her finding out. As if she has been stripped of clothes they want to cover her with kindness, lend her things, and touch her hair" (172–73).

Settle suggests that it is the guards themselves, more than any other direct cause, that bring violence to Paint Creek. Mother Jones, during speeches in Charleston and Montgomery throughout August and September of 1912, pled for the guards' removal, condemned their presence, and forecast the violence that would occur if they stayed. The Mining Investigation Commission appointed by Governor Glasscock recognized that the United Mine Workers' efforts to organize West Virginia mines had serious economic disadvantages for owners, but insisted that miners had a right to organize and that the use of guards was a "vicious" practice that intensified the volatile situation on Paint Creek.[20] Even Lawrence Lynch, whose 1914 analysis occasionally anticipates post-World War I political fear and suspicion, maintained that violence was caused in large part by the guard system. Howard B. Lee and Fred Mooney[21] also saw the coercion and mistreatment used by guards who first arrived on 10 May 1912 as a primary cause of Paint Creek violence.

Settle's guards are for the most part hot-tempered and hard-drinking, not-very-bright thugs like Anderson Carver, or candy-ankled kids looking for a little excitement. Guard Mooney

McKarkle, a native of the hollows, decides to run away from both his job and Paint Creek after witnessing the behavior of fellow guards. Mooney, "victim" of the wood splinter Samuel Tremble's bullet sends flying crazily into his leg, recovers quickly enough to ride by Dan Neill's side the night the guards intrude on a union meeting at Jake Catlett's and become embarrassingly entangled in garments hanging from clotheslines. Mooney had thought of the guards as knights, and imagined "Chancellorsville and Waterloo and the Rough Riders" (177). But he quickly comes to see that they are only "a bunch of pool-playing white trash full of white mule like hung around the courthouse and bragged" (190). He listens to them tell crude jokes about "Dago women" with "wells instead of slits, you disappear inside and go to glory." Again and again he hears the guards shout for blood: "Let's git us ourselves a Dago! Git him on company property. Bushwack him." Some want Carlo Michele because they believe he is spreading socialist propaganda. Anderson Carver prefers Eddie Pagano. "Worst one is that Eddie Pagano," he says. "Everybody knows him, sniffing around the ladies." But who it finally is does not matter greatly. "Hell," an unidentified guard shrugs, "I can't tell one Dago from another" (190).

Settle's figure Goujot (pronounced Go-show) is "Butcher Tony Goujot" of history, ex-sergeant of the regular army and holder of the Congressional Medal of Honor. Howard B. Lee writes, "The strikers said that of all guards on the two creeks, 'Old Tony' was the most heartless and brutal."[22] With historical correctness Settle makes her own Butcher Goujot even more dangerous than the young guards who whoop and holler "full of piss and vinegar" (191) in front of the Company Store and around the hollow. Even before Goujot marches Carlo Michele to his death, we see him commit indecencies and atrocities. Sensing union activity, he dismounts from his horse and walks into Jake Catlett's barn. Mother Jones immediately recognizes his "big loud mouth," for she had dealt with him in 1902. "You goddamned rednecks are having a meeting and that ain't legal!" he shouts. Accused by someone in the room of acting outside the law, of not being deputized, Goujot laughs, "We deputized each other, you goddamned redneck" (182).

Later, seeing a young French boy break away from the strike-breakers' line and run, a scab who thought he was coming to Paint Creek to cook, Goujot shoots him in the leg. He then announces, "First man breaks ranks gets a bullet in his laig" (255). After the women leave the Godley area and the transportation are pushed into the mine, Goujot and his men fire at the daisies that have been placed on mine props at the Godley entrance as a warning to scabs not to enter. They do not quit "until the daisies were shredded and the fragments of both funeral baskets bounced in the dirt and shale, shot full of holes" (257). Finally, as Goujot and his men ride to their murderous destination in Italian Hollow, draped all over a train engine and dressed in their typical black coats with black slouch hats, Settle tells us they look "like black flies, swarming over the engine, black flies with rifles" (265). These are deadly flies, and Goujot is the most deadly of all.

The detectives' violent nature is perhaps best realized through Settle's juxtaposition of gentle John Lacey from Nigger Hollow with the Baldwin detectives who repeatedly fire into the body of Carlo Michele. John Lacey happens to be in the woods looking for his stray cow Samantha when he comes upon the murder, and knows he must find cover and flee. But even as he senses danger for himself, he worries about the physical safety and comfort of the cow: "He went on driving Samantha slowly so she wouldn't drag her full bag on the underbrush carefully so her thick udders wouldn't get torn" (272).

Settle's novel is not, as Anatole Broyard suggests in his 1980 review, "a morality play" with a too simple opposition between good and evil, labor and management.[23] We soon realize, after completing even the first of the book's four sections (sections divided by the gradual progression of hours from June 7 to June 8), that Rosellen Brown's assessment of Settle's intentions is far more perceptive and correct: Brown claims that Settle illuminates the strike "so exhaustively, so authoritatively, that her technique— a dozen voices speaking of their own involvement—convinces us that it is the only plausible way to pay honor to the complexities of social history."[24] Settle's analysis of Appalachia and of American labor history is complicated at every turn. John Sayles's film *Matewan* looks like a Western (although a very good one) next to Settle's work.

Should we be surprised that Settle searches for subtle, indirect causes of violence to document the more visible and direct? She essentially spent twenty-two years trying to understand why one man hit another in a jail on a Saturday night in West Virginia.[25] Asked how the idea of writing a narrative from the time of Cromwell to the late twentieth century, of writing *The Beulah Quintet*, came to her, she said, "I had a picture of one man hitting another in a West Virginia drunk tank one Saturday night, and the idea was to go all the way back to see what lay behind that blow.

At first I went back all the way to 1755, then I realized that wasn't far enough, and I went back further still, to Cromwell's England, in *Prisons*."[26] Such a commitment helps us better understand the complexity of motive and cause in each separate volume of the quintet.

Settle in part blames the class distinctions emerging about this time in the region's indigenous population.[27] Forced by luck and circumstances into new classes after Northern land acquisition, Settle's long-time residents of Lacey Creek begin, consciously or unconsciously, to put class affiliation above kinship and family. Eller, talking about pre-industrial Appalachia, writes,

> Family . . . as the central organizing unit of social life, brought sub-stance and order to that sense of place. Strong family ties influenced almost every aspect of the social system, from the primary emphasis upon informal personal relationships to the pervasive egalitarian spirit of local affairs. Familism, rather than the accumulation of mate-rial wealth, was the predominant cultural value in the region, and it sustained a lifestyle that was simple, methodical, and tranquil.[28]

In Settle's world families are dying: class distinctions and a market economy are preventing the communication possible in a former time, the calming of tempers, the support, the sense of identity that kinfolk once supplied.

As we have seen, the Laceys, Catletts, and Neills have all once owned rich land. Although their wealth was never even, and some groups always worked for others, class awareness was sel-dom apparent, and never a matter of great concern. Old Mr. Lacey had felt sorry for Lewis Catlett, a squatter on his land who had boldly built a cabin at the mouth of a hollow. So he had sold him some of the side hollow land, land later discovered to possess a five-foot coal seam. "We liked having some people around," he would explain. "They'd had an even harder time than we had. The war had left them about half starved" (40). After the buy out, Mr. Lacey sold his only mine other than Seven Stars—Godley (named after his friend Mr. Godley)—to Godley himself. He sold it "because [Godley] was a gentleman. They raised carnations together." Even though Godley, in turn, had to sell to Imperial in 1907 to prevent being "wiped out in the panic if he hadn't" (12), the community thrived under his care and affection (although Mother Jones teasingly had called him a "capitalist paternalist son of a bitch" [55] when she organized the Kanawha Field in 1902). Godley could reason with Mother Jones in 1902; Godley had taken the workers now huddled in United Mine Worker tents camping when they were boys, had sung songs with them, blown taps, started baseball teams, built a bandstand. And now he was dead, and so were many former friendships and bonds of kin.

Jake Catlett and Beverley Lacey hesitate to talk to each other in spring 1912, although they miss their former closeness and secretly yearn for advice and wisdom. As he sits on his porch, worried about the tensions that are developing, Jake watches the Big House, Beverley's house. "Lord God, he must have sat out there and watched it a thousand times from his front porch." But on this night he makes his mind up to wait for the lights to go out and visit his friend, his distant relative Beverley Lacey: "Beverley was as near to him as his own brother, nearer . . . Him and Beverley had something, a stillness together. They had shared their hours ever since he'd followed Beverley around like a pup, and Beverley never did chase him off, not like Jethro" (195). Convincing himself that his decision is the right one, Jake boldly thinks, "He wasn't going to explain to nobody" (196).

Under the pretense of returning a wire cutter, Jake finds his way in the darkness to the Lacey house. Jake and Beverley talk together and listen to each other. Beverley explains, "Dammit I don't understand anything anymore. We never had a walkout at Seven Stars. Father negotiated with the union in oh two. I'm ready to negotiate a contract with you, you know that." And Jake can only reply, "It ain't that simple no more, Beverley. You only got one mine" (213). Beverley finally concludes, "Company policy against solidarity and us in between. That's how I see it." Settle adds, "That was how Jake saw it too, sitting up in the library with Beverley, but he knew he wouldn't see it that way down the hill or on his own porch" (214). Jake warns Beverley that there will be trouble if scabs are marched into Godley, but Beverley can hardly understand his meaning. Frustrated, Jake thinks about talking with Dan Neill next: "I'm goin' up thar and talk to Dan Neill. Dammit, he's my own cousin. Blood's thickern water." But he confesses his fear of such a meeting out loud to Beverley. "If my boys find out what I done they'll accuse me of goin' over. Well, I don't give a damn. I'm goin to talk to him" (216).

Fury builds in Captain Dan Neill of the Baldwin Feltz: fury of his past, of his grandfather's land loss, of his father's suicide in the face of bankruptcy, of being shamed by Mother Jones in front of his own troops. He knows this: "[H]e knew he ought to find Jake, talk to him. He wanted to talk to somebody, somebody who knew who he was" (221). Dan Neill's fury gathers direction after he sees Lily, dirty and crying, wrongly imagining that she has been raped by Eddie Pagano. While Dan searches for the felon, he finally does meet up with his cousin Jake. Dan thinks he can "defuse Dan Neill, boy who he known ever since he'd peed in his lap" (266). He assures Dan that nothing is going on, puts his hand on Dan's shoulder, and says, soothingly, "I sure did set store by your pappy son . . . don't you worry about a thing" (267). Sensing Dan's angry determination, Jake reaches for still more words. "May the good Lord take a likin' to you." But it is too late. Dan can no longer be moved by his cousin's words, and seems now just a figure "carved out of wood" (268). The comfort of family and the possibility of communication among cousins and friends has all but disappeared in the 1912 community of Settle's Lacey Creek.

By subtle use of very careful genealogy, Settle reveals the central irony that these people placing themselves so firmly within different classes and fighting one another are related by blood. Lewis Catlett had married Sara Lacey; Dan Neill's grandmother Melinda was Brandon Lacey's daughter; Beverley was raised by a Catlett. Mooney McKarkle will marry a Neill; and after all is over, Captain Dan Neill himself will marry Althea Lacey. Amusingly, all Settle's families—the Laceys, the Catletts, the McKarkles—are descendants of Jonathon Church, of the English Revolution in Settle's book *Prisons*. In *The Killing Ground* we once again meet many of these same people, or their descendants, as Mooney's daughter Hannah returns to Lacey Creek. And in *Charley Bland* (New York: Farrar, Straus, Giroux, [1989]) Settle continues to make connections: for example, Anderson Carver—called "Broker" Carver since the 1929 Crash—steps into her fiction again. Yet ironically, Settle's closely related characters all insist on class distinctions at the time of the strike. We, however, if we're not careful, forget the relationships among them, and must be reminded.

Settle pushes hard into the issue of class by trying to determine what makes her West Virginians—what makes all of us, perhaps—so arrogant, so ambitious, so proud that they forget where they come from, forget kin, need and create "hillbillies" below them on the social class ladder, and choose to live only in a very ephemeral present. Dan Neill, crazy about Lily Lacey, hates the "black Dago Wop" she spends her time supposedly "educating," and sees her as a victim, as he is, "of invasion and circumstances" (71). Essie, wife of union leader Jake Catlett, makes sure to wear her hat, not her poke bonnet, to the home of friend Ann Eldridge Lacey. She is proud of her friendship with this wealthier woman, and sometimes decorates her hat with grouse feathers or violets from Ann Eldridge. "It showed every one of them that she wasn't no servant. She was a friend and helping out wasn't the same" (48). She hates every stranger who has come into the valley: "It was all their fault, nothing but Englishmen and Yankees and Dagoes and field niggers and eastern Virginians and all the white trash both sides of the river" (50). And Beverley Lacey plants rambler roses to protect his daughters' white skirts and dresses.

Even some of the Paganos—Steve and Carlo Michele himself—are committed to upward mobility. Steve urges Carlo to bring a gun with him from Italy so that Steve can "swagger around like the mountain boys" (96). Steve "would call his own father and mother Dagoes or Wops when they did anything old-country" (93). Carlo Michele was set afire by the idea of coming to America after having caught a glimpse of gilt and red damask through a window of a beautiful building on a street unlike his own. He suffered and saved "in order that someday he could wear a sky-blue cape, draw a red damask curtain, unwrap a woman from clouds of lace and fine linen, drive an automobile and belong to the English tennis club" (116). When he reads letters from An-nunziata to his grandmother, he hears about the promise of land and dreams it into being. He refuses to listen to his grandmother: "No. There is no land. It is not like that. You go to bed a donkey. You wake up a donkey" (117). The Italian women in the barn think they are better and cleaner than the mountain women, and the mountain women, of course, think the opposite.

Settle proposes the thesis that it is the American dream that defeats family strength and true democracy every time. The title of her quintet, as Shattuck notes in his introduction to the Ballantine edition of *The Beulah Quintet*, comes from the well-known gospel hymn whose words are adopted from Isaiah 62:

> O beulah Land, sweet Beulah Land,
> As on the highest mount I stand,
> I look away across the sea
> Where mansions are prepared for me,
> And view the shining Glory Shore,
> My Heaven, my Home, forevermore.

The Beulah hymn somehow works its way into each of Settle's West Virginia volumes. In *The Scapegoat* the women Mother Jones organizes sing it as they march to Godley mine, keeping time to the hymn "with their dishpan drums, and their spoons" (253). It is land, Beulah Land, that our ancestors first dreamed of; it is land that defined America for them, and in some form still defines it for us. But, as Shattuck so perceptively notes, "The land one struggles to reach and to prepare for future generations holds out the promise of a better life. Alas, the counterpart truly is too often forgotten: land corrupts as well as inspires."[29]

The dream of land and the bitterness of land lost, the promise of American wealth—houses on the sides of hills rather than the mouths of creeks—has set the people of Lacey Creek against each other, against their friends and families. And Dan has inherited this burden of anger and frustrated ambition. Disappointment in that dream is behind the act of violence committed against Carlo Michele.

Ironically, Carlo Michele himself had bought the American dream. Asleep in the Paganos' tent that fateful morning, he, too, wanted to be rich. Perhaps he was still dreaming when the foot of Goujot kicked him awake. Disappointment in the dream explains why people such as Dan pull triggers they never meant to pull, why a gentlemen like Mr. Roundtree accepts Northern policies he finds repellent, why Beverley Lacy agrees to put a gatling gun on his porch.

Settle's final image is one she has used in other books to make us think about the American dream. Eduardo, escaping the detectives with the help of Lily and Mr. Roundtree, sits in the dining car of a train and is served "a half of a yellow fruit that he'd never seen before, sitting in a silver bowl" (278). In *The Clam Shell*, a semi-autobiographic account of Settle's days at Sweet Briar, the narrator's father, while living on Cheat River as a boy, had seen two rich coal operators eating in a dining car, "eating from half-moons of silver a fruit he had not seen before, halfmoons of yellow." An Appalachian Adam, "he yearned to follow the train and taste the fruit that flashed by in the sun." He is pathetic in the novel, for the fruit "became his grail, a half-eaten grapefruit on a silver chalice, and he followed it successward, down the river."[30] But Eddie in *The Scapegoat* has already made an important discovery: "His first taste of grapefruit was bitter. At home he would have spat it out" (278). We don't know what will happen to Eddie. Robert Huston thinks he is "a budding Mafioso or car dealer."[31] But we might argue through the imagery that he has already seen bitterness and divisiveness brought to Paint Creek by the American dream, and that he *will* find the courage to spit it out.

Settle's recording of characters' thoughts continues to complicate her version of American history, to remove easy answers, judgments, and assessments. George Garrett recognized her unusual ability with character: "The places, things, people (above all the sculptured, three-dimensional, realized, known and named people) are as knotty and gnarled, as complex and eccentric, as 'difficult' as any living things/beings can be, demanding the best that a reader has to bring and without the comfort of clichés of thought, feeling, or lingo."[32] Watching what she does with the historical figure of Mother Jones, for example, we better understand the process Garrett describes, and we also better appreciate the rare variety of historical novel Settle writes: "True being is not timeless. Rather we come upon it when the stream of individual consciousness coincides briefly with the stream of time shared with others. . . . [Settle's characters] remain *in time*."[33]

Labor organizer Mary Harris Jones, born in 1830 (although official records have never substantiated this date) to Irish peasants in Cork, aged eighty-two at the time of the book's key episode, is largely the woman of history and time. What she does and what she says on Lacey Creek coincide with historical fact. She did arrive in Paint Creek in early June, taking a train from Montana after hearing news about unrest in West Virginia: "I cancelled all my speaking dates in California, tied up all my possessions in a black shawl—I like traveling light—and went immediately to West Virginia. I arrived in Charleston in the morning, went to a hotel, washed up and got my breakfast early in order to catch the one local train that goes into Paint Creek."[34] Mary Rose first sees her quietly alight from a train, "a little old lady in black bombazine with a frilly black hat and a lace jabot" (19), the typical Victorian garb we see in photographs. Mary Rose even notices her shawl: "Lily said she was the most famous union organizer in the United States, but I don't believe that. Famous people don't ride the day coach with their things in a shawl" (20). She organizes the women, telling them to carry babies and washbasins and cooking spoons, and to hold a "prayer meeting" by the mouth of Godley because she knows, of course, that picketing by the men is illegal. Historically, in strike after strike Mother Jones would use this device.

Famous lines from speeches Settle had read, as well as key episodes recounted in Mother Jones's autobiography, are worked into the pages of *The Scapegoat*, sometimes broken into parts, compressed, or slightly altered, giving the book further authenticity and the important sense of time Shattuck praises. In *The Scapegoat*, for example, Settle has her fictionalized Mother Jones make fun of Lily Lacey by using a distinction originally appearing in the actual Mother Jones's 1 August speech on the levee at Charleston. Knowing Lily does not belong in the barn with mountain women and immigrants, in spite of her idealism and adoration of Eugene Debs and Mother Jones herself, she accusingly says this: "That's not a woman. That's a lady. Let me tell you! Modern parasites made ladies. God Almighty made women!" (200). The historical Mother Jones had used similar words to describe the four thousand women who marched with her at three in the morning in 1900: "They weren't ladies, they were women. A lady, you know, was created by the parasitical class; women, God Almighty made them."[35] In both the novel and her speeches, she calls the guards "bloodhounds," Governor Glasscock "Crystal Peter," and alludes to a story about an owner who says Dagoes should be used as mine props.

A famous scene in the *Autobiography,* based on an actual episode from the Paint Creek Strike, appears in a modified form in Settle's novel. In her *Autobiography* Mother Jones tells about a dangerous trip she made to Eksdale with thirty-six miners in a buggy pulled by a mule. Not long after they had set out, men began shooting at them from the tracks. Mother Jones climbed out of the buggy, up onto the tracks, and toward a group of boys huddled around a machine gun. Supposedly, she "walked up to the gunmen and put [her] hand over the muzzle of the gun" (157). A gunman named Mayfield could not be cowed by her bravery, nor her explanation that her class had brought out the metal that made the gun, and therefore it was her gun, not his. He threatened her entire company with death. She pointed to the hills and lied, "Up there in the mountain I have five hundred miners. They are marching armed to the meeting I am going to address. If you start the shooting, they will finish the game."[36] Mayfield quivered and allowed them to advance. In Settle's novel Mother Jones tells Goujot about the men in the hills to chase him off Jake Catlett's property and away from a planned union meeting. "If you don't get these men out of here I got eight hundred armed men up in these hills won't leave a goddamn one of you alive" (189). And later Mother Jones covers the front of Goujot's rifle as he tries to force the women and Mother Jones herself to leave Godley mine.

Settle's Mother Jones is the brave, defiant, dramatic, sometimes dangerous, sometimes sentimental, sometimes vulgar figure that writers like Dale Fetherling, activist Elizabeth Gurley Flynn, Howard Lee, Clarence Darrow, Fred Mooney, Linda Atkinson, and even juvenile writer Irving Werstein have admiringly described.[37] She is the woman Gene Autry sang about before cowboy fame in his 1931 cut of "The Death of Mother Jones" that begins this way:

> The world today's in mourning for the death of Mother Jones
> Gloom and sorrow hover around the miners' homes.
> This grand old champion of labor was known in every land
> She fought for right and justice, she took a noble stand.[38]

Settle clearly admires her; Settle's personal stationery from Bridge Building Icons (211 Park St., Burlington, Vermont) displays a picture of Mother Jones on the front, with a mine machine behind her, holding a famous text from her 1902 organizing days ("Pray for the dead and fight like hell for the living!"), surrounded by a halo and the Greek inscription for "Holy Mary."

But in spite of all the admiration Settle holds for this very amazing and good woman, she insists on looking at the dark consequences of her political fervor, registering Mother Jones's thoughts (something even her autobiography avoids), and revealing that good, like evil, is rarely simple. Although Mother Jones often claimed she was opposed to violence, in Settle's novel she is directly responsible for convincing religious fanatic Samuel Tremble that the union is on the side of God. She converts him with her rhetoric, but also shares responsibility for the wound that Mooney McKarkle receives from Samuel's gun, the wound that sets the tragedy on its way.

In one of the most poignant moments in the first sequence of the book, Mother Jones has a brief revelation that the clear political divisions she has been seeing, and creating, are not so clear after all. While she stands with several miners and looks down from a ridge at the guards by the Club House, a puff of smoke irritates her eyes and makes them water. "When she turned back she had a flick of a vision, like a glimpse of her death or the intrusion of a dream. Down below on the road, and there with her on the cliff, were the same men; the black coats, the slouch hats, the guns, the still, straight backs. They seemed to be one mirror image, waiting, not ready yet. She knew it was a weakness of age. She had to make herself see the difference" (66). Jake proceeds to point at the guards and give them names. "The names had helped. She could see them now as the thugs they were, and let fury clear her mind" (67). We know, of course, that the revelation was not a weakness of age, but the arrival of wisdom.

At times, her actions and decisions seem callous and are meant by Settle to seem this way. When Jake tells Mother Jones about Mr. Cordell's brag, "We use Dagoes for mine props," she feels initially sick. But within a moment she recovers and thinks, "That'll come in handy in a speech—get more foreigners to sign on with the union." The narrator concludes, "She believed in putting everything to use" (60). Although Jake Catlett is sometimes wrong about his information, he clearly identifies Mother Jones's weakness in his thoughts: "It was easy for the old woman to breathe fire and brimstone. She wasn't kin to anybody and she hadn't been raised with anybody" (54).

The worst instance of her "putting things to use," however, occurs after the tragic death of Carlo Michele. Mother Jones is saddened by Carlo's death, but her final response is organizational rather than personal. "Mother, what air we agoin' to do?" asks Jake after the funeral. " 'Use it,' she told him" (275).

Mary Lee Settle has the ability to read history and to record it with accurate attention to detail. But she also has the ability to imagine its complications; the perception that forces us to relinquish easy, conclusive assessments of historical situations; and the most profound understanding of American democracy—both its failings and its promise—of perhaps any writer working in America today. Settle's democratic style, giving everyone a voice, forces us to see parts of ourselves in many of the Paint Creek characters. Our arrogance, our own commitment to the American dream, our lack of compassion for people of other classes, other races, other regions, other families, our tendency to use information to our advantage, our disloyalty to our families, our pretension, our refusal to adopt a lifestyle of unambitious, simple ways, our callousness, our love of money and more money—our own iniquities, in other words—appear in the faces of people we have never met from a time and world not our own. But Settle allows us no scapegoat, and, instead, makes us look hard at ourselves and ask if we would have been in any way responsible for the death of Carlo Michele had we lived on Paint Creek in 1912, when coal was King.

Notes

1. Mary Lee Settle, *The Scapegoat* (New York: Random House, 1980), 271. All subsequent citations in the essay are to this edition.

2. The event is documented in such early sources as Lawrence R. Lynch's "The West Virginia Coal Strike," *Political Science Quarterly* 29, no. 4 (December 1914): 634.

3. Howard B. Lee, *Bloodletting in Appalachia* (Morgantown: West Virginia University, 1969).

4. *Report, Investigation of Paint Creek Coal Fields of West Virginia*, 63rd Cong., 2d sess., 1914.

5. Roger Shattuck, introduction to *The Beulah Quintet* (New York: Ballantine, 1981), xiii.

6. Ibid., xiii–xiv.

7. Philip S. Foner, *Mother Jones Speaks: Collected Writings and Speeches* (New York: Monad Press, 1983), and Edward M. Steel, *The Correspondence of Mother Jones* (Pittsburgh: University of Pittsburgh Press, 1985).

8. Many references to Mother Jones, for example, reflect Settle's awareness of the 1925 *Autobiography of Mother Jones*, ed. and ghostwritten by Mary Field Parton (Chicago: Charles Kerr & Co.).

9. "I never read a single secondary source, or any book published after 1649, when I was working on that first volume," Settle said in an interview for *Contemporary Authors*, ed. Frances C. Locher, 89–92 (Detroit: Gale Research Co., 1980), 467.

10. Ronald D. Eller, *Miners, Millhands, and Mountaineers* (Knoxville: University of Tennessee Press, 1982), 16–17.

11. Ibid., 56.

12. Ibid., 138.

13. Ibid., xxv.

14. "The Poverty of Abundance Revisited," *Appalachian Journal* 15, no. 1 (Fall 1987): 24.

15. James Still, *The River of Earth* (1940; reprint, Lexington: University Press of Kentucky [1978]), 21.

16. John Alexander Williams, *West Virginia: A Bicentennial History* (New York: Norton, 1976), 143.

17. Eller, *Miners*, 162.

18. Foner, *Mother Jones Speaks*, 153.

19. *The Dollmaker* (New York: Macmillan, 1954).

20. *Report of West Virginia Mining Investigation Commission, Appointed by Governor Glasscock on the 28th Day of August, 1912* (Charleston: Tribune Printing Co., 1912).

21. *Struggle in the Coal Fields* (Morgantown: West Virginia University, 1967).

22. Lee, *Bloodletting*, 21.

23. "Books of the Times," *New York Times*, 22 October 1980, 29.

24. "Trapped in the Mines," *New Republic* 183 (27 December 1980), 37.

25. This idea is the premise of *Fight Night on a Sweet Saturday* (New York: Viking, 1964), later rewritten into the fifth book of *The Beulah Quintet* called *The Killing Ground* (New York: Farrar, Straus, Giroux, 1982).

26. Locher, *Contemporary Authors*, 467.

27. During a presentation to a 1988 National Endowment for the Humanities Summer Seminar group ("Appalachia: Myth and Reality," Boone, North Carolina, 11 July–5 August), Ronald Eller mentioned that if he had his book on mining and timber to write over, he would "Put greater emphasis on the growing sense of class" (25 July 1988, Center for Appalachian Studies).

28. Eller, *Miners*, 38.

29. Shattuck, *Beulah Quintet*, xi.

30. *The Clam Shell* (New York: Delacorte Press, 1971), 40.

31. Robert Huston, "Blood Sacrifice," *Nation*, 231 (8 November 1980): 70.

32. George Garrett, "An Invitation to the Dance: A Few Words on the Art of Mary Lee Settle," *Blue Ridge Review* 1 (1978): 19. Garrett is also the author of *Understanding Mary Lee Settle* (Columbia: University of South Carolina Press, 1988).

33. Shattuck, *Beulah Quintet*, xvi.

34. Parton, *Autobiography of Mother Jones*, 148.

35. Foner, *Mother Jones Speaks*, 164.

36. Parton, *Autobiography of Mother Jones*, 158.

37. Dale Fetherling, *Mother Jones the Miners' Angel* (Carbondale: Southern Illinois University Press, 1974); Elizabeth Gurley Flynn, *The Rebel Girl: An Autobiography, My First Life (1906–1926)* (1955; reprint, New York: International Publishers, 1975); Clarence Darrow, introduction to the *Autobiography of Mother Jones*; Linda Atkinson, *Mother Jones: The Most Dangerous Woman in America* (New York: Crown Publishers, 1978); Irving Werstein, *Labor's Defiant Lady* (New York: Thomas Y. Crowell Co., 1969).

38. Gene Autry, "The Death of Mother Jones" (original version 1931), album *Poor Man, Rich Man, American Country Songs of Protest*, Rounder Records, Somerville, Mass.; see also Archie Green, *Only a Miner: Studies in Recorded Coal-Mining Songs* (Urbana: University of Illinois Press, 1972).

"Music at Every Meeting": Music in the National League of American Pen Women and the General Federation of Women's Clubs, 1920–1940

Laurine Elkins-Marlow

Introduction

Most histories of music have been written in terms of the superlative, focusing on the greatest and most innovative composers, the most celebrated performers and conductors, and the largest and most influential musical organizations in the most sophisticated cultural centers. A perusal of the index of any general history of music reveals that the majority of figures discussed are men. Women are mentioned as patrons, as teachers, as performers, but rarely as composers.

Yet as one begins to study women composers, a totally different picture emerges, particularly if one is fortunate enough to have access to personal papers that include collections of programs, clippings, and correspondence. There appears another musical world—the world of women's music-making in communities large and small, a tremendous network of performances and musical organizations, threads interwoven across the United States and across national boundaries, lines of communication established and kept vital through the National Federation of Music Clubs, the General Federation of Women's Clubs, the National League of American Pen Women, and women's musical fraternal organizations.

The role that these groups have played in the history of American music has been largely overlooked, except for occasional comments such as the following, made in 1932 in a non-academic publication: "The National Federation of Music Clubs promotes every kind of musical endeavor, with 400,000 or more members in 4,762 clubs. The General Federation of Women's Clubs is even larger, a very large portion of its 14,500 clubs sponsor choruses or orchestras or both, of their own members, and many of them have given support to musical endeavors outside of their own membership." Elks, Masons, Shriners, deMolays, Rotary, Kiwanis, Lions clubs "which may also have groups" were also enumerated as supportive of music.[1]

A strong commitment to music is implied in the title of an organization called "The National Federation of Music Clubs." Less obvious is the tremendous support given music by the other two women's organizations: the National League of American Pen Women (NLAPW) and the General Federation of Women's Clubs (GFWC), both founded before 1900. By the 1920s, each had developed into a powerful national network of local chapters or branches, an administrative hierarchy culminating in an established national office, with regular publications on national and statewide levels, and definite goals for outreach and development. Although NLAPW was a professional organization of artists, musicians, and authors, and GFWC was an association of diverse social and special interest clubs, both placed emphasis on music at local and national levels, such that concerts became a regular part of meetings and conventions.

Each was large and powerful. In 1931 NLAPW claimed to be the world's largest literary organization of women, with a membership of more than 2,000 professional authors, writers, artists, sculptors, and composers in 53 branches in almost every state of the Union.[2] The GFWC's strength was evident as the Washington Arts Club in 1920 proposed the building of a "peace carillon—a musical peace tower to commemorate at the nation's capitol the victory over imperialism and the part played in it by American Manhood." The estimated cost of the carillon was $200,000; with a tower to house it and a proper memorial building, the cost would approach $2,000,000. The Arts Club proposed that "it could be erected by the federated clubwomen of America as their national headquarters, and as tribute . . . A dollar each from federated clubwomen would make the building possible."[3] For a variety of reasons, this was not done, but such an idea is tribute to the group's strength. By 1942 there were 16,500 clubs affiliated with the GFWC, graphically demonstrated on a "pin map" of the United States on the cover of the War Service Programs Volume.[4]

The National League of American Pen Women

The NLAPW was first organized in 1897 as the League of American Pen Women by Marion Longfellow O'Donoghue (a journalist for major Boston and Washington newspapers who had been barred from the all-male Washington Press Club), Margaret Sullivan Burke (the first woman admitted to the Press Gallery as a regularly accredited telegraphic correspondent), and Anna Sanborne Hamilton (*Washington Post* social editor and special proofreader for the United States government). Formed originally for the purpose of "bringing together women journalists, authors, and illustrators for mutual benefits and the strength that comes of union," NLAPW admitted composers about 1910, first as writers of musical texts, then recognized as composers of music. Prospective members were obligated to show payment for and submit samples of professional work to membership committees on both local and national levels.[5]

The best-known composers of the day became members.[6] A major objective of the group was performance: conventions regularly featured music, and additional concerts in various cities were sponsored by NLAPW over the years.

An early project that received attention in the press was "The American Women Composers First Annual Festival of Music under the auspices League of American Pen Women," held in 1925 in Washington, D.C. Extant programs indicate that songs and chamber works were performed at the Men's City Club on 28 April, followed by major works for chorus and orchestra given at Memorial Continental Hall the next two evenings. Performers included the United States Navy Band Orchestra, the Washington Choral Society, the Rubinstein Club, and the Marine Band Orchestra, as well as a number of vocal and instrumental soloists.[7] This author has found no record of additional festivals in this implied series, but performances of large works became a regularly scheduled part of the biennial conventions.

In 1930–1932, six "National Concerts" were given in major cities, including Washington, D.C., New York, Pittsburgh, and San Francisco.[8] The main features of these concerts were the compositions which had won first prize and first and second honorable mention in the most recent national NLAPW composition contests, supplemented with compositions from the outstanding local composers in each particular Branch.[9]

The NLAPW sponsored regular contests for its authors, artists, and composers, with winning selections featured at the conventions. The Music Award was given each year for a different specified genre.[10]

Branch meetings provided additional performance opportunities. Composers tended to live in the large towns and cities, and some branches could claim no musician members. Nonetheless, all were encouraged to recognize the musical as well as literary achievements of women. For instance, Grace Warner Gulesian, music chairman in 1940, urged that

> at least one meeting during the season, in every Branch, be a musical program. Have a member talk on the work that American Women Composers are doing. There are several books in the libraries on this subject. . . . On that same Club afternoon, compositions of Club members . . . , composers living in that Region, and other worthwhile musical works by N.L.A.P.W. members could be performed. If there is a chorus in your city, have them sing some choruses written by N.L.A.P.W. members. Have your schools use good songs written by members of our organization.

She also observed "The widespread suppression of musical activity in Europe because of the holocaust of political tyrannies, has laid upon America a new responsibility to hold more firmly to artistic traditions and to develop a greater musical future. Europe has carried the brilliant torch of culture for centuries and has handed it to America to keep burning."[11]

Many branches throughout the country devoted meetings to the topic of music. Notable were the annual musicales of the Knoxville, Tennessee, branch. In 1932 an all-Penwoman program of eleven composers was given "under direction of Professor Mayer of the University."[12] Professor Mayer apparently had a long association with the group, as he arranged the fourteenth annual musical in 1940, featuring works of nine women composers.[13] A survey of Branch Histories shows that musical performances were also a frequent part of activities in the Chicago; Worcester, Massachusetts; Waterloo, Iowa; and Green Mountain, Vermont, branches.[14]

Throughout the years the principal institutional showcase for Penwomen-composers was the biennial convention. Under the leadership of Music Chairman Dorothy DeMuth Watson, the 1932 and 1934 conventions were particularly notable for their musical emphasis. The so-named "Music Festival of [the] Composer Group" in 1932 featured a major musical presentation nearly every day of the biennial convention. Concerts were held at American University, the Congressional Club, the Willard Hotel, the Women's City Club, the Congressional Country Club, the American Association of University Women's Clubs, the Sears-Roebuck Galleries at 1106 Connecticut Avenue, the Federation of Women's Clubs, the Polish Embassy, the Arts Club of Washington, during four church services, and at several private homes. In all there were twenty-two concerts with music by twenty-one composer members performed by an assortment of vocal soloists, instrumentalists, The Chaminade Club, the American University Mixed Glee Clubs, and the seventy-voice choir of the Mt. Vernon Methodist Episcopal Church, South.[15]

Two years later, the convention's musical activities were organized as the "Golden Jubilee Music Festival, given during the League's biennial convention in Washington April 21–27 in honor of Mrs. H. H. A. Beach,[16] who has devoted 50 years to music." Concerts were again presented in a variety of locations—the Willard Hotel (official convention headquarters), the Congressional Country Club, the U.S. Chamber of Commerce Auditorium, the East Room of the White House, the Clubhouse of the A.A.U.W., Wilson's Teachers College, and Barker Hall of the Y.W.C.A. There was also a broadcast from the United States Marine barracks by the United States Marine Band.[17] Works for a variety of instrumental and vocal combinations written by twenty composers were heard.

Special activities for NLAPW composers continued to be a part of convention planning. For instance, the 1940 biennial convention included a composers' banquet and concert; musicales at the opening of the National Art Exhibit, at the Congressional Club, the Washington Club, the Y.M.C.A., and the Women's City Club; a soirée to meet Washington composers; an "autograph session" for composers at a local music store, and performances of NLAPW members' music at Sunday morning church services.[18]

The General Federation of Women's Clubs

The General Federation of Women's Clubs was established in 1890. Comprised of a wide variety of organizations such as garden clubs, social clubs, Junior Leagues, literary and music study clubs, political action clubs, and youth auxiliaries for all of the above, the GFWC had a huge membership, which, when mobilized, could exert considerable impact. The official publications of the GFWC, *General Federation News* and its successor, *the Clubwoman*, continually brought worthy causes to the members' attention. GFWC philanthropic and educational activities included

creation of libraries, parks, and playgrounds in many cities, upgrading standards of education, establishing scholarship funds
for women, and lobbying for legislation regarding child labor
laws, woman suffrage, fair treatment of Indians, and healthful
conditions in factory and marketplace. Many of these major projects were successfully completed even before women were en-
franchised.

Musical activities were first administered under the Art Department, an integral part of the GFWC since its founding. In 1910 a
separate Committee for Music was established for the purpose of
promoting "the intelligent comprehension of one of the greatest
factors of strength in the homes of the nation."[19] Federated clubs
were urged to make music a part of each meeting, and were
exhorted in articles in the *General Federation News,* fliers, and
pamphlets to examine and enrich the musical life of their communities. The response was enthusiastic: the Rhode Island Music
Committee soon reported, "Almost every club opens its meeting
with a "club sing."[20] The wider effect of the music program was
felt within the decade as women's clubs donated instruments to
military bands and placed pianos and victrolas in army camps and
Y.M.C.A.'s during World War I.[21]

A particularly devoted and ambitious early Music Chairman
who served in the 1920s was Anne (Mrs. Marx) Oberndorfer of
Chicago. In addition to her regular contributions for *General
Federation News,* she wrote articles for such magazines as *Ladies
Home Journal* and had a regular column entitled "Music for Every
Home" in *Fruit, Garden, and Home,* a periodical reaching many
small towns and rural communities. She also produced a Chi-
cago-based radio broadcast series entitled "Hearing America
First," using GFWC material available for club use.[22]

Mrs. Oberndorfer established high musical standards and challenging objectives for the GFWC. She introduced her plans for the
1924–25 year with these inspiring words: "Realizing that music
must be a force in the life of every citizen in the country and that
our music work must be so correlated to our other club activities,
that it will be a vital part of the daily life of the community," this
division suggested a program for every month of the year:

September—planning the music selections for the year so that progress will be correlated.
October—a musical symposium where the music of the community
shall be discussed
November—national music shower where music shall be collected to
be donated to public institutions

December—community Christmas carols
January—the MacDowell Memorial Week
February—the celebration of Lincoln's and Washington's birthdays by
    Colonial and Civil War progress
March—music memory contest in schools
April—Sunday school hymn memory contest
May—National Music Week
June—community opera given outdoors
July—Citizenship Day music
August—summer concerts

She reported that 600 clubs had celebrated the MacDowell Memorial Week the first year it was suggested, and twice that many the year past, and that ten thousand clubs had used the program on Lincoln and Washington's birthdays.[23]

By the 1920s the GFWC had established music loan libraries offering programs, outlines for papers, books for reference, sheet music, player piano rolls, and phonograph records. Topics for study included Indian music, Negro music, music in Colonial days, pioneer music, the Civil War period, present day composers of America, Edward MacDowell, and American women composers. The popularity of these is indicated by this announcement: "Programs will only be sent when definite dates for their use are given. They must be returned immediately after using as the demand for these programs is very great."[24]

The GFWC was also devoted from early on to outreach to youngsters, sponsoring clubs, scholarships, and contests. Of particular note is the musical memory contest, which involved coordination of a number of facets—preparation and distribution of study materials, judging, and awards. As Mrs. Oberndorfer reported: "The music memory contest has become a national institution and the music supervisors and instructors who have been carrying on this work claim that the influence of the women's clubs has been of tremendous importance."[25] In 1924 prizes of $50, $25, and $15 were to be given to children of grammar-school age for the best paper sent in on music selections broadcast 14 March. Any child in America might enter, and any child with a score of 95% was to receive $5. Similar prizes were offered for high school students.[26] Children also enjoyed the benefits of the GFWC loan programs: "The Loan Libraries of Player Piano Rolls for boys and girls will be sent to any club in towns and cities of any size. . . . It is hoped that this library will be the nucleus of a National Music Memory Contest."[27]

The GFWC's commitment to artistic enrichment was further demonstrated by the regular inclusion of concerts, lectures, and art exhibits at conventions. For instance, music preceded each evening's session of the Salt Lake City meeting held 12–18 June 1921, performed by an assortment of musicians—girl's glee club, harp, solo voice, male quartet, Indian songs performed in costume. A concert was presented by the local Orpheum Club. An afternoon session devoted to "The Building of the West" was augmented by musical examples. For the concluding session of the convention, delegates were part of an audience of 30,000 to hear a performance of Haydn's *The Creation* by the Salt Lake City Oratorio Society and soloists of the Chicago Opera company accompanied by a 45-piece orchestra.[28]

The 1924 Biennial in Los Angeles featured music at each day's major session, planned to coordinate with each topic. For instance, a set of "Prison Sonnets" was sung at the public welfare program when prison reform was stressed, the words written by a former prisoner, the musical setting supplied by Mrs. Oberndorfer. On Fine Arts Day a number of distinguished speakers addressed the convention—Arthur Farwell, Charles Wakefield Cadman, Carrie Jacobs Bond, and Ossip Gabrilowitsch.[29] (These were figures of stature perhaps comparable today to Leonard Bernstein, Artur Rubinstein, and Aaron Copland.[30])

There was even more music scheduled for the 1926 convention in Atlantic City, 24 May–4 June. Each day's activities began with the singing of six state songs by their delegates at 8:45 A.M. (42 state groups were heard in all), followed at 9 A.M. by a session of assembly singing, recitation of The Club Litany or The Lord's Prayer, and salute to the flag. The program listed eighty individual musical compositions to be performed by thirty-two musicians and three ensembles. Unnamed in the program, and thus uncounted, were the pieces performed by two other large performing groups, the club choruses vying for the choral award, and the repertoire of contestants in a music memory contest.[31]

By 1928, the leadership had passed to Mrs. Eugene B. Lawson of Tulsa, Oklahoma, who wrote in *General Federation News:*

It has long been the desire of the Music Division that music be a part of every club program. Just how nearly the goal has been reached can be seen in the following condensed report: [further condensed for this article to seven citations from an original thirty]: "Idaho reports: Each club has given a portion of its time during the past year to the furtherance of music. . . . North Dakota has recorded music in every club, with practically every club giving one purely musical program. . . . Delaware supports eight clubs with active chorus organizations. . . . California is justly proud of 142 choral bodies in two districts, totalling a thousand singers. . . . Massachusetts has organized a women's symphony orchestra. . . . The past year Minnesota held choral contests in eight districts, with the state contest at Crookston. . . . Seven hundred women participated, representing 75 towns. . . . North Dakota is doing splendid Music Memory Contest Work with public schools, 27 counties participating. . . ."[32]

Committed to higher education, the GFWC established scholarships early in its history. In addition, in 1929, the New Jersey Federation of Women's Clubs built a music building costing more than $100,000 for the New Jersey College for Women at New Brunswick. The GFWC had been instrumental in the founding of this school and had already donated a science building "debt-free."[33]

GFWC programs were tremendously important in the cultural life of America's smaller communities located far from the major cultural centers: "That the music activity and interest in our country is not confined to the cities and larger communities is attested by the fact that by far the larger number of contacts made by the Music Division has been with the towns of 5,000 or less inhabitants, records and piano rolls often being called for from nonmusical clubs."[34]

The programs of the GFWC continued to flourish in the early years of the Depression. In 1933, National Chairman Mrs. H. S. Godfrey put forth the following club aims:

1. to encourage ensemble singing at each meeting
2. to sponsor "Composer Days"
3. to sponsor concerts by guest artists
4. to present programs on American women composers
5. to support music in the community
6. to establish a choral group in each club.[35]

In support of these aims, GFWC Chairman for American Music and Folksong Gena Branscombe[36] compiled fourteen programs of music for those performing resources most likely available within a club's membership—pieces for piano, solo voice, women's voices, violin, various small instrumental ensembles, and "story poems with musical settings." Half of these programs were devoted to works by fifty-eight women composers, and the other seven included works by these and thirty-five American men.[37] Also available to club members were four programs of American folk songs and Indian songs, Spanish California folksongs, Negro spirituals, and various songs from the mountains and plains of the East and West.[38]

Branscombe urged that 1934 be designated "American Music Year," and inspired clubwomen to view this project in terms of preservation of heritage as well as responsibility to the future. She wrote:

> Going from these tuneful beginnings our gifted and well-trained composers have given us atmospheric art songs, sturdy ballads, instrumental pieces, chamber music, choral works ranging from short part-songs to large oratorios, symphonic works, and operas that have proved the outstanding success of a Metropolitan [Opera] season.
>
> In order to do their best work, composers must have the certainty that their compositions will be performed. Publishers also must be assured that major American works will be used and copies paid for, or they will not dare to sink money in the printing of such works.
>
> By pledging ourselves to perform some American music on every club program, and arranging to give a well-prepared performance of one large American work each season, we will be giving practical encouragement to our composers and publishers, while enriching and developing the musical consciousness and appreciation of our audiences.[39]

Branscombe's exhortations and those of previous music chairmen were brought to fruition in the National Golden Jubilee Chorus of one thousand voices that sang at the 1941 convention. Branscombe described her experience as conductor of this group as follows:

> One of the nicest things that has happened to me was when the General Federation of Women's Clubs had me to conduct their national chorus of one thousand women which sang at Atlantic City to celebrate fifty years of women's achievements. Choruses came from every state in the Union but two. From a program planned a year in advance, the fine co-operative local conductors drilled their singers, using uniform instruction sheets giving all interpretive details. I flew to different parts of the country for three different regional rehearsals, and the whole chorus came together for one joint rehearsal at Atlantic City. They entered the great rehearsal hall by states—Oregon, Arkansaw [sic], California, New Jersey, Minnesota, New York, Alabama. . . . On they came.
>
> And that night they sang with a sensitivity of nuance, a complete integration of tone, intelligibility of diction, as though they'd been an intimate chorus of twenty women.[40]

This impressive chorus was a fitting symbol of all the GFWC had accomplished for music in its first half-century. The program included six compositions by Americans (three of them women), folk song settings, and selections by "the masters"—Mozart, Haydn, and Handel. The concert concluded with Handel's "Hallelujah Chorus."

In the early 1940s the musical activities of the GFWC mirrored society's concerns. Music study outlines available to clubs were on topics of patriotic music, war songs, music in America, Latin American music, and sacred music. Clubs were urged to sponsor fireside and lobby sings in community centers and public places, to be active in music as a patriotic service in civilian defense and war work, and to emphasize folk and art music of the Central and South American republics.[41] The only musical events listed in the outline form program of the 1942 Convention, held in Fort Worth, Texas, 27 April–2 May are "Massed Chorus," "Western Hemispheres Night—Folk Songs and Dances of the Americas," a presentation on "Recent Developments in the Field of Music and Musical Interchange" as part of a Pan American Forum, and a cowboy band appearing as part of a Chuckwagon Supper at the River Crest Country Club.[42]

Conclusion

The lessened emphasis on music at conventions of both groups in the early 1940s can be attributed to wartime travel and financial limitations but also may have resulted from reaction to the length and complexity of convention formats. The NLAPW seems to have adopted more modest aims for financial reasons. It was proposed that the 1941 budget for national awards be divided among the divisions as follows: letters, 50%, arts and music, 25% each. The National Award for music was to be $50, with an allowance of $75 for expenses. That this would constitute a reduction from the usual is implied in the somewhat defensive "NOTE" printed at the end of the proposed budget:

> To put on a concert or series of League concerts is expensive, even when composers donate their services and expenses. The reason that the Music Department was built up, so that practically every well-known composer was a member, was because concerts were given in difficult cities and $500.00 and even more spent annually on the Music Department—sometimes on one concert alone. Therefore it is hoped that other moneys will be contributed by those musically interested.[43]

In the case of the GFWC there may have been a trend toward

more streamlined convention proceedings, as outlined in an article criticizing the "crazy-quilt" of convention activities and ad-
vocating a "New Deal in Conventions." With regard to music, the
author wrote: "too many conventions give too much morning
time to musical programs and other entertainment, with the result that when the 'meat' of the proceedings is on, it is too late to
get much in the press. Why not get down to bed-rock earlier and
relax in song later?" and "I recall one state convention to which a
college president drove many miles to address an evening session. When he arrived he was told that an hour's musical program
would precede his talk. The look of disgust on his face was not
unwarranted, and his wife did not hesitate to speak of the ar-
rangement as an 'imposition.' Let us not forget that entertainment
can be as exhaustive as a work program, and if the two must be
mixed, let it be 'MOST sparingly'."[44]

The achievements of both the NLAPW and the GFWC in their
first half-centuries are impressive indeed, especially when one
considers their existence in a time before music was widely taught
in public schools, before the establishment of many of our community and civic symphonies when orchestras were still concen-
trated in the large cities of the nation, before the growth of state
and community colleges and their adult education programs,
before Time-Life and Reader's Digest boxed sets of classical record-
ings, before the days of public radio, before television and "Live
from Lincoln Center," and before widespread well-stocked public
libraries. Indeed, many of the abovementioned cultural institutions are the direct result of GFWC effort, because members who
were not themselves musicians were nonetheless influential in
establishing symphony orchestras, concert series, and other
cultural institutions in their communities.

Both the GFWC and the NLAPW showed a strong commitment
to women composers in providing numerous performance opportunities for composers at meetings and conventions. Both worked
to bring the music of women and the importance of the role of
women in music to a larger public through public recitals,
broadcasts, lectures, and other programs. The NLAPW, as a professional organization, provided its members additional encouragement through monetary awards in its annual composition
contests. The GFWC's aims were more varied, with many of its
contests and programs directed toward generating musical enthu-
siasm throughout society, and its advocacy of music embracing
folk musics of the Americas and the world as well as compositions
in the "classical" European tradition.

A number of women were active in both organizations. Pen-women served the Federation as music chairs or members of advisory boards, composed state songs and music for Federation pageants, and conducted GFWC choruses. Among these are Gena Branscombe, Grace Warner Gulesian, Harriet Ware Krumb-haar, and Phyllis Fergus Hoyt.

Although written in the 1920s, the words of Mrs. Oberndorfer summarize well the accomplishments of these important decades:

> But the most important achievement of all is the fact that three million club women have changed their point of view regarding music. They realize that it must be given a fitting place upon their club programs; that professional artists must be paid; that English is a good singing language; that we have the greatest Folk Music in the world in America; that our local musicians are oft times better than our American artists; that music must be made a vital part of the community and last, but not least, that whether we have technical training or not, we are all musical and have an important part to play in the building of the American School of Music, which will be the greatest the world has ever known.[45]

Notes

1. Augustus Delafield Zanzig, *Music in American Life: Present and Future. Prepared for the National Recreation Association* (New York: National Recreation Association, 1932), 242–43.

2. Harriet Chace, second vice-president, "The National League of American Pen Women," *Bulletin of the N.L.A.P.W.* 7 (March 1931): 5.

3. "Carillon of Women's Peace Memorial Proposed by Arts Club," *General Federation News* 1 (October 1920): 1, 5, 8.

4. *General Federation Clubwoman, War Service Programs* 23 (October 1942).

5. "The League, Yesterday," in The National League of American Pen Women, Inc. brochure (Washington, D.C.: n.p., n.d. [ca. 1980s]).

6. Among the more famous members were Amy Beach, Gena Branscombe, Annabel Morris Buchanan, Mabel Daniels, Eleanor Everest Freer, Mary Howe, Mana-Zucca, Mary Carr Moore, and Harriet Ware: composers of sufficient stature to be included in standard reference works like the *New Grove Dictionary of American Music*.

7. Programs, The American Women Composers First Annual Festival of Music for 28, 29, and 30 April 1925, in the Gena Branscombe Collection, to be in the New York Public Library at Lincoln Center.

8. "National President's Report, 1930–32," *Bulletin* 8 (June 1932): 2.

9. "Music, Art and Letters," *Bulletin* 7 (November 1930): 3.

10. The following partial list of winners was compiled from various records of the NLAPW:

1928—$100 Award (given by Cyrus McCormick) to Gena Branscombe for "Pilgrims of Destiny," choral drama, "Best Composition in the Music Contest of the NLAPW for 1928"

1930—$100 to Mary Howe for "String Quartet"

1931—$100 to Mabel Wood Hill for "Clothes of Heaven," accompanied song

1932—$100 to Mary Carr Moore

1934—Dorothy Radde Emery for choral work, "Ode to St. Cecilia"

1935—Mary Carr Moore for "Quintet for Piano and Strings"

1936—Persis Heaton Trimble for song, "Fairy of Spring"

1938—Seven separate awards—for string ensemble ($30), quartet of mixed voices, accompanied ($20), song, tone poem, Christmas hymn, composition on a Chinese theme or scale, song or piece with lyric by a NLAPW member ($10 each).

11. Grace Warner Gulesian, "Say It with Music!" *NLAPW Official Bulletin* (NLAPW) 15 (November 1940): 11–13.

12. "Branch News, Knoxville," *Bulletin* 8 (May 1932): 24.

13. Lilian C. B. McA. Mayer, "Knoxville Branch [News]," *Official Bulletin* 15 (December 1940): 21.

14. Branch Histories Collection, The National League of American Pen Women, National Headquarters, Washington, D.C.

15. "Program of the Sixth Biennial Convention, 23–28 April 1932 at the Willard Hotel, Washington, D.C.," as printed in *Bulletin* 6 (May 1932): 12–17.

16. Mrs. H. H. A. (Amy Cheney) Beach (1867–1944) was known as the "dean of American women composers." Hers was the first symphony by an American woman to be written and performed by a major orchestra, the Boston Symphony. She was listed along with major American composers of her generation in books published through about 1930. Her art songs achieved great success, and so great was her popularity that many music clubs were named in her honor. Beach has been the subject of several dissertations. A major study of her life and works is in preparation.

17. Phyllis Fergus Hoyt, National [music] Chairman, "Golden Jubilee Music Festival," *Official Bulletin* 10 (June 1934): 11–12, 19.

18. Nell V. Smith, Publicity Chairman, "The 1940 Biennial," *Official Bulletin*, 14 (June 1940): 4–5.

19. Mildred White Wells, *Unity in Diversity. The History of the General Federation of Women's Clubs* (Washington, D.C.: General Federation of Women's Clubs, 1953), 179.

20. "Summary of Work Done by State Federations," *General Federation News Supplement* 2 (July/August 1921): 2.

21. Wells, *Unity in Diversity,* 179.

22. Anna [sic] Oberndorfer, "Music Chairman Outlines Department Work for Year," *General Federation News* 5 (July/August 1924): 12.

23. Ibid.

24. Anne Oberndorfer, "Music Loan Library Rules Announced; Programs Available," *General Federation News* 5 (December 1924): 3.

25. Oberndorfer, "Music Chairman Outlines Department Work," 12.

26. "Music Memory Contest by Radio WMAQ Planned," *General Federation News* 4 (March 1924): 12.

27. Oberndorfer, "Music Loan Library Rules Announced," 3.

28. "Program of GFWC Council, Salt Lake City, June 12–18," *General Federation News* 1 (June 1921): 1, 8.

29. "Music at Biennial to Surpass Anything Previously Planned," *General Federation News* 4 (June 1924): 6; and "Noted Artists Take Part at Biennial," *General Federation News* 5 (July/August 1924): 7.

30. For the composer Carrie Jacobs Bond there is no contemporary parallel—she wrote the still-popular songs "I Love You Truly" and "A Perfect Day," which sold more than eight million sheet music copies, five million records, and were issued in sixty versions.

31. "Program of the 18th Biennial Convention of the General Federation of Women's Clubs to be Held at Atlantic City, May 24th to June 4th," *General Federation News, Biennial Clip Sheet Number* 6 (May–June 1926): 1–3, 18–21.

32. "A Singing Federation," *General Federation News* 9 (September 1928): 9.

33. "New Jersey Federation Sees a Vision Fulfilled," *General Federation News* 9 (January 1929): 9.

34. "A Singing Federation," 9.

35. Mrs. H. S. Godfrey, "Department of Fine Arts," *The Clubwoman* 8 (February 1933): 18.

36. Gena Branscombe (1881–1977) is often mentioned along with Mrs. H. H. A. Beach and a handful of other women as the most outstanding composers of their sex in America. Born in Canada, Branscombe spent her entire professional life in the United States, and most of it as choral conductor and composer in New York City. A tireless proponent of American music, she succeeded Beach as the second president of the Society of American Women Composers in the 1920s, and is also the subject of a dissertation and a forthcoming biography.

37. Of these, the names that might be most familiar to the present-day musical layperson are Louis Gottschalk, Edward MacDowell, Stephen Foster, George Gershwin, and Charles Griffes.

38. *Handbook, General Federation of Women's Clubs, Department of Fine Arts, Division of Music* ([Washington, D.C.]: General Federation of Women's Clubs, 1930–1932), 2–16.

39. Gena Branscombe, "American Musical Works Performance Essential to National Development," General Federation of Women's Clubs, Department of Fine Arts, one-page notice, (1934) in the Gena Branscombe Collection, to be in the New York Public Library at Lincoln Center.

40. Gena Branscombe, untitled speech beginning, "It is a pleasure for me to be here. . . ." (after 1950), in Laurine Elkins-Marlow, "Gena Branscombe (1881–1977): American Composer and Conductor," (Ph.D. diss., The University of Texas at Austin, 1980), 156–57.

41. *General Federation of Women's Clubs War Service Programs* (October 1942): 9.

42. "Program of the Annual Convention of the General Federation of Women's Clubs," *General Federation Clubwoman* 22 (April 1942): 16.

43. Grace Thompson Seton, chairman, "Concerning Awards and Award Patrons," *Official Bulletin* 15 (December 1940): 34–35.

44. Louise Cattoi, "Speaking of Conventions," *General Federation Clubwoman* (May 1938): 11–12.

45. Oberndorfer, "Music Chairman Outlines Department Work," 13.

Contributors

CHIARA BRIGANTI, assistant professor of English at Carleton College, was educated at the University of Pisa, the University of California-Davis, and Penn State University. She is completing a book on the incest paradigm and its implications from the point of view of narrative theory in Dickens, Charlotte Brontë, and Austen.

PHYLLIS CULHAM, professor of history at the United States Naval Academy, has published several articles on aspects of Græco-Roman antiquity. She recently co-edited the book, *Classics: A Discipline and Profession in Crisis?* with Lowell Edmunds of Rutgers University.

MINNA DOSKOW, professor of English and former dean at Glassboro State College, has been director of the honors program and professor of English at the University of Baltimore. Her publications include articles on William Blake, Heller, and writing by women.

JOYCE DYER has published several articles on Southern literature. She is currently at work on a critical study of Kate Chopin's *The Awakening* to be published by G.K. Hall/ Twayne. A recipient of two National Endowment for the Humanities grants to pursue her interests in Appalachian literature and the literature of coal, she lives in Hudson, Ohio, and teaches at Western Reserve Academy.

LAURINE ELKINS-MARLOW received her master of music and Ph.D. degrees in musicology from the University of Texas-Austin. She is an independent scholar of women's music, particularly orchestral works by American women composers, and has written a biography of the Canadian-American composer-conductor Gena Branscombe. She has taught music at Suffolk County Community College and since 1989 has been visiting lecturer at Texas A & M.

WAYNE FRANITS is an assistant professor of fine arts at Syracuse University. A specialist in seventeenth-century Dutch painting, he is the author of several articles and book reviews and is completing a book on women and domesticity in seventeenth-century Dutch art and culture.

LESLIE K. HANKINS did her graduate work at the University of North Carolina-Chapel Hill. She has published articles on Virginia Woolf and film theory and given papers on Katherine Anne Porter, Eudora Welty, Sherley Anne Williams, Alice Walker, and women in western film.

CLAIRE HIRSHFIELD received her Ph.D. in European history from the University of Pennsylvania and is currently professor of history at Penn State University, Ogontz Campus. She has published a monograph on Anglo-French relations circa 1900 and several articles on Victorian and Edwardian England.

SELMA KRAFT is professor of art history at Siena College in Loudonville, New York. She is currently chair of the Department of Fine Arts and co-ordinator of Interdisciplinary Studies.

ALICE SHEPPARD received her Ph.D. in psychology from Clark University. She has served as a lecturer and research associate at Susquehanna University and currently teaches at State University of New York at Geneseo. She is completing a book, *Cartooning for Suffrage*, to be published by the University of New Mexico Press.

KATHERINE STANNARD is professor emerita of psychology at Framingham State College in Massachusetts. Her interests include the psychology of artists and applications of Jungian psychology to the arts and popular culture.

JOYCE W. WARREN teaches English at Queens College, the City University of New York. The author of *The American Narcissus: Individualism and Women in Nineteenth-Century American Fiction* (1984), she edited *Ruth Hall and Other Writings* by Fanny Fern and wrote a biography of Fern, *Fanny Fern: An Independent Woman* (forthcoming).

LESLIE WILLIAMS teaches art history at the University College of the University of Cincinnati. Her work on visualizing Victorian schooling has recently appeared in the *Bucknell Review*. She is completing a book on the images of children during the Regency and Victorian periods.

MARA WITZLING teaches art history in the Department of the Arts, University of New Hampshire. She has written on medieval manuscripts and also women artists. Her collection of writings by women artists, *Voicing Our Visions,* will be available in 1991.

Index